THE ORDER OF OMEGA

KRISTEN MARTIN

BLACK FALCON PRESS

For information contact :

Black Falcon Press, LLC

http://www.blackfalconpress.com

Library of Congress Control Number : 2016903007

ISBN: 978-0-9968605-2-9 (paperback)

Cover Illustration by Damonza © 2016

10 9 8 7 6 5 4 3 2 1

To my mother, Barbara Marvel—
for loving me and supporting me no matter what.
You are truly the best mom out there. I love you.

1

The sound of crunching glass beneath her blood-stained combat boots reminded Emery of a much happier time. Stepping out into the first Christmas snow in Northern Arizona, her family curled up by an outdoor fire pit, watching as the blazing sun fell behind a wide canvas of mountains. It was one of her happiest memories, a time where she'd felt as though everything had finally come together. Every aspect of her life had been perfect. Nothing had been missing.

But she was far, far from that place. And she wasn't sure she'd ever get to go back.

Emery broke her gaze from the shards of glass on the floor, focusing her attention on the blank faces staring back at her.

Torin. Mason. Warren.

They'd all survived the lethargum attack, thanks, in large part, to her. Orange dust speckled their uniforms from the sanaré bomb that had lit up downtown Chicago just two hours prior. From a physical standpoint, Mason's headshot wound had healed quickly, but the mental damage had taken a turn for the worst.

Torin had rushed Emery, Mason, and Warren to his apartment, claiming that he had some sort of technology that would speed up the healing process. Emery had sat with Mason's head on her lap as Torin fastened a strange looking device, almost like headgear but in holographic form, around his head. Orange currents buzzed at lightning speed as they scanned the top of Mason's head down to his chin. Within minutes, Mason's eyes had shot open, his face frozen in terror. It'd taken some coaxing, but eventually he'd calmed down.

Since then, the four of them had sat in Torin's apartment, not moving or talking, stunned by the events that had just taken place. Emery decided it was time to break the silence. "Well, that was eventful." She raised an eyebrow at Torin, mentally egging him on to respond, but he didn't. Instead, he averted his eyes and bowed his head to the floor.

"Can someone fill me in on what just happened?" Mason interjected. "In case you failed to notice, I was shot. In the head. By *Theo*." He twiddled his thumbs, his eyes flitting back and forth between Emery and Torin. "By my own *team*."

Emery's stomach turned. "I wanted to tell you when we were hiding behind the trashcan . . ."

"Tell me what?" Mason asked through clenched teeth.

"That we were fighting for the wrong side," Emery blurted out. "Everything Theo told you about the Seventh Sanctum was a lie. The members of the Federal Commonwealth are the creators of Dormance. They're the ones who want to control all of mankind." She stole a glance at Torin before continuing. "And had it not been for Torin and his impeccable timing, they probably would have succeeded."

Torin's eyes grew wide as if he'd just heard the world's biggest lie. "That's not entirely true. It was all Emery's idea. I just did what I was told."

A burning sensation crept across her cheeks.

"Hold on," Mason interrupted. "I still don't understand what just happened."

Emery eyed him warily. "It's a lot more complicated than you realize. Trust me. I'll find more time to explain later, but not right now." She walked over to Torin and grabbed him by the arm, then led him toward the fire escape she'd used earlier that day.

"Wait, what are you doing?" Torin asked as she dragged him along behind her.

"There's somewhere we need to go. You two stay here," she demanded, pointing her index and middle fingers at Warren and Mason.

Mason opened his mouth to object, then closed it. "It's not worth it," he muttered as he fell onto the couch, the toe of his boot knocking against what remained of a coffee table.

Emery swung her legs over the windowsill, then slid down the fire escape, Torin's feet dangling just a few inches above her head. When they'd both landed safely on the pavement, she turned to face him, lowering her voice to a whisper. "I left something behind in Dormance. Something important."

Torin's face fell. "What do you mean?"

As she opened her mouth to answer, a loud buzzing sound filled the space between them. Torin held up his hand as if to pause the conversation, and reached into his pocket for his phone. Disbelief crossed his face.

"This can't be right."

Emery moved closer to him, straining her eyes to see. "Who is it?"

"It's a call," he said quietly, "from Dormance."

Their eyes met for a brief moment. But before he could answer it, the buzzing came to a stop.

Emery grabbed the phone from his grip, her eyes scanning the device. "What happened? Who was it?"

"I'm not sure. The call dropped."

"Can you trace it back somehow?"

"Emery," he said, as if he were trying to explain something to a small child, "the call was from Dormance. We deactivated Dormance. Meaning it shouldn't exist. And we certainly shouldn't be receiving calls from anyone there. Because they don't exist either. It's impossible."

"Unless," Emery started as she handed the phone back to him, "it didn't work and we did something wrong." She shook her head and kicked the pavement with the toe of her boot. The realization dawned on her. "We messed up. We didn't deactivate Dormance."

A wave of confusion washed over Torin's face. "What are you talking about? Of course we did. I was there. I heard the confirmation."

"No," Emery argued, her heart picking up speed. "We must have missed something."

Torin threw his head back, blinking a few times before returning upright. "You sound mental, you know that?"

Emery waved her hand absentmindedly in the air as if the insult had landed on deaf ears. She took a few steps forward in a zig-zag pattern, then back again in the opposite direction. Her eyes met his as a coy smirk crossed her face. "I know what we need to do. But you're not gonna like it."

Torin shook his head, as if he could read her mind. "No. Nope. Not happening."

"Listen to me. You have to send me back."

"I take back what I said. You don't just sound mental, you *are* mental!" His boots clacked against the pavement as he paced back and forth. "How can I send you back to Dormance?"

"Don't you see? There is no way you could have received a call if we'd fully deactivated Dormance. Which means it's still active. You have to send me back."

"But what if something happens? What if you get stuck there?" Torin asked, clearly searching for any reason that might change her mind. "What if there's retaliation? What if it's a giant black hole?"

Emery rolled her eyes. "Everything will be okay," she coaxed as she searched her pockets for the crystal dials. "I promise."

Torin shook his head, eyes wide with fear. "It's too dangerous. You know I can't let you go."

"Torin," she reprimanded as she extended her right palm. "Give me the dials."

He stood his ground, unflinching, but after a few seconds of her seemingly endless death stare, gave in. Emery watched as he reached into his pocket and pulled out the dials, smiling as they fell from his fingertips into her open palm. She closed her hand securely around them, then walked briskly across the street to find the nearest platform. Torin wasn't far behind her.

"Can you still connect to the holodevice in the common room?" she asked through hurried breaths.

He drew his phone from his pocket and fumbled with it for a minute. "Working on it. You know, if you'd just slow down a little . . ."

"We don't have time to slow down," she called over her left shoulder. "Come on, Porter, keep up."

After walking another block, they finally arrived at a T-Port on the corner of Fifth Street and Main. Emery hopped onto the platform and dropped the crystal dials onto her wrists, her foot tapping impatiently as she waited for him to catch up.

"Okay, I can't be one hundred percent sure, but I think I'm connected now," he panted as he approached the platform. "Wait, what are you doing?"

"Send me back," she ordered. "I'm ready." She closed her eyes before he could try to talk her out of it. She heard him sigh, then waited for the familiar gust of air, the tingling in her legs and feet.

But nothing happened.

She opened one eye with caution. Her surroundings hadn't changed. Torin was still standing right in front of her, looking dumbfounded.

She curled her fists, her fingers sliding against her sweaty palms. "Try it again?" she asked, taking a deep breath to calm her nerves.

"I can't," he muttered as he gazed up from his phone. "There's an error."

"What kind of error?" she asked impatiently.

"One that says the portal is closed . . ."

As soon as the words left his mouth, Emery's phone began to buzz uncontrollably. Although she didn't recognize the number, history had proven more than once that ignoring it wouldn't make it go away. She accepted the call, waiting as patiently as she could for the voice on the other end.

"Hello?"

Static.

"Hello? Is anyone there?"

"Emery? Is that you?"

Her breath caught. She immediately recognized the voice on the other end of the line.

It was Naia.

2

Emery had never been so happy to hear another person's voice.

"I'm so happy you answered," Naia gushed. "Is everything okay? I haven't been able to get through to anyone, not even Theo. What's going on?"

Emery's face paled. She closed her eyes as scenes from earlier that day raced through her mind. Theo holding a gun to Mason's head. The bullet tearing through Mason's skull. His limp body crumpling to the ground. Raising her gun and pulling the trigger. Theo's body collapsing next to Mason's.

She'd shot Theo. And Naia didn't know.

Emery swallowed, trying to keep her voice from shaking. "I'm sorry, Naia. It's not a good time. I have to go."

"Emery, wait—"

She disconnected the call before Naia could finish. Her body trembled as she sank to the ground. Guilt surrounded her like dark clouds on a stormy night. *Naia doesn't know. Which means she couldn't have been helping me. The devices in my boots, the capsules in my training sessions. I'm a fool.* As the realization hit her, Emery tried to hold back tears, but it was no use. She'd almost forgotten Torin was still there, about to witness her emotional breakdown.

Torin knelt down beside her and reached for her shoulder. Then, with a gentle squeeze, asked, "Are you okay?"

It hadn't fully hit her until now. *I'm a killer. I'm a murderer. With more than one victim. I'm all alone in this.*

Emery wiped the tears from her eyes as she shook her head. "I'm a bad person." An image of Rhea's smiling face paraded around her thoughts. It was quickly replaced by her roommate's lifeless body—first in the hospital room, and then later, in the underground hallway in Dormance. *She didn't deserve to die.* Emery squeezed her eyes shut, hoping that the images would flee from her mind. But they stayed, tormenting her. Haunting her. The permanent ghost from her bleak past.

"You are *not* a bad person," Torin reassured, bringing her back to reality. "You did what you had to do. And the world is a better place for it."

She gazed up at him with wide eyes. "I killed people, Torin. I shot Rhea. I murdered Theo and a dozen others. That's not an easy pill to swallow."

"I know it's not," he agreed as he patted her on the shoulder, "but you'll get past it. Everything is going to be okay." He gently brushed his fingers across her cheek. "What did Naia have to say?"

"She asked if everything was okay. Obviously, she doesn't know that the Federal Commonwealth's strategy backfired. She probably thinks everyone is still alive and well. Including Theo."

"Oh, I see." Torin sighed as he sat down next to her, his hand covering hers. "You know, she's going to find out eventually. Maybe we should call her back. I bet she can help us reopen the portal."

Emery caught her reflection in a puddle on the ground. Bloodshot eyes stared back at her, cheeks puffy and flushed. She shook her head as she slowly lifted herself from the pavement. "Not yet. Now's not the time."

"Then when?"

Ignoring his question, Emery took a deep breath, hoping that a few minutes would be enough to help her get her thoughts in order. "We need to go to my house." She made her way around Torin to the platform, his fingers grazing her arm as she passed. Without saying a word, he stepped onto the platform next to her. A wave of heat hit her cheeks as she recited her home address and, a brief whir later, they found themselves standing in the driveway of her home in Arizona.

Words caught in her throat as she gazed at her surroundings. Her house looked bigger—a lot bigger—

than she remembered. Donning the exterior were some interesting gadgets that hadn't existed in Dormance. Solar panels lined the roof in neat rectangles and just below that was the garage . . . at least, it *should* have been the garage. A sleek glass entrance now sat where the once drab paneled door used to be.

Emery inched closer to the garage and peered into the tinted glass. It wasn't like she expected to see any cars since the 7S world used teleportation to get around. If she were being totally honest with herself, she didn't know what she expected to see. It was surprising, to say the least.

On the other side of the glass was a greenhouse with foliage of all shapes and sizes planted in neat, orderly rows. She craned her neck, expecting to see the usual suspects— tomatoes, peppers, cucumbers, squash—but to her surprise, there wasn't anything of the sort. Instead, there were plants she'd never seen before. Tall orange stalks blossomed outward into multiple hexagons and within each hexagon were hundreds of microscopic ovals. Each one was filled with a clear liquid.

She observed these strange plants as best she could from a distance when Torin appeared beside her. "Cool plants," he admired as he pressed his face against the window, his breath fogging up the glass.

Emery drew herself away from the sight and examined the remainder of the house. "It's strange. We didn't have a greenhouse in Dormance." She meandered over to the entryway, scanning the overhang and windows for any other new features, but nothing caught her eye. She turned her attention to the front door. It opened with ease. *Alexis must have left it unlocked . . . again.* Emery entered the foyer with Torin close behind her, both of their shoes gliding along the marble surface.

"Hello?" she called out. Although a response wasn't expected, it was worth a shot, but her greeting was met with silence.

The layout of the house was more or less the same— the kitchen, living room, and her mother's bedroom downstairs, her room and Alexis's room, plus the loft upstairs—but the décor was completely different. The style of her home in Dormance had been on the more rustic end of the spectrum. The décor here, in the 7S house, was the complete opposite of that. A metallic platform, undoubtedly used for teleporting to the first and second floors of the house, had taken the place of the once steep staircase. The walls joined at sharp angles, like something out of a modern art museum, and all of the doors were made of titanium. The walls were painted a stark grey, but the paint didn't appear to be water-based or oil-based. Instead it had a pewter look to it, but not harsh enough to look like actual metal.

It feels more like a bomb shelter than a house, she thought sullenly.

She slid her hands along the smooth walls until she reached the archway that led to the kitchen. This setup was quite different, seeing as the refrigerator, oven, and microwave weren't in their usual places. Emery narrowed her eyes and surveyed the kitchen. Actually, those items were gone and in their place were pod-like structures. A large holoscreen covered the wall where the oven used to be. Emery walked over to the pods, gingerly reaching out to touch the foreign objects. She turned to Torin with giant question marks in her eyes. "So, I take it people don't cook anymore?"

Torin laughed. "They do, in a sense, but why would you when you have SmartMeal?" He walked over to one of the pods and swiped his hand in a clockwise motion across the screen. The device lit up as a shadow of a female figure appeared on the screen. "Welcome to SmartMeal. Would you like to order breakfast, lunch, dinner, snacks, desserts, or beverages?" a pleasant voice asked.

Torin tapped his finger against his chin as if he were weighing the most important decision of his life. "Let's see. We'll go with lunch."

"From what restaurant?" the voice asked as different locales and food categories populated the screen.

"You in the mood for pizza?" he asked with a smile.

Emery nodded in awe as she waited for him to continue.

"Sam's Pizza," he confirmed.

"Please state your order for Sam's Pizza."

"Two slices of cheese pizza and two glasses of lemonade."

The machine processed the order and a confirmatory beep sounded to signal it had been received by the restaurant. Not even two minutes later, their food materialized right in front of them.

Emery picked up the slice of pizza cautiously, turning it over in her hands to examine it. When she decided it was safe to try, she took a generous bite, nodding her head thoughtfully as the cheesy goodness swarmed her taste buds.

"Pretty cool, huh?" Torin swiped his hand in a counterclockwise motion to power down the machine, then picked up his meal and carried it over to the dining room table.

Emery followed, glancing back at the machine along the way, then sat down next to him as she took a large gulp of her lemonade. "Don't we have to pay for the food?"

Torin bobbed his head from side to side. "Technically we already did."

"But I didn't see you—"

"It's a monthly fee," he interrupted. "Your handprint is like your credit card. 7S actually came up with the idea. Each household chooses a meal plan—basic, regular, or premium—and pays a monthly fee for the service," he explained through mouthfuls. "Pretty neat, huh?"

Speechless, Emery picked up the remainder of her pizza. It was difficult to wrap her head around how much more advanced everything was in the 7S world, and it was hard not to feel completely out of place, like she'd traveled through time from the Renaissance era onto a planet of martians. Regardless, she wasn't going to let a few new technological advancements intimidate her.

Her thoughts scattered as the reason they'd come to her house in the first place resurfaced. Without warning, she jumped up from her seat and darted out of the kitchen and into her mother's bedroom. She rummaged through multiple dresser drawers, paying little attention to the socks and undergarments she was flinging across the room. *Nothing.* The nightstand was her next target. No mercy was given as she shuffled through the multitude of electronic gadgets and pieces of jewelry.

Torin appeared in the doorway, clearly amused at the sight before him. "What exactly are you looking for?"

Emery stopped mid-rummage, forehead crinkling as her mind went blank. "Actually . . . I don't know."

Torin grinned as he took a few steps into the bedroom. "I don't know about you, but I've found that it's pretty hard to find something when I don't know what it is I'm looking for."

Emery sighed as she plopped down onto the bed. "I guess I'm looking for a clue of some sort." She looked at him expectantly, hoping that she wouldn't have to explain further.

"I wish I could help. I also wish I knew what in the world you're even talking about. Want to fill me in?"

Emery bowed her head to collect her thoughts. The flurry of activity recently made it difficult to keep everything straight. "Remember earlier today when I mentioned that I'd left something valuable behind in Dormance?"

He nodded.

"Before I left for Darden, my mother gave me a ring. It was shaped like an outline of a fish—"

"You mean like an alpha symbol?" he cut in.

Emery couldn't help but narrow her eyes. "Exactly like an alpha symbol." It was almost uncanny that he'd been able to describe the ring so accurately without ever having laid eyes on it. She sucked in a breath before continuing. "I tucked the ring in a closet drawer in my dorm room at Darden at the beginning of the year, but the last time I looked for it—right before deployment—it wasn't there."

"So you lost it. No big deal. People lose things all the time."

"Not me. I hardly ever lose things." The words came out a little harsher than she'd intended. "Everything has its place and I know exactly where to find it. I know for a fact that I didn't move that ring from that drawer. What's even weirder is that I've had these strange dreams," she pulled the pendant out from underneath her shirt, "where I found this."

"Whoa." Torin took the pendant in his hands, his fingers tracing the horseshoe shape. "What do you think it means?"

"I have no idea. But both of these symbols were on the mainstation in Dormance."

He shook his head, his focus shifting between Emery and the pendant. "So, let me get this straight. You think that since your mom gave you the alpha ring and you found this pendant, there might be a clue here, at your house, explaining why?"

Hearing him say it out loud made her feel worse. It did sound a little out there. "I don't know. But the one thing I do know is what my mom said. She said the ring represented new beginnings," Emery recalled. She could still hear the way her mother had said it, almost as if there had been a hidden layer of meaning. Or maybe she was reading too much into it. After all, she *had* been off to a "new beginning"—starting a new life at Darden. Perhaps that's all her mother had really meant.

She unclasped the pendant from around her neck and held it in both hands. Her thumbs traced the shape over and over again. *What am I missing?*

"Well, I'll start looking for . . . something. A clue, I guess," Torin said as he headed for the door. "How about I tackle the upstairs and you stay down here?"

Emery nodded absentmindedly, her eyes fixated on the pendant. "Sounds good," she murmured. By the time her stare had finally broken, he was gone. She walked further into her mother's bedroom, eyes scanning the perimeter. "What am I missing?" she repeated, aloud this time, even though there was no one there to answer her question. She squeezed her eyes shut, firmly grasping the pendant in her right hand. "Alpha and Omega."

Emery almost lost her footing as she opened her eyes. Trees upon trees suddenly surrounded her, their thick branches swaying in the breeze. Although the sudden change in scenery was disorienting, she knew exactly where she was. Prescott, Arizona. The same place her mother had taken her and her sister camping when they were little. Giggles erupted and filled the air around her. Emery turned toward the sound. In the distance were two small figures who were chasing each other and squealing with delight.

Two little girls.

Her breath caught as she blinked a few times, trying to make sense of the scene before her. She looked down at her hands, noticing a beautiful two-carat wedding ring adorning her left ring finger. *My mom's wedding ring.*

A young version of herself, approximately five years old, ran toward her, followed by an even younger Alexis.

"Mom!" Alexis screeched. "Emery got hurt!"

Emery gaped at Alexis as she shifted her gaze to herself as a child. Five-year-old-Emery stomped her foot and turned her right leg outward so that her calf was clearly visible. Her mouth crinkled into a pout. "See."

Emery remembered this moment as if it'd happened yesterday. Her mother had taken them camping in Prescott, like she did every fall when the weather finally cooled down. She and her sister had been playing a little ways away from the campsite and she'd accidentally fallen into a patch of poison oak. Luckily, Alexis had stayed back far enough to not be affected with any symptoms, but the leaves had brushed against Emery's right calf and she'd immediately broken out in a rash.

Emery brought herself back to the present moment. What was so strange about this particular situation was that her mother was nowhere in sight—and *she* was wearing her wedding ring. *Somehow I'm in a flashback. And I'm seeing it from my mother's point of view.*

"Not to worry," Emery said, the voice of her mother's and not her own. "Follow me."

This is incredible, she thought to herself as she took the two little girls' hands into her own. She led them over to a dense area of trees and pulled out a strange silver device that resembled a spout. She lightly hammered the spout into the tree, smiling as her younger self and Alexis intently watched the spout turn a deep orange. Shortly after, sap began to flow out of the tree. Emery collected it in a small container and then knelt down so that she was eye-level with the infected area on her younger self. She poured some of the sap onto her hands and smoothed it onto the rash.

Five-year-old Emery breathed a sigh of relief as the sap worked its magic.

"It's zagume," Emery heard herself say, although the voice wasn't her own. "Now this is the really cool part. Watch."

Within a minute, the rash had completely vanished and her normal shade of olive-colored skin returned.

"All better!" Alexis said as she clapped her hands. "Mom fixed Emmy."

"Thanks, mom!" her younger self squealed as she leaned in for a hug.

Before she could say anything, Emery found herself floating away from the campsite, away from her younger self and sister. She extended her hand forward, reaching for them, wanting to stay in the moment. Tears pricked her eyes as the two little girls slowly disappeared before her. Everything faded to black. As she wiped her eyes, a familiar setting came into view. A bed. A nightstand.

I'm back in my mother's bedroom. She took a deep breath as she brought her hands into view. Her knuckles were a ghastly white from clutching the pendant. She let go and watched as the pendant fell to the floor, spinning on its side before falling over completely. *What just happened?*

Emery stumbled backward until her heels hit the edge of the bed. Her body collapsed onto the mattress. Another tear fell from her eye, and she quickly wiped it away. She missed her mother and sister so much. Not knowing where they were or if they were safe was almost too much to bear. Her throat thickened with grief as terrible situation after terrible situation plagued her mind. What if they were still trapped somewhere? What if they were in pain?

Don't think like that. They're fine. Emery inhaled a shaky breath as she sat up, her eyes immediately going to the abandoned pendant lying on the floor.

"How did you do that?" she whispered to the inanimate object. "What were you trying to show me?"

Before she could reflect any further, Torin appeared at the doorway. He must have immediately sensed her distress because he rushed over to her and sat down, his eyes full of questions. His gaze followed hers until it landed on the pendant.

"Did I miss something?" he asked.

Emery shook her head. Try as she might, she couldn't quite make sense of what had just happened. "Yes."

"Do you want to talk about it?"

Emery tilted her head back, eyes trained on the ceiling. "I honestly wouldn't even know where to begin."

"Well, whatever *it* is, it seems to have made you a little distraught."

"You have no idea."

Torin popped up from the bed. "Well, seeing as you don't want to talk about it, let's do something to occupy your thoughts. Let's keep looking for this mystery clue."

Emery gave him a small smile. It was hard not to admire his enthusiasm.

"Okay," she agreed.

As much as she wanted to fill him in on her out-of-body experience, she couldn't seem to find the right words—if any words at all—and until she figured it out herself, how could she explain it to someone else?

With a sigh, Emery brought herself to a standing position and scooped the pendant from the floor. She secured it around her neck, determined not to think about the strange phenomenon for the rest of the day.

But after two hours of searching the remainder of the house and coming up empty-handed, she still couldn't shake the nagging feeling that the flashback hadn't just been a coincidence. It had something to do with her mother, and it had been trying to tell her something. She wasn't sure how to even begin to figure out the answer, but somehow she would.

She had to.

3

Torin watched as Emery drifted into an even deeper sleep on the couch. Her chest rose and fell, eyelids fluttering as her mouth parted to release small breaths. She looked so peaceful, so relaxed—and yet, Torin knew the tranquility wouldn't last long.

They'd been at her house in Arizona for three days now, and every night they'd spent there had started off the same. Emery would drift off to sleep, followed by a period of peace and quiet, followed by night terrors so intense they shook her awake. Her haunting screams were enough to chill him to the bone. The girl had demons—that much he knew—but still he yearned to know more about her.

He lay on a leather recliner, his eyes threatening to close, when his phone buzzed. He glanced at the holoclock on the wall. It was eleven o'clock at night. *Who in the world is calling me so late?* Torin groaned and leaned forward, swiping the phone from the edge of the coffee table. His eyes grew wide as they landed on the number lighting up the screen. He'd recognize that number anywhere.

Someone from 7S Headquarters was calling him.

A rush of energy surged through him as he sprang from the chair and darted into the nearest bedroom, closing the door quietly behind him. He cleared his throat and tested his voice to make sure he didn't sound half-asleep before answering. "Hello?"

A holoimage of a male's shadow appeared as a raspy voice on the other end greeted him. "Mr. Porter."

Torin froze at the familiar voice. It was the Commander. "Sir," was all he could manage.

"Porter, is there a reason why you haven't checked into headquarters this week?"

Although he didn't exactly sound angry, Torin could pick up on a slight edge in the Commander's voice. The question confused him because the last he'd heard of was his suspension from the Seventh Sanctum, so why would he need to check in? "To my knowledge, sir, my suspension hasn't been lifted."

The Commander cleared his throat. "Ah, yes. Well, after that stunt you pulled, we really didn't have much of a choice, now did we?"

He's speaking in past tense. Torin narrowed his eyes, wishing that he could see the Commander's face for clarity. *Oh, please, please give me my job back.* "I don't understand, sir."

The Commander sighed. "You know too much, you've done too much and, to be honest, we could really use you. You have a very special skill set that is hard to come by. As much as I hate to admit it, and despite recent events, somehow you've proven yourself."

Those words were music to his ears. A wide grin stretched across his face. "So, does this mean—?"

"*Sergeant* Porter, you are hereby officially reinstated at the Seventh Sanctum. Your duties as Sergeant will begin this coming Monday . . ."

But Torin had stopped listening after the first sentence. Instead, he was parading around the bedroom pumping his fists in the air. *Sergeant! I've been promoted!*

He'd been a Corporal for years. If he'd known that getting suspended was all it'd take to get promoted, he would have hatched that egg a *long* time ago. *Better late than never.* "Thank you, sir, for this incredible opportunity," he said as evenly as he could. "I will see you on Monday." A small laugh dared to escape, but he quickly covered his mouth to silence his glee.

"Roger that."

There was a moment of silence before the line clicked off. Once he was certain the Commander could no longer hear him, Torin threw his phone onto the bed. He broke out into a sort of jig, his feet moving in a way that only a leprechaun was capable of.

He'd proven himself. He was worthy. Finally.

He rushed back out to the living room where Emery lay fast asleep, faint snores escaping from her lips. He considered waking her to share the good news, then thought better of it. With a quick glance at the holoclock, he realized that she'd been asleep just long enough to where she *should* be having night terrors. But she was still.

Peaceful and calm.

Torin fell onto the recliner and leaned back as far as it would go, sinking into the worn leather headrest. How could he sleep at a time like this? Things were finally looking up. He was here with Emery, he'd gotten his job back, and he'd even been promoted . . . and for breaking the rules, no less.

But still, something in the Commander's voice told him that what he'd just agreed to would be a major undertaking. Something had the Commander, and probably the rest of 7S, on edge, but he was completely out of the loop.

No use worrying about it now. I can worry about it on Monday.

For now, he would focus on the good news, and the look on Emery's face when he told her that same news tomorrow morning. They could both use some after their failed searches at her house.

He glanced over at her again, surprised at how quickly one look at her could quiet his mind. It was almost as if someone entered his brain and flipped a switch—awake one minute, exhausted the next.

That's enough excitement for one day.

His eyelids grew heavy, but he continued to focus on Emery before finally surrendering to a deep sleep. Little did he know, it'd be the first time in days he'd sleep through the night without a single disruption.

4

How could such a miniscule object hold so much value? Victor spun the alpha ring around his pinky finger, the diamonds catching in a faint glimpse of light. He rose slowly, his attention so consumed by the ring that he didn't even notice the oversized leather chair roll toward the other end of the room.

With one last look at the ring, he lifted his gaze to the massive window before him. The view was breathtaking. Rolling hills covered the abounding landscape, thousands of pine trees scattered across the uneven terrain, the sky a magnificent cerulean blue with not a single cloud in sight. Although he hated to admit it, it was times like these that made him wish he hadn't turned out this way. Evil. Deceitful.

A dictator.

Victor pushed his thoughts aside and diverted his attention to the task at hand: the omega pendant. He recalled both his excitement and greed as he'd watched Emery unearth the pendant from the hallway in Dormance. His eyes had practically glazed over at the sight of it.

It was the last piece of the puzzle, and it was the majority of the reason he'd created Dormance instead of leaving half of mankind to waste away in a comatose state. He'd searched and searched the 7S world for both the ring and the pendant to no avail. It made sense that they'd be in the one place he refused to access. He could have retrieved them himself, but that would have meant putting himself in Dormance and relinquishing control of everything, if only for a few brief hours—a risk he hadn't been willing to take.

Fortunately, he'd been able to track Emery's every movement through her microchip. When she'd found the pendant, his heart had swelled with joy, but he'd also felt a stitch of fear. Even though she knew nothing of him— what he looked like, how his voice sounded, what his plans were—he couldn't help but feel like, somehow, she was onto him. And if she wasn't, there was no doubt in his mind that she would be soon.

After watching her day in and day out for almost a year, it was no secret that she was a clever girl, one who was unnervingly fast at piecing things together. Even more frightening was the fact that he'd completely lost tabs on her after the explosion in downtown Chicago. The portal between Dormance and the 7S world had somehow been disconnected and, despite his countless efforts, he hadn't been able to get in contact with Naia to reopen it. He was walking blind in a world where he was *supposed* to have complete control.

Victor reached into his suit pocket, his fingers running over the screen of his phone. He closed his eyes and murmured a plea before attempting to dial Naia yet again. When the call failed, Victor flung his phone at the wall, seething as it sank into the far corner of the room.

Even though Emery had an embedded microchip, the technology was useless. The main control station in Dormance had been disconnected, meaning that his control station in the 7S world wasn't connected to anything. Both stations had to be in an active state in order to work. And with the portal being closed, there was no way he could gain control over the microchips; however, there *was* a way around it. And it involved both the alpha ring and the omega pendant.

Some time ago, he'd learned from the leader of 7S that the ring and the pendant were required to activate both machines in a case such as this. Well, he hadn't so much learned this information as he'd forced it out.

Ten years ago. That's when it'd all started. He'd spent years interviewing and gathering members for his organization, the Federal Commonwealth. Recruits were to be taken by force from their homes due to their knowledge of Alpha One, a simulation program to train soldiers. Despite technology having been halted for years, Alpha One had received private funding, which had allowed it to keep its operations afloat. The technology within Alpha One was truly remarkable, and could give him the power to fulfill his dreams of building a world-class society. The leader of 7S had plenty of inside information about Alpha One, so Victor had ordered he be removed from his home at once to join the Federal Commonwealth.

But getting him to voluntarily offer information was much more difficult than Victor had imagined. At first he'd wondered why, but after doing some digging, he'd discovered that the man's *wife* had been the creator of Alpha One. Going after her proved to be even more difficult, so Victor had stuck with what he had. Plus, threatening the man's family was a much better tactic than trying to force information out of someone who would never give in.

There were a few times where he'd had no choice but to resort to physical means to get answers. In one particular instance, he'd left a nasty scar etched in the man's left cheek. Regardless, he'd gotten the information he needed.

Back then, he was the one in power, the one in complete control. This was the first time in a long time he'd felt helpless.

There has to be another way to get the pendant from her.

Victor paced back and forth across the room, racking his brain for an idea—any idea—that might solve his predicament. He stopped in his tracks as his eyes landed on the bottom drawer of his desk. With a grunt, he knelt down and placed his hand on the drawer's scanner, watching as a green ray of light analyzed his fingerprints.

The drawer immediately popped open, the contents making him shiver with delight. Victor pulled the items out—one self-embedding microchip and one remote with the capability to control up to five hundred microchips. Too bad the remaining microchips were in Theo's office in Dormance. Fortunately, all he needed at the present moment was one. Years ago, he'd stored these items in case of an emergency and, needless to say, this certainly counted as one.

Now for the difficult part. Trying to embed a second microchip into Emery's neck wasn't only highly unlikely, it wasn't at all feasible. He'd have to capture her, remove the old microchip, and implant the new one. Too messy.

He could target one of her close friends—the hacker, perhaps—but that would likely raise suspicion. Plus, he'd be in need of said hacker's assistance at a later time. What use would the boy's mind be if Victor had control of his every thought? No, if he was going to get that pendant, he'd have to be discreet. He'd have to make her trust him. *I have to gain access to her inner circle.*

The idea hit him like a bolt of lightning on a stormy night. There was only one other organization that knew about Dormance besides the Federal Commonwealth.

The Seventh Sanctum.

Once Emery realized she hadn't completely deactivated Dormance, she'd undoubtedly enlist 7S for their help and resources. And what better way to make her trust him than to gain access through the leader of 7S?

5

"How many days has it been?"

Mason looked up from his desk with a somber expression, his lips barely parting as he spoke. "Eight."

Warren raised an eyebrow. "Have you tried calling her?" he asked as he wandered over to the aquarium in the middle of the room. He tapped on the glass, smiling as the colorful fish darted in panicked patterns throughout the water.

The 7S administration had been gracious enough to let both Mason and Warren camp out at headquarters for the time being, seeing as they didn't have anywhere else to go. They couldn't get back into Dormance, nor would they want to, and Mason was wary of teleporting back to Arizona since he'd never done it before. Plus, he wanted to go back to his hometown with Emery—together—but she'd made her intentions perfectly clear when she'd chosen Torin to go with her instead.

Mason had gone back and forth between calling her and not calling her more times than he could count, but every time he picked up the phone, his pride managed to get in the way.

"If she wants to talk, she'll call," Mason replied as he spun his phone on the desk, watching it twirl round and round. Before he could say another word, Warren was standing beside him, his hand halting the phone mid-spin.

"Listen to me. You haven't talked to her in eight days. Not to mention, she's off with another guy doing god knows what. Yeah, she turned you down, but you guys clearly have some kind of connection. You need to call her," he commanded, stuffing the phone in Mason's face.

Mason pushed his friend's hand away, his irritation growing. "It's fine. Like I said, if she wants to talk, she'll call."

Warren ran his fingers through his neatly combed hair. "Man, I'm just looking out for you. Can you honestly say that you're not even the slightest bit concerned?"

Truthfully, Mason *was* concerned. Emery was all he could think about for the past one hundred and ninety-two hours. He constantly wondered where she was, what she was doing, who she was with, why she hadn't called. Or maybe she had called and he'd missed it? He scrolled through his phone again, just to be sure, then sighed.

Nope. Wishful thinking.

It was hard to wrap his head around why she'd picked Torin to join her, someone who, in his opinion, was a complete stranger, especially considering everything he and Emery had been through as of late. He'd almost been *killed* and yet, she'd still flocked to Torin. It didn't make any sense.

"I've been meaning to ask," Warren began as he fidgeted with a button on his shirt, "what do you think of Torin?"

Mason shrugged. "I don't really have an opinion of him," he lied. "Why?"

Warren rolled his eyes. "I guess what I'm really asking is whether or not you think he's harmless."

Mason furrowed his eyebrows. "What exactly are you getting at?"

Warren walked along the outer edge of the desk, his fingers trailing the smooth titanium. "You very well know what I'm getting at. What if Torin isn't who he says he is? What if he's the bad guy?"

"He's not the bad guy," Mason sighed. "Don't fill my head with that garbage. You're better than that."

"Or what if," Warren continued, ignoring his plea, "Torin's fallen for Emery and is trying to win her over?"

Mason shifted in his chair, suddenly feeling uncomfortable. Sure, the thought had occurred to him, but hearing it out loud made it feel like an actual possibility.

"So, I'll ask again. Do you think he likes her?" Warren pressed.

"How would I know? It's not like I'm friends with him—"

"Doesn't matter," Warren interrupted. "Think about it." His expression turned serious. "Do you think he likes her?"

"Of course he likes her," Mason blurted out. "How could he not? How could anyone not?" He slammed his hand on the desk, the coolness of the metal lessening the sting.

Warren jumped at his sudden outburst. The tension between them was palpable, but still, he continued to pry. "So you're telling me that you're just going to stand by and let this happen? You're not going to go after Emery?"

Mason rose from his chair, his hair disheveled, eyes bewildered. He was trying to keep his temper at bay, but Warren was making it difficult. His friend had a tendency to poke and prod until, eventually, no stone was left unturned. Mason decided to cut him off right then and there. "Stop putting these ideas in my head. I've got enough on my plate already."

Warren shook his head, then lowered his voice to a whisper. "These ideas were already there, my friend. I'm just bringing them to the surface."

"Well, I wish you'd stop," Mason snapped. He'd spent so much time over the past week reassuring himself that everything with Emery was fine. Yet here was Warren, unraveling each and every thread of that reassurance.

"You have to do something and you know it."

Mason wrinkled his forehead as he made eye contact. "I know I'll regret asking this, but I'm going to do it anyway." He let out a long sigh. "What would you do if you were in my shoes?"

Warren's eyes gleamed with malicious intent. "Stop him before he takes the one thing that is precious to you. It's time for you to take Torin down."

6

Emery awoke in her old room to the sound of dishes clanking and the smell of coffee brewing downstairs. She rolled out of bed, glancing briefly at the full-length mirror to make sure she wasn't completely unpresentable. Her crimson hair was frizzy and unkempt. She smoothed it down to calm the flyways and fashioned it into a low ponytail. Stifling a yawn, she walked out of her bedroom, shielding her eyes from the bright sunlight beaming through the windows.

She and Torin had been in Arizona for a little over a week and they still hadn't found anything. They'd searched her house inside and out, including the garage, or in this world, the greenhouse, the attic, and the backyard, and yet, they'd still come up empty-handed. She felt just as clueless now as she had when they'd first arrived.

What was even more concerning was that no one had shown up at her house in the time they'd been there. She had no idea where her mom and sister were, let alone how to get ahold of them. She hadn't heard from her best friend, Riley, either, which was strange. It was like everyone from her past was missing.

Like they'd disappeared into thin air.

And even though she was convinced that Dormance was only temporarily deactivated, it was strange that *she* was here, in the real world, and her family wasn't.

Where could they be?

Bile rose in her throat as thoughts of her family and friends trapped, tortured, and dead flooded her mind. Emery knew she needed to get back to Chicago to sort everything out, but something was keeping her from leaving. Maybe it was the hope that her mom, sister, or Riley would burst through the front door and things would go back to the way they once were. Or maybe it was the nagging feeling that she was missing a huge piece of the puzzle and the only way to solve it was to stay. Regardless, her patience was nearing the end of its rope, and she could tell that Torin was starting to feel the same way.

"Morning, sunshine," Torin chirped as he slid a mug of coffee across the kitchen counter. "A dash of cream and two packets of sugar, just the way you like it."

"How thoughtful," Emery replied with a smirk as she tightened her robe and slid onto the barstool. "No name-brand coffee today?"

Torin gestured toward SmartMeal. "Trust me, it is name-brand. I just wanted to add a special touch by pouring it into one of your homemade mugs."

Emery looked down at her mug to examine it more closely. Pink and white ceramic stared back at her with large block letters that spelled out: BEST MOM EVER. It was the mug she'd handcrafted for Mother's Day in second grade.

She knew her mom treasured everything she and her sister had made while they were growing up, from popsicle-stick figurines to paper Christmas ornaments, but she was a little surprised that the mug had been sitting in their kitchen cabinet instead of in storage. A longing smile touched her lips at the memory of her childhood, but the feeling was quickly replaced by a sense of sadness.

Where are they? Why haven't they come home?

She traced the shape of the pendant from the outside of her robe, and that's when an idea hit her. She'd been able to go back in time and see her family in Prescott at the campsite, if only for a brief time. Maybe it was possible to do that again.

She jumped up from her chair, taking her mug of coffee with her. "Be right back," she said as she hurried toward her mom's room.

"Okay," Torin called after her, waving absent-mindedly as he bit into a slice of toast.

Emery shut the door quietly behind her and turned the lock in place. She unclasped the omega pendant from around her neck and held it in both hands like she had before. "Okay, you can do this. You can figure this out."

She took a deep breath and closed her eyes, hoping that it was enough to jumpstart the pendant's . . . abilities. But when she opened her eyes, the same lavender bedspread stared back at her.

Why isn't it working?

Emery closed her eyes again and squeezed them shut as tightly as humanly possible. After waiting a few seconds, she peeked through one eye. Still nothing. Same lavender bedspread.

A wave of uneasiness washed over her. *What am I doing wrong?* She thought back to her first flashback and retraced her steps throughout the room. Feeling stumped, she took a seat on the bed. As she gazed at the pendant, a memory resurfaced. *I said something.*

A small ray of hope illuminated within her. With the pendant tight in her grip, Emery closed her eyes and, in a voice that was barely audible, said what she thought were the magic words. "Alpha and Omega."

She was right. Those were the magic words. Her eyes fluttered open. Once again, she was standing in a place that was immediately recognizable. Pleasanton Beach.

Her family had taken many trips to the quaint beach town in Rhode Island where the days were filled with bicycle rides along the coasts, stops at ice cream parlors, and evening bonfires roasting marshmallows. Emery's favorite part had always been early in the morning when she'd go hunting for seashells with her mother. Pleasanton Beach was known for having rare species of fish, birds, and aquatic life. Emery would pick up any shell she could get her hands on to add to her collection, but her mother seemed particularly interested in one type: a beautiful deep green and fan-shaped shell.

Emery could see her mother and sister down the coast less than half a mile away. Her gaze shifted to the ground, and she noticed her feet were small, the size of children's feet, and adorned with pink jelly sandals. Wavy auburn hair cascaded over her shoulders. There was no question about it. *I'm the kid version of myself.*

Without a moment's hesitation, Emery swiped the nearest seashell from the sand and darted over to where her mother and sister were splashing in the waves. "Mom!" she heard her squeaky non-adult voice call out. "Look what I found!"

Her mother flashed her a bright smile as she scooped Alexis out of the water and placed her on her hip. Her sister squealed with delight. "What'd you find, princess?" her mom asked as she strode toward her.

Emery could feel herself blush. It was strange to hear her mother talk to her with such affection. It dawned on her that she hadn't seen her mother in over six months.

She opened her mouth, desperately wanting to ask the same questions plaguing her mind as of late. *Where are you? When are you coming back? Are you safe?*

Emery swallowed her sadness as she held her hand out for her mother to see. In her palm just so happened to be a fan-shaped seashell in a deep shade of green, the same kind her mother was so fond of.

Her mother let out a small exhale as she set Alexis on the ground, then knelt down so that she was eye-level with Emery. "Did you pick this one out just for me?"

Emery bobbed her head up and down.

"That's my smart girl," Sandra said as she traced the outline of the shell with the tip of her finger. "You know, this is a very special kind of seashell. Do you know why?"

Emery shook her head.

"Well, these are called achioshells and they can only be found on this beach. They also have special powers."

"Really?" Emery asked, her eyes lighting up. "What kind of powers?"

"The kind that make you feel better. The kind that make you happy." She put her hand out so Emery could take the shell back. As she reached out to take it, she realized that her mother and sister weren't as close to her as before. They were slowly fading off into the distance, becoming mere shadows in a distant memory.

"How does it work?" Emery called out, hoping that her mother could hear her. "Please, help me figure this out!"

But her mother just stood there, her sundress dancing in the ocean breeze, hand clasped tightly with her younger sister's. Emery knew the flashback was coming to an end. She closed her eyes, wishing that she could stay. "Please don't make me go back without you," she whispered.

She kept her eyes closed, knowing that the minute she opened them, she'd be back in Arizona, in her mother's room, alone. And sure enough, that's exactly where she found herself the minute her eyelids fluttered open. She looked down at her hands, the omega pendant tight in her grasp. With a sigh, she unwound the necklace from her hands, then clasped it back around her neck. She didn't even notice Torin standing in the doorway.

"Hey," he said, startling her. "I was calling for you, but you weren't answering. Are you okay?"

Emery could feel a wetness on her cheeks, and she quickly wiped it away, hoping he hadn't noticed. "Yeah, I'm fine. Just missing my mom and sister, that's all."

"Do you want to talk about it?"

Emery opened her mouth to respond, but the words wouldn't come. As much as she wanted to tell Torin about the strange powers the omega pendant had, something told her not to do it. Not yet, anyway.

It was almost as if these flashbacks were something that had been designed just for her. It sounded crazy, but until she could figure out what it all meant, she'd have to cope with her delusional thoughts. There was already enough nonsense going on; no need to tell Torin and make things any more confusing than they already were.

"Your coffee's getting cold," Torin said with a small smile as he picked her mug up off the nightstand. "Come on, let's brew you a fresh cup."

Emery nodded reluctantly and pulled herself up from the bed. She followed Torin into the kitchen, the rich scent of hazelnut filling her senses. It was clear that Torin's running in on her in her mother's bedroom had made him uncomfortable because he began to busy himself with random chores, like folding dish towels and scrubbing the interior of the sink as he babbled on about some new attraction in Chicago.

Emery sipped on her coffee, slightly amused at his behavior, but fully aware that the level of awkwardness between them was steadily rising. She'd made things awkward and he didn't know how to react. *Poor guy*. It was then that she realized they'd stayed long enough. Clue or no clue, it was time to go.

"Gather your things, Mr. Porter," she ordered as she rose from the barstool. "I believe you have some people you'd like to introduce me to."

+ + +

Emery hopped off the T-Port behind Torin and followed him to the luminous building that was 7S Headquarters. Just as they were about to approach the gigantic double doors, Torin abruptly veered off to the left and entered a different building entirely. Emery quickly changed direction and followed suit, her eyes catching the holosign perched right above the building.

It read R3.

Her curiosity piqued, she followed Torin into the establishment, and holy smokes, was it a sight to be seen. On one side of the room were walls alive with holoimages of crashing waves and palm trees, white sandy beaches, and fragments of seashells covering the ground. The walls on the opposite side showcased holoimages of bonsai trees and peaceful zen gardens. The further she moved into the building, the more she could smell the salty air and physically *feel* the mist from the ocean waves on her face. Her mind and body relaxed almost immediately. She took a mental snapshot of the view before closing her eyes. If she were being honest, it was the first time in months she'd felt completely and utterly relaxed.

The clearing of a throat interrupted her peaceful state of mind. Her eyes shot open to find Torin standing directly in front of her. A dot on each one of his temples blinked from white to blue and back again. In his hands were an additional two dots, just like his. He extended his hands out to her, dots blinking, and without saying a word, she nodded. Emery kept her focus on his aquamarine eyes as he secured the circular devices onto her temples.

Almost immediately, the sound of waves crashing onto the shore and seagulls flying overhead filled her senses. She closed her eyes briefly, but when she opened them, Torin was no longer in front of her. No one was. She was completely by herself, standing on a sandy shore with the waves rolling up onto her feet.

It was so peaceful. So serene.

Emery took a seat on the ground and kicked her legs out in front of her. Her feet were adorned in gladiator sandals that she hadn't been wearing when she'd walked into R3, and a vibrant orange and pink sundress fluttered around her legs. It was the most comfortable thing she'd worn since . . . well, since she could remember.

She leaned back on her elbows to get the perfect view of a cloudless summer sky. Oxygen filled her lungs and nose, making its way through every vein in her body. She smiled at the feeling. Not only did she feel calm and relaxed, she felt *happy*. The minute Torin had placed those dots on her temples, she'd traveled to her happy place, where everything felt right and nothing could go wrong.

After a few minutes of deep breathing and meditation, the beautiful scene surrounding her began to fade. Slowly, shadows of people started to appear, and so did the walls with the holoimages. Not wanting to head back to the real world just yet, she gently pressed the devices on her temples, hoping that they would let her stay and give her a little more time at her sanctuary, but they didn't. *How cruel.*

"You were in there for a long time," a voice from behind her said. Startled, she whirled around to find Torin sitting in a holochair. "You must have had a lot of anxiety built up. Feel better?"

Emery sighed as she took a seat in the chair across from him. "Of course I have a lot of anxiety built up. Don't you?"

Torin's lips slid into a smile. "Apparently not as much as you."

"That was amazing. I wish I could go back . . ." She hesitated, realizing she didn't quite understand what she'd just experienced. "So, what was that exactly? And what is this place?"

Torin cocked his head toward the entrance. "R3. Any guesses for what it stands for?"

Emery shrugged. "No. All I know is that I could do that every single day. I felt so . . . happy."

"That's sort of the point. Relax, refresh, rejuvenate—that's what R3 stands for." He leaned forward in his chair and propped his elbows onto the table. "It's a place people can go to feel happy. To rid them of their anxiety. To make them feel at peace again." He made an exploding motion with his hands as if he'd just performed the greatest magic trick in the history of the world. "Pretty neat, huh?"

"Yeah, it's amazing," Emery said with a laugh. "I have to ask though, are doctors okay with this? It seems like this would take away a lot of their business."

"What a random concern." He raised an eyebrow. "The answer is yes and no. It's actually a treatment a lot of doctors recommend to their patients."

"In Dormance, doctors would just prescribe us a pill and require that we come back once a week," she said half-jokingly, even though it was wholly the truth.

"This is better than loading people up with drugs and chemicals, don't you think?" He blushed as if he'd said too much.

"Well, of course it is." Emery shifted in her seat, wondering why he suddenly seemed so defensive. "I just wish I could have stayed there longer, that's all."

"That's why there's a time limit," Torin explained, his expression darkening. "Just like any drug that makes you feel good, too much can be a bad thing and create its own set of complications. Which is why one hour a day is the maximum. Just think, if people stayed in there all the time, they'd never come out. They'd never face reality."

"Too much of anything is never a good thing," Emery agreed with a nod. "How long was I in there for?"

Torin grinned. "The full hour."

"Are you serious?" Emery asked with wide eyes. "I felt like I was in there for *maybe* ten minutes."

"Ever heard the expression, 'Time flies when you're having fun'?"

She rolled her eyes. "Of course I have."

"Same principle," he said with a shrug. "Time also flies when you're happy."

Emery considered this before asking her next question. "So why did we come here instead of going straight to headquarters?"

Torin hesitated, his eyes flitting from her to his hands and back again. "You have to understand, I just got my job back at 7S. I haven't seen my colleagues in a while and I was feeling a little . . . anxious."

When he didn't continue, Emery asked something she immediately wished she could take back. "Is everything okay, Torin? I mean, are you happy?"

She didn't mean to catch him off-guard, but there he was, breaking eye contact and adjusting his posture. He cleared his throat before answering. "I'm not unhappy, just . . . complacent, I suppose."

Emery knew she shouldn't pry, but she felt concerned. "What does that mean?"

Torin shook his head as he rose to his feet. "Nothing for you to worry about. I'm fine," he said unconvincingly. "Come on, let's get these introductions over with."

As he headed for the door, Emery felt a pang of despair for her friend. Normally, their conversations were light-hearted and rarely serious. But the one that had just taken place was probably one of the deepest moments she'd ever shared with Torin. As soon as they'd started to venture into unchartered waters, he'd suddenly tied up the sails and steered the ship into a different direction. Emery made a mental note to keep chipping away at his exterior to discover what was really underneath all those layers.

She made sure to stay back a few paces as she followed Torin into headquarters, her combat boots gliding along the slick floor. As tempted as she was to ask questions regarding who she was about to meet, she didn't want to pry more than she already had.

Her thoughts were interrupted as her phone buzzed. A deep pit formed in her stomach when she realized who was calling. It was Mason.

She'd been so wrapped up in looking for answers at her house that she'd completely forgotten about him. He was probably worried or angry or a combination of the two. *I'll call him back in a little,* she thought as she declined the call and stuffed the phone back into her pocket.

She'd see Mason soon enough. There were other things that needed tending to first, like meeting 7S leadership and not making a complete fool of herself.

Emery watched as Torin pressed the button for the service elevator. "It baffles me that elevators still exist when you have T-Ports stationed all over the country."

Torin smirked. "Trust me, it's not what you think."

"Really?" She followed him into the metal box. "Because it sure looks like an elevator to me."

"It's a cover." He winked. "You'll see." He pressed the button for floor seven, slid his phone into his back pocket, then turned to face her. "Have you talked to Naia yet?"

Since they'd been together every second of every day for the past week, she wasn't sure what had prompted this question. He very well knew that the answer was no. She shook her head silently, her eyes dropping to the floor.

"You don't want to wait too long—"

"First things first," Emery interrupted, hoping to avoid a lecture. The last thing she needed right now was anyone interfering with the jumbled mess that had recently become her life.

A loud ding echoed in the empty space as the elevator doors opened. Emery scanned her surroundings as she stepped out of the elevator behind Torin. The soft padding of their footsteps was the only audible sound in the vast chamber. Technology-ridden desks sat at the far end of the room, but there were no chairs, no people, to accompany them. She narrowed her eyes as she tried to make out the other shapes in the lackluster lighting. If they hadn't just come from outside, she wouldn't have been able to tell that it was still daylight.

Darkness surrounded them as they moved forward, although she couldn't figure out what, if anything, they were walking toward. Except for the abandoned desks, the room was empty and had only one exit—the elevator that had just slammed shut behind them.

They reached a slate-colored wall that appeared to be made of stone, but when Torin laid his hand on it, the stone morphed into a sort of transparent layer. Lining the other side were rows and rows of bright white walls, all parallel to one another.

"Whoa," Emery breathed as she stepped forward to place her hand against the wall.

Torin smacked her hand down. Immediately after, he murmured, "Sorry," his eyes apologetic for the unnecessary force. "You haven't been coded into the system yet, so it won't recognize you. The system would think we were intruders, or that you were holding me against my will, and we wouldn't be able to gain access."

"Gain access to what?" As soon as the words left her mouth, she felt the ground tremble beneath her.

A green ray of light scanned Torin's fingerprints and retinas, then scanned his entire body. Once he was confirmed for entry, the ground split out at all sides, leaving them standing atop what remained—a disc-shaped piece of stone. A clear bubble made out of flexible glass emerged from all sides of the disc, encapsulating them with no way out.

Emery grabbed onto the sleeve of Torin's shirt, her balance wavering as the disc lowered six feet into the ground. It positioned itself onto a track and locked into place, then began to move forward at a terrifying speed.

Blindingly white walls whizzed by her as the disc moved forward along the track. Small blue lights blinked at random intervals along each wall in horizontal lines. Emery narrowed her eyes, realizing that the wall wasn't actually a wall at all—it was completely made up of white wires. The blue lights indicated where one wire ended and where another began. She gazed in awe at the wire-filled walls as the disc slinked along the track.

The ride was smoother than expected and, after three short minutes, came to a stop in front of a platform and yet another wall. With the touch of a button, Torin disconnected the dome overhead and jumped off the disc. He held his hand out to Emery for support. She graciously took it as she leapt over the gap to where he was standing. Torin positioned himself in front of the wall, just like he had moments before, and waited for the scanner to identify him.

Emery almost expected the ground beneath her to tremble again, but was relieved when a door within the wall popped open instead. "If that isn't maximum security, I don't know what is," she joked as Torin ushered her inside. She was about to crack another joke, but the sight before her stopped her in her tracks.

The room they'd just entered was no more than twenty feet in length, but the height seemed to go on for miles. She gazed up at the seemingly endless ceiling, her mouth agape. It was a building within a building, and it reminded her of a shopping mall, except it was taller than it was wide.

Much taller.

Numerous floors with countless offices lined the halls, people bustling to and fro. Emery focused her attention on one of the workers, a disheveled young man clad in all white, as he made his way through a crowd on the fourth floor. Her eyes followed him until, suddenly, he disappeared from sight.

"Where did he go?" she asked in a panicked tone, straining her eyes as she searched for the man. Her gaze followed Torin's arm, his finger pointing to the seventh floor.

"Oh, right. Teleportation," she laughed, her heartbeat slowing. "You probably think I'm an idiot."

Torin smiled. "On the contrary. You've been introduced to a lot of new things in a short period of time. At least you figured it out on your own without me having to tell you." He nudged her in the side, his face lit with childish joy, then grabbed her by the hand and pulled her over to another platform. "As I'm sure you've already guessed, there are multiple T-Ports on every floor. That's how everyone gets from point A to point B."

This platform was smaller than the others, and Emery quickly calculated that it was probably meant for just one person. Her legs brushed against Torin's in the small space, their chests almost touching. His breath warmed her face and she could have sworn she felt his heartbeat speed up.

Emery lowered her eyes, her cheeks blushing a rosy shade of pink. She didn't know why, but she couldn't help feeling drawn to him. *He's just a friend*, she reminded herself, casting her attraction aside.

"The Commander's Office," Torin instructed. He grabbed her hand, squeezing it tight as the familiar tingling sensation took hold. First her feet, then her legs, chest, and arms. She closed her eyes as the cool gust of wind whirred them up to the seventh floor.

When she opened her eyes, they were standing in front of a massive oak door. The sight jarred her for a moment—she was so used to seeing metal everywhere that wood seemed like an outdated resource.

Torin knocked on the door three times, his hand heavy against the small silver knocker. A young man, no older than twenty-five, opened it with a stern expression on his face. "May I help you?"

Torin pulled out his identification badge. "We're here to see the Commander."

"Do you have an appointment?" the man drawled, his words dripping with apathy.

He reminds me of Theo.

Instantly, Emery flashed back to Theo's fallen body in the middle of downtown Chicago, gun in hand, barrel smoking. She quickly broke eye contact with the man and gazed down at her boots instead. A tear threatened to fall from her eye, but she shook her head and squeezed her eyes shut, forcing the image to dissipate. As much as she despised Theo for leading her under false pretenses, she despised herself even more for what she'd succumbed to.

For killing him.

Torin's firm tone interrupted her thoughts. "No, we don't have an appointment," he said to the man. "Please inform the Commander that *Sergeant* Porter has requested to see him."

The man eyed them suspiciously, then turned away. With his back facing them, he muttered something into his headset, nodded, and turned back around to face them. With reluctance, and a look of humiliation, he mumbled, "Right this way."

Emery and Torin followed him down a long corridor until they reached an enormous desk covered in electronics. Phones, tablets, and other devices Emery had never seen before were scattered all over the surface. A burly man stood facing a window, looking out at a breathtaking view of pine trees and snow. She wondered how this was possible, seeing as the entire building was enclosed with no way to view the outside, but her question was quickly answered as the landscape shifted from pine trees and snow to sand and sunshine.

They were holoimages, just like the ones she'd seen at R3.

"Those are beautiful hologrounds," Torin said, breaking the silence. "Are they photos of real places?"

The hologround shifted to an image of a cabin. A *very* familiar cabin.

Before the Commander could answer, Emery let out a gasp. She'd seen those photos before. Her mother had *taken* those photos.

That was her family's cabin. In Northern Arizona.

The man turned around to face them, his eyes landing on Torin. "Yes, my wife—"

"—took them," Emery finished, her eyes wide. Even though she hadn't seen him since she was a child, her father looked exactly as he had in the photo she'd uncovered in her room in Dormance, right before she'd left for Darden.

Before her entire life had changed.

She rushed over and opened her arms for a hug, unable to believe her eyes. "Oh my god. I can't believe this. Is it really you?"

Her father's expression matched hers and, for a moment, everything seemed to move in slow motion. The Commander met her warm embrace, rocking her back and forth in his arms, both of their eyes squeezed tightly shut. Emery wished more than anything that she could stay in that moment a little while longer, but she forced herself to unwrap her arms, her gaze drifting upward to her father's unshaven face. "This is surreal. I thought I'd never see you again. And if I head correctly, *you're* the Commander of the Seventh Sanctum?"

Her father nodded, his eyes glistening in the office light. "This is more than I ever could have asked for." He gave a grateful smile to Torin, who was standing there looking bewildered and confused. He turned his attention back to his daughter. "I'm so happy that you're safe. I've been so worried about you." He pulled her in once more for a hug. "I didn't know when I would see you again."

Emery whirled around to face Torin, her eyes brimming with tears. "It's my dad!"

Torin leaned into the nearest chair, his mouth agape. "Well, what are the chances of that?"

"Slim to none," the Commander answered as he walked toward him. "I'm guessing you had no idea that Emery was my daughter. But still, I want to thank you for bringing her to me, Sergeant." He stuck his right hand out, clasping Torin's in a firm handshake.

"You're correct, sir. I can't take any of the credit. This is merely a coincidence. I honestly had no idea."

The Commander smiled. "Regardless, you're both here. Can I get you anything? Are you hungry?"

"I could go for some food," Emery responded as she bounced over to where Torin was standing. "Do you guys have those SmartMeal things here?"

"We sure do. Let me show you around. We can end the tour at the dining hall." They walked to the front of the office as Emery filled her father in on everything he'd missed over the last ten years.

Torin walked awkwardly in front of them until he reached a nearby platform. "See you down there." He waved, and Emery watched as his body materialized and disappeared right before her eyes.

She glanced over the railing as a figure emerged from the platform on the first floor. "That is still so mind-boggling." She turned to face her father, her smile fading as soon as she saw the serious expression on his face.

"I have something important I need to tell you," he urged in a hushed tone.

Emery frowned. The confident, strong man she'd just witnessed moments ago had disappeared. "What is it, dad? What's wrong?"

He grimaced. "As much as I need to talk to you, we can't do it here. It's not safe."

Emery tried to hide her smile. "Come on. What could be safer than this place?" she teased, gesturing at the massive structure surrounding them.

Her father wiped one hand over his brow. "I'll find a time and location and send it to you." He pulled his phone out of his pocket to emphasize his point.

Her face fell. "Dad, you're starting to worry me. Is everything okay?"

"It will be." He forced a smile. "Now, you head on down there. I'll meet you in just a few minutes."

Without another question, although she had many, Emery did as she was told and stepped onto the platform. "Floor One," she commanded, watching as her father's face vanished.

Moments later, she arrived on the first floor, her eyes level with Torin's. "I almost thought you'd changed your minds," he joked as he helped her off of the platform. "Did I miss anything?"

Emery opened her mouth to respond, but decided against it. It was probably best to keep her mouth shut for now . . . if only she knew what it was her father was hiding.

7

Torin ambled behind Emery and the Commander, his eyes glued to the backs of their heads. He couldn't help but smile every time Emery turned to look at her father—the crinkle at the corners of her eyes, the way she threw her head back as she laughed. Happiness radiated from every inch of her being. It was hard to believe he'd been working for Emery's *father* all this time; but what was even more difficult to wrap his head around was just how intimidated he'd felt every time he'd been in the Commander's presence. It all seemed so trivial now. As much as he hated to admit it, the Commander wasn't the evil monster he'd made him out to be. He'd just been a lonely old man. But not any longer.

How suddenly that had changed.

Torin continued to follow them, his mind wandering off to Emery-land. Normally she wasn't one to open up, but lately she'd confided in him more than he ever could have hoped.

Without warning, his thoughts flitted to Mason. Poor Mason, who was probably agitated somewhere, wondering why the girl he'd fallen for had chosen him, of all people, to accompany her on this seemingly never-ending journey. Come to think of it, Torin didn't actually know *why* she'd chosen him over Mason—but he wasn't complaining. He was happy she'd chosen him. Absolutely *delighted*, in fact.

The Commander continued the tour of the Seventh Sanctum headquarters, gesturing to the many rooms surrounding them as he explained what each one was for. While Emery seemed engaged throughout the tour, she seemed even more interested in reconnecting with her father. Who could blame her? She hadn't seen the man in over ten years.

As happy as he was for Emery, Torin couldn't help but feel a pang of sorrow. The sight of them together reminded him of his foster family. A memory resurfaced, one of the few in which his parents had actually been in town for.

His tenth birthday.

It was a crisp autumn day in the suburbs of Illinois and the leaves had just begun to fall from the trees. He was outside in the backyard, playing in the piles, laughing as they crunched underneath his boots. His mother called out to him, beckoning for him to come inside. With one last leap from the pile, he ran toward the white Victorian-style house onto the front porch, whizzing past the navy-blue shutters and through the front door. There, standing in the doorway, were his mother and father, each with one hand underneath a plate, atop of which sat a two-tier chocolate birthday cake. Ten flames flickered in the breeze.

"Happy birthday to you. Happy birthday to you . . ."

The words were music to his ears. At the orphanage, birthday celebrations had been rare. With such limited supplies, the administration had to make do. At most, the children received a sticker of a smiley face, a parachute man, or a plastic bazooka, but that was it.

No cake. No candles. No birthday song.

Torin reveled in the moment as his foster parents finished singing. His mother knelt down so that she was eye-level with him. "Make a wish, sweetie, and blow out the candles."

With a deep inhale, the scent of chocolate and raspberries infiltrating his senses, Torin made his wish. *I wish for my parents to never leave me.* He closed his eyes and exhaled.

His dad clapped his hands together, then ran into the kitchen to grab plates and silverware.

Torin opened his eyes and gazed up at his mother. Her eyes were calm, a sea of blue staring back at him.

"Did you wish for something good?" she asked.

He nodded his head. "I wished for—"

"Shhh." She brought her index finger to his mouth, then smiled. "Don't tell anybody your wish. If you tell, then it won't come true."

How wrong she'd been. Whether he told someone or not didn't matter because the next day, his parents boarded the plane that would come crashing down and kill them both.

Torin shook his head in the hope that he'd also shake the memory far, far away. It was no secret that his past had left him with some pent-up issues. Being passed around from orphanage to orphanage hadn't helped either. For almost his whole life, he'd wondered if feeling the way he did was normal. It was hard to know who he was when he didn't even know where he came from. He'd had a few identity crises throughout his life, and he couldn't help but feel that another one was fast approaching.

His gaze landed once again on Emery. In a sense, she was a lot like him. She hadn't seen her father in over ten years and, for most of her life, she'd probably felt that a part of her had been missing, too. In a sad, twisted way, they were just two people, trying to discover their true identities and where they belonged in this crazy, damaged world.

His concentration broke as Emery looked over at him, the corners of her mouth turning upward, but the smile didn't reach her eyes. And yet, he smiled back.

He knew who she was. She was strong, beautiful, and confident, even though she sometimes hid behind a stubborn, shelled exterior. She was smart and witty, but above all, she was compassionate. The things she'd done the past year undoubtedly haunted her, this he knew from the many night terrors he'd witnessed over many sleepless nights.

He knew her better than she knew herself.

He sighed as she broke eye contact and turned her attention back to her father. Yep, he had her all figured out. Now, if only it were that easy to figure himself out. It was the same question that had plagued him his entire childhood and most of his adult life; the same words that kept him awake at night.

Who am I?

8

Victor pressed his back against the wall as inconspicuously as possible on the third floor of 7S Headquarters. For such a secure building, it was frightening how simple it'd been to sneak in behind Emery and her hacker friend. The lag time in the closing of the doors after each security scan was almost comical.

He'd made sure to keep a safe distance so as to not raise any suspicion. There was, however, a brief moment of panic as he'd watched the pair disappear inside an encapsulated dome that took off along a set of tracks at a startlingly high speed. Fortunately, he'd located a concealed side entrance and, even though it'd taken him twice as long to arrive, he'd eventually made it to the undisclosed headquarters.

From the third floor, Victor's eyes followed Emery, her friend, and the Commander, who had just appeared atop a T-Port on the first floor, drinks in hand. If she hadn't already, Victor knew that she'd figure out sooner or later that her father was the Commander in Chief of the Seventh Sanctum. He could only hope that the Commander hadn't revealed any information that might lead his daughter to start piecing things together.

Victor grimaced as Emery leaned in to give her father a hug, then proceeded to leave, her friend following close behind. No whispering. No panicked expressions. So far, it looked like both he and his agenda were in the clear.

The Commander stepped onto the nearest platform, then teleported up to the seventh floor. Victor knew that a man of his caliber didn't go home at night—he had sleeping quarters in his office. He checked his watch, his eyes widening at the late hour. The hallways had thinned out considerably with each passing minute.

When the hall was finally empty, Victor emerged from his discreet hiding place and headed for the nearest platform. He quietly ordered the machine to transport him to the seventh floor. His surroundings whirred around him and, after a split second, he found himself a few feet away from the Commander's office. He tiptoed over to the massive door, then flattened his body against the wall.

And now, I wait.

Fifteen minutes ticked by until the door opened, where a young man wearing a headset emerged. Every muscle in Victor's body tensed as he prepared his next move. Just as the man lifted his hand in front of the scanner to lock the door, Victor leapt from the shadows, taking the sides of the man's face in his hands. With one swift movement, he cracked the man's neck, grinning as the limp body fell to the floor. He knelt down to check for a pulse, his ears on high alert for any sounds coming from the office or the hallway, but there was only silence. No pulse. He lifted the man's hand to the scanner, smirking as the light blinked green. *Access granted.*

With caution, he pushed the door open. His eyes darted across the room, frantically browsing for any sign of movement. When he was sure it was empty, he pulled the man's lifeless body inside and laid him parallel to the wall, then closed the door gently behind him. He blinked a few times as he slid along the wall, pausing for a moment so his eyes could adjust to the darkness of the room. Around the corner, he could see a sliver of light.

A shadow flickered from underneath the door as padded footsteps made their way across the room. Floorboards creaked, followed by the rustling of blankets as the Commander situated himself in his bed. Victor smiled and silently commended himself as the lights switched off. *Impeccable timing, as always.*

For twenty minutes, he kept his eyes glued to the door until faint snores filled the inside of the bedchamber. His fingers slid into his coat pocket as he pulled out the self-embedding microchip and remote. Making as little noise as possible, he tiptoed across the office to the door that led to the Commander's bedroom. The doorknob creaked loudly as it turned. He turned the light on the remote to the lowest setting and peeked inside, the glow landing on the Commander as his body rose and fell with each breath.

He was fast asleep.

Slinking over to the side of the bed, Victor placed the microchip on the pillow next to the Commander's head, then retrieved the preprogrammed code and activated the embedding sequence. The microchip beeped quietly while legs, like those of a spider, protruded from the center. The spider-like device crawled over to the Commander's neck, positioning itself lightly underneath his hairline. The Commander flinched in his sleep as the legs latched onto his pores, then dissipated as it sunk under the skin's surface. The words EMBEDMENT COMPLETE flashed across the screen of the remote.

"Long time, no see, *Commander*. I'll see you in the morning," Victor snickered as he patted him on the shoulder, "as your new Secretary of Defense."

9

Emery awoke to her phone buzzing noisily on the coffee table next to her. She sat up from the couch in Torin's living room, rubbing her eyes as she tried to focus on the blurry letters. Torin had insisted that she sleep in the bedroom, but her stubborn nature had overridden his plea.

She quickly gave up trying to figure out who was calling and answered the phone with a half-yawn. "Hello?"

"Emery?" Mason's voice echoed on the other end of the line.

She stopped mid-yawn. *Crap*. "Hey, um, sorry that I haven't had a chance to call you back—"

"I'm honestly shocked that you answered," Mason interrupted. "I know you've been gallivanting around town with Torin. I bet that's where you are right now. Isn't it?"

Emery rolled her eyes at the hostility in his voice. Before answering, she took a minute to survey her surroundings. The curtains were drawn just enough so that only a sliver of light shone through, and there were take-out containers littering the coffee table. Her stomach gurgled at the thought of the wonton soup and chicken fried rice she'd indulged in last night. It had tasted good at the time, but in hindsight, she probably should have gone with something less filling, like a salad. *But who orders salads from Chinese restaurants?*

She reached for her water bottle and took a swig, contemplating how to respond to Mason's hissy-fit. "Yes, I'm at Torin's. I crashed here last night and I slept on the couch. No big deal."

"Actually, it kind of is a big deal, especially when you haven't spoken to me in weeks."

Emery sighed. "Don't be so dramatic. It hasn't been that long."

"It's been almost fourteen days."

At this, she leaned back into the couch, her chest rising as she inhaled. Had it really been fourteen days? Where had the time gone? Surely it hadn't been almost two weeks since she'd spoken to him. Then again, anything was in the realm of possibility these days.

"Listen Mason, I'm really sorry. I've just had a lot on my mind and a lot that I've needed to sort through. I hope you can understand where I'm coming from—" The static on the other end of the line interrupted her apology. She furrowed her eyebrows, trying to make sense of the noise. "Wait, where are you?"

"Both Warren and I have been staying at 7S Headquarters," he responded. "I really didn't have anywhere else to go."

A pang of guilt hit her in the stomach, although she didn't know why. It wasn't like Mason was her boyfriend. *Neither is Torin. And yet, I invited him to come with me.* "I'll fill you in on everything," she promised, her choices replaying over and over again in her head. "How about tomorrow? We'll go grab a bite to eat or something."

There was a long moment of silence before he spoke. "Yeah. I'd like that."

"I'll call you later tonight and we'll set something up."

Mason's voice caught. "I look forward to it."

As she was about to say goodbye, the line clicked. She brought the phone away from her ear and looked down at the screen. The words CALL ENDED stared her in the face. She brushed her annoyance aside as she stood up from the couch, but before she could organize her thoughts, a figure emerged from the bedroom.

"You're up before me," Torin observed as he made his way into the kitchen. "That's a first."

"Har-har," she responded as she plopped onto a barstool.

"Did you sleep well?" He quickly ordered breakfast from SmartMeal, then slid a plate of toast and a glass of cold milk across the counter.

"Better than usual," she responded as she took a bite. "That couch is surprisingly comfortable."

"Happy to hear it," he said with a grin. "So, what do we have planned for the day?" He maneuvered his way around the kitchen counter and sat down on the barstool next to her.

She didn't know how to tell him that she needed to meet with her father . . . in private. It felt weird keeping things from Torin, especially when he'd been so supportive and helpful the past couple of weeks. It felt wrong to not include him, but her father had made it clear that he'd wanted to speak with her alone. She checked her phone again, hoping that her father had sent a message regarding when and where to meet, but her inbox was empty.

I need to talk to him. Today.

"If it's alright, I'm going to head over to 7S this morning, maybe grab coffee with my dad before he gets too busy." Before Torin could invite himself, she continued, "It'd be nice to have some father-daughter time."

Torin struggled to hide the disappointment on his face. "Okay, yeah. That sounds nice," he said, then quickly added, "for you and your dad. Not for me." He blushed. "If you don't mind, I might tag along—not to coffee," he reemphasized, "but to headquarters. I have a few things I need to check on."

"Fine by me," Emery responded as she munched on her last bit of toast. It was easy to forget that Torin actually worked for the Seventh Sanctum . . . for her father. *How bizarre.* "I can be ready in twenty minutes. Does that work for you?"

He smirked, his boyish nature returning. "Make it fifteen."

She smiled, happy to see his disappointment hadn't lasted long. "You've got yourself a deal."

It actually ended up being a good thing Torin had wanted to tag along because Emery still didn't have access to many of the corridors within 7S Headquarters. She gazed up at his head of shaggy brown hair as the moving disc came to a stop. The ride into the interior of the building felt longer than she remembered, or maybe it was just the anticipation of finally finding out her father's secret. She fidgeted with the zipper on her jacket, her nerves getting the better of her.

When they arrived at the ground floor, Torin leaned in to give her a hug, which was a little out of character, even for him. "Have fun with your dad," he said hurriedly as he split off to run his errands.

"Bye!" Emery called after him.

His figure faded into a mere shadow, then disappeared altogether in the morning rush hour.

She sighed as she stepped onto another platform, and directed it to take her to the seventh floor. The ride was brief, as per usual, but as she stepped off the T-Port, the hair on the back of her neck rose. It made sense that the seventh floor was never as crowded as the other hallways, seeing as it was the Commander—ahem, *her father's*—floor, but today, something felt different.

Something was . . . off.

Her throat thickened as she strode over to the oak door that led to her father's office. She gently tapped the silver knocker three times, expecting the young male assistant to greet her like last time. Instead an older gentleman, whose hair was the color of a crisp winter's snow, greeted her. His face was rugged and wrinkled, like a leather bag that had sat out in the desert sun for far too long. His eyes were a deep grey, the irises so large and so whole, that they almost swallowed his eyes.

She felt herself shiver as a cool draft swept across the back of her neck. "Hello. I'm here to see the Commander." Her words came out far quieter than she'd anticipated.

The old man grinned, almost demonically, before gesturing for her to step inside. "Do come in."

At that moment, all Emery wanted to do was turn around and run. This man, whoever he was, looked at her as if he'd known her his whole life. Another chill ran down her spine.

Who is he?

Cautiously, she stepped inside the doorway and started down the hall toward her father's office, the man's footsteps in time with her own. She picked up the pace as she approached her father's desk. He stood at the window with his back to her, in the same position as last time, watching the holographic images switch from one scene to the next. She cleared her throat, hoping to catch his attention. When that didn't work, she inched a few steps closer. "Hey, dad. Sorry I'm a little late."

He turned toward her almost robotically, his eyes empty and devoid of emotion. She stepped backward in shock, unable to pinpoint why he looked so . . . different. When she reached out to grab his arm, he briskly stepped to the side, his eyes locked on the man standing behind her.

"It's okay," he answered, his focus unwavering. "Emery, I'd like to introduce you to my new Secretary of Defense, Chief Victor Novak."

The only word she heard was *new*.

The white-haired man walked toward her, extending his hand for a firm handshake. Emery hesitated ever so slightly before meeting his grip with equal force. She looked him up and down as nonchalantly as she could. She wasn't sure why, but she didn't like him. The way he slithered over to her reminded her of a serpent just before the moment it attacks its prey. With that image etched into her mind, she quickly released his hand, then rubbed her palm along the side of her pants.

"This must be your daughter," Chief Novak drawled. "Emery, is it?" As her name rolled off his tongue, she noticed his eyes went straight to the pendant clasped around her neck. He stared at it for a minute too long, admiring it as if he wanted it for himself.

Goosebumps rose all over her arms and legs. *Stay calm. Don't freak out.* "If you could please excuse us for a moment, I need to speak to my father in private." Her eyes narrowed as she directed a harsh stare at Victor.

"Take your time," he murmured. "I'll be at the front. Commander, please don't forget that our next appointment is at 0900." He slinked toward the front door out of sight. When she was sure he was out of earshot, Emery turned back toward her father. "What a strange old man. Please tell me that he was appointed *by the people* and that you didn't hire him."

Her father moved away from the window, then sat down in his plush leather desk chair. "Correct. Victor was appointed by the people. He's great company and he's damn good at what he does."

His movements were less robotic now, and Emery relaxed a little. "So, I never heard back from you, which had me a little worried since you told me you had something important to tell me." She paused, waiting for a flicker of recognition to cross his face, but there was nothing. "You said you'd send me a time and place to meet you, remember?"

Still nothing. Not even an ounce of recognition.

Don't panic.

"So, what is it you wanted to talk about?"

Her father stared at her like a statue, not a single muscle moving throughout his entire body.

"Dad?"

He was still for a few more seconds before finally picking some strange gadget up from his desk. "Consider it taken care of. Chief Novak has it handled."

Her stomach twisted into knots. "Chief Novak has what handled?" she pressed. *Why is he brushing off our conversation like it's nothing?* She knew she hadn't mistaken the tone of his voice the other night. There was something serious he'd wanted to share with her. Something urgent.

"I said to consider it taken care of. If we're finished here, I need to head to my next appointment." He stood up from his desk and gathered his tablet and a few other indiscernible gizmos. "I'll see you soon." He gave her a hasty nod, then walked to the front where Chief Novak was standing just out of earshot.

"It was nice to meet you," Victor called out to her as he opened the door for the Commander. "I'm sure we'll bump into each other again soon."

Emery crossed her arms defiantly, her lips pursed. "We certainly will," she murmured. *"Chief"*.

10

She's onto me.

Victor walked briskly alongside the Commander, amazed at how well his self-made technology worked. It was normal to expect a kink or two in the controlling mechanism, but that wasn't the case this time around. The Commander was easier to control than ever.

When Victor had overheard Emery asking her father about his "secret", he'd controlled the response with the touch of a button. Surprisingly, hearing the question come out of her mouth had put his mind at ease—it meant that her father hadn't told her yet, which in turn meant she still didn't know. And as long as Victor had him under his control, there was no way she'd ever find out.

A wicked smile touched his lips. *Everything's still on track. No disruptions. No setbacks.*

He continued to walk alongside the Commander until they reached the end of the hallway. Victor hit a combination of buttons on his remote to power down his robotic boss, waiting for his eyes to close and his head to lower, then shoved him into the nearest utility closet.

He leaned against the cool metal wall, his mind reeling back to the past twenty minutes, to his first real sighting of the omega pendant. It was just as beautiful as he'd imagined—a sterling silver horseshoe lined with dozens of tiny emeralds. He smiled as he recalled the way the emeralds had bounced off the light. It had taken everything in him to not reach out and tear the necklace from the girl's throat; but his temptation had dissipated as his eyes had traveled from the pendant to Emery's face. *That look.*

It'd been a look of complete and utter distrust, but there had been something else there as well. Something Victor knew quite well.

Loathing.

It was the same look he'd received at school as a young boy. The same look all the teachers and counselors had given him. The same look his parents had given him. The experiences during his childhood hadn't even been close to smooth sailing, quite the opposite in fact. His father had been a mechanic, his mother an alcoholic. Instead of raising him while his father was away at work for ten hours a day, his mother would drink herself into oblivion. Whiskey, tequila, scotch. Full cabinets one night, and empty the next. It was a vicious cycle.

She was never abusive, but Victor wouldn't have put it past her. She was either blacked out or too disoriented during her waking hours to pay him any attention. Sadly, this wasn't even close to the tip of the iceberg—no, that had come when his father had been diagnosed with a rare case of lymphoma. At the time, only two percent of the world had been diagnosed.

There hadn't been, and still wasn't, a cure.

The treatment had been brutal on his father. Multiple rounds of chemotherapy with no health insurance and the woman he loved drinking herself off a cliff. Eventually, his father had become so weak that he was unable to fulfill his duties at work. Working on cars called for too much physical exertion that his father just couldn't keep up with. In the end, Victor could only watch, as a helpless young boy, as his father and what remained of their family unit disintegrated right before his very eyes.

Helpless.

It was the one emotion he never cared to feel again. The one emotion that filled him with rage every time an image of his frail, dying father drifted across his mind—which was less and less often, but it still happened every now and again. Back then, he'd been powerless to do anything and so, every move he made, every decision he took would lead him to never feel that way again. It simply wasn't allowed.

Once his father had passed, Victor's need for control became stronger than ever. To have the ability to fix things and make everything right—to do the very thing he couldn't do in his past. This was all that mattered, and Alpha One was his answer. More than that, it was his calling.

He sighed as he tried to push those thoughts far from his mind, but it was no use. A flood of anger suddenly washed over him as he reached into his inner coat pocket and pulled out the alpha ring. He'd been so close to getting what he'd wanted until Emery's friend—*Torin, was it?*—had come along. He'd had everything all mapped out, down to the last detail. Thankfully, Theo had done most of the dirty work; all that was left to do was reap the rewards.

Full control was just within his reach, right beneath his fingertips.

Of course, they'd experienced more than a few setbacks, but that was to be expected. Strangely enough, though, those setbacks all seemed to revolve around one particular person.

Emery.

And who had been in charge of Emery's training? Her overall candidacy? *Naia.* His eyes narrowed at the possibility of being two-timed by such a young and naïve girl. While he'd never been particularly fond of Naia, he was almost certain that she wouldn't do anything stupid—

like putting his entire operation at risk. She was one of his own, an integral part of his team.

Wasn't she?

Doubt clouded his mind as fear settled in. *What if I've been played? What if all of this is her fault?* He allowed the fear to stay only for a moment before shaking the thought far from his mind.

He had to stay focused on the task at hand. His plan to make Emery trust him wasn't going as smoothly as he'd wanted. He'd hoped that having her father, someone she trusted and admired, introduce the two of them would give him some ground to stand on, but it seemed that she'd seen right through the deception.

"It'll just take some time," Victor muttered to himself. He turned the alpha ring over in his palm, the diamonds glimmering in the overhead light. He placed the ring back into his pocket and stepped onto the nearest platform, his mind swirling with images of the omega pendant and the alpha ring united for the very first time.

11

Mason's heart fluttered as Emery strolled out of the giant sliding doors of 7S Headquarters. His knees ached from sitting on the same bench for the past hour in the hopes that he'd eventually catch a glimpse of her. He'd expected Torin to be with her, but, surprisingly, she was alone.

He jogged over to her, instantly realizing that she was pretty shaken up over something, albeit he didn't know what. "Hey," he breathed, as he lightly placed his hand on her shoulder.

She looked up from the ground, her eyes brimming with tears. "If you're here to scold me, I'd prefer if you didn't."

He smiled and wiped a tear from her cheek. "Hey, I'm not here to scold you. What's wrong, Em? You can tell me."

She shook her head and fell onto the ground, even though the bench was just a few feet away.

"Really? The bench is literally right there."

When she didn't move, he leaned down and scooped her up, her legs dangling over the sides of his arms. "Come on, it'll be ten times more comfortable than the ground." He carried her over to the bench he'd previously occupied and set her gently on the surface. She buried her face in her hands. With each passing second, her breathing grew heavier and heavier.

"Emery," he soothed, unsure as to why she was so worked up, "please tell me what's wrong."

"You're going to think I'm crazy," she managed through uneven breaths.

"You know me, I love crazy," he urged. "Bring on the crazy. Even if I wanted to, you know I couldn't go anywhere."

At this, she looked up at him and laughed, the smile stretching all the way to the corners of her eyes. It was the first real smile he'd seen in ages and the closest he'd felt to her since their initial meet-and-greet one summer ago. He latched onto that smile, onto that feeling, hoping that it'd carry him through whatever was about to come out of her mouth.

"Where do I even begin?" She let out another shaky breath as her expression turned serious. "Remember a couple of weeks ago, when I told you that we were fighting for the wrong side? That Theo wasn't who he said he was?"

Mason nodded. "I remember."

"Well, it turns out the Federal Commonwealth is the one who wants to control all of mankind. That's why Theo was on the rooftop with the lethargum—you know, that green fog that killed everyone. We launched the sanaré and it brought everyone back to life, except for Theo and the eleven other members of the FCW, because I'd sliced the wires connecting their pods to the mainframe just moments earlier." She sighed as if telling him all of this was physically exhausting her. "The Seventh Sanctum soldiers have been the good guys all along. They've been trying to stop the Federal Commonwealth from wiping out mankind."

Mason bit his lip as he absorbed the information. As hard as it was to believe, it helped clarify a few things—like why they *had* to have embedded microchips, and why the whole thing was such a blasted secret, *and* why Theo would shoot him when they were supposedly on the same team. "How did you find all of this out?"

"Torin," her face lit up as she spoke his name, "he was the one who told me. He reached out to me in the middle of training—"

A surge of jealousy raged through him. "Wait, you were talking to Torin the whole time during training?"

A shade of scarlet crept across her cheeks. "Well, not the whole time—"

"You were talking to him and you decided it'd be best not to share it with anyone?" His words came out far harsher than he'd intended. "Not even me?"

Emery's face paled. "Who could I share it with, Mason? I had no idea you were a part of the initiative and vice versa. *And*, even if I had known and had decided to tell you, my memory would have been wiped clean and we wouldn't even be having this conversation right now." She crossed her arms defiantly. "My hands were tied."

"You could have told me once we'd been deployed, right?"

"Well, maybe, but—"

"So, why didn't you?" he pressed.

Emery stared at him, her mouth agape. She struggled to find her words. "That was such a whirlwind and you know it. I had no idea we were going to be deployed right after we received our final judgments. Hell, I didn't even know that you were a part of the initiative until you materialized right in front of me in the middle of downtown Chicago!"

Mason bolted upright from the bench. *Control yourself.* He began to pace back and forth, hoping that the movement would calm him down—he couldn't allow his temper to get the best of him. Not right now.

He took a deep breath before saying, "You're right. I'm sorry." He sat back down on the bench and ran a hand through his golden hair. "We shouldn't focus on that. We need to move past it." As the words left his mouth, he knew that he was trying to convince himself more so than her. "So tell me what's happened since we've been here."

Her mouth pressed into a grim line. "Long story short, I need to retrieve something from Dormance. Somehow, that world is still active, but I can't seem to find a way back in."

Mason scratched his head, trying to follow her train of thought. "Retrieve something? What did you leave there?"

"A present from my mom." She kicked a small rock with the toe of her boot. The pebble catapulted through the air like a bomb from a cannon. "It's a fish-shaped ring, like an alpha symbol, embedded with tiny diamonds."

Mason raised an eyebrow. "That sounds like a nice keepsake and all, but do you really want to risk going back there for it?" She shot him a look that made him quickly add, "I mean, do you really need it?"

"I do. The symbol on that ring and this one," she pulled out the omega pendant for him to see, "were both on the mainframe in Dormance."

"The same mainframe you thought you'd deactivated?"

She nodded as she tucked the pendant back underneath her shirt. "There were indentations in the control station, like it was a sign to place the ring and the pendant there. Almost like keys or something. But I don't know what it is the ring and pendant do. They could unlock something. Blow up something. Who knows?" She looked at him hopefully, her irises engulfed in a haze of grey.

"Well, if your mom is the one who gave you the alpha ring, then she ought to be able to help, right?"

A sigh escaped from her lips. "That's why I spent the past two weeks at my house. I'd hoped that she and my sister would come home, but they never did. I searched the house for clues, for a sign, for anything—but there was nothing." Her head dropped as she kicked another pebble into the air. "I failed."

"Don't talk like that. You didn't fail. Just think of it as a minor bump in the road," he said as optimistically as he could. "Remember, behind every dark cloud is a ray of sunlight waiting to shine through."

A hint of a smile touched her lips. "I suppose you're right. Thanks."

"No problem. So, what else did I miss?" he teased in hopes of lightening the mood.

Emery cocked her head. "Well, my dad's the Commander in Chief of the Seventh Sanctum."

"Seriously? This whole time?"

"Yep."

"And you didn't know?"

"Nope. The last time I saw him was when I was six years old. I really thought I'd never see him again." She bit her lower lip as a flash of pain darted across her eyes. "It's strange though. He said he wanted to talk to me, but when I went to visit him this morning, he waved it off like it was nothing."

"Maybe it was nothing."

Emery shrugged. "I'm not so sure."

The pieces were finally coming together. "Are you thinking that what he wanted to tell you has something to do with the ring your mom gave you?"

"I don't know," she sighed. "And now I'm not sure I ever will."

Those last words hung thick in the air. They sat in silence for a few minutes. As much as Mason wanted to help Emery and give his full, undivided attention to her problems, there was only one person repeatedly infiltrating his thoughts: Torin.

Maybe Torin has something to do with this.

Just as he opened his mouth to express his concern, Emery rose from the bench. "I should get going," she said as she threw her bag over her shoulder. "Thanks for listening and for talking me through everything."

Mason swallowed, his mouth going dry. He smiled in an attempt to mask his disappointment. *Don't let her go. Not yet.* He cleared his throat as she turned to leave. "Hey, Em?"

She turned back around, her face filled with mixed emotions. Loneliness? Hope? Confusion? He couldn't tell. "I don't want you to be alone right now. Not after everything you just told me."

Emery cast her eyes toward the ground.

"Let's go do something. Grab a bite. See a movie," he offered. "Let me be there for you."

At this, Emery's head popped up. "You always have been."

A swell of warmth filled his chest like a rolling tide on a warm summer day.

She took a step closer to him and grabbed his hand, her fingers looping with his. "Come on, I know a great Italian place that's just around the corner."

Relief set in as Mason followed her to the restaurant. She was okay. They were *okay*. He held onto the feeling for as long as he could, trying to be present in that moment for as long as possible. If experience was any indicator, their time together was bound to be cut short far too soon.

12

It was eleven o'clock in the evening and Emery was wide awake. She'd been trying to doze off for at least an hour, but the thoughts in her head wouldn't keep quiet. She gently brought herself upright and tapped her feet on the floor.

Faint snoring caught her attention. Mason was fast asleep on the couch, his arm thrown over the back and his leg dangling off the end. She scooted to the edge of the bed and stood up, her knees cracking in the process. She froze, hoping that the sound wouldn't disturb him, or worse, wake him up, but his soft snoring continued.

After their conversation earlier that day, Mason had insisted that they spend the evening together. The Seventh Sanctum had provided both Mason and Warren with accommodations at the hotel that was connected to headquarters. The guilt piled up every time she thought about the way she'd ditched him over the past two weeks, so she'd obliged to his request in hopes that spending some time together would eradicate any tension or negative feelings he had toward her. She knew that opening up to him would be a step in the right direction, so that's exactly what she'd done. She'd told him about everything that had happened last year, from starting school at Darden, to Theo calling her and inviting her to join the Alpha Drive, to her interactions with Torin in the 7S world. For the most part, her opening up seemed to have eased the tension, and they were almost back to how they'd been before, but it was clear they still had a long way to go. She could tell that Mason was still upset she'd invited Torin to go back home with her instead of him. For some strange reason, he seemed to *want* to hold onto it with no sign of ever letting go. Getting back to the place they were at before wasn't impossible; it would just take time.

Even though her day had been consumed by Mason, Emery found that Torin was never far from her mind. The one thing Torin provided her with that Mason didn't was a feeling of security. While this had been evident for a while, her feelings had been solidified just a few hours prior.

She and Mason had just finished a meal at an Italian restaurant and as they were exiting the establishment, a man had suddenly grabbed her arm and pulled her toward him. Caught completely off-guard, Emery had yelped as she was pulled toward the stranger, her eyes honing in on

Mason's panicked expression. Instead of coming after her immediately, Mason had just *stood* there.

Frozen. In shock.

Fortunately, she knew how to take care of herself, and she'd broken away from the man's grip. The owner of the restaurant had gotten involved shortly thereafter and had escorted the persecutor off the premises. They'd left the restaurant in silence and it was then that all she could think about was Torin and what he would have done in that situation. He wouldn't have hesitated, not even for a second. He would have gone after that man with fire in his eyes and more rage than a bull seeing red.

Then again, Torin did have his faults. For starters, he was incredibly closed off and a difficult egg to crack. Every time she gazed into those aquamarine eyes, she couldn't help but feel like there were oceans between them—a separation so vast and so deep, they'd never be able to land on the same shore.

In the end, what it really came down to was *trust*. Mason had been her friend long before Torin and yet, there was just something about Torin she was naturally drawn to.

But what exactly? Was it the air of mystery surrounding him? Or something more surface-level, like the fact that he was from a completely different world than she was?

The more she got to know Torin, the more she felt as though she'd known him forever—yet there was still so much he seemed to keep hidden. And that right there was the fatal attraction.

Can Torin be trusted?

True, he'd singlehandedly helped her defeat the Federal Commonwealth, and he hadn't lied to her as of yet, at least not that she was aware of. To her, Torin felt like a *partner*, a trustworthy companion. *So why am I doubting him?*

An idea came to her so quickly that it almost felt like she'd gotten the wind knocked out of her. She pulled the omega pendant out from underneath her shirt, admiring the emeralds embedded within the shape. She ran her thumb on the outer edge of the pendant. "I need answers," she murmured. "Alpha and Omega." She took a deep breath and closed her eyes. Silence surrounded her for a long moment. Then, a familiar voice filled the airwaves.

Naia's voice.

Emery's eyes shot open. She gasped as she took in the scene before her. She was in Dormance. Or was she? It was hard to tell.

Naia sat at her desk, busily typing away onto the control station. "Hey, Naia," Emery said with a wave. When Naia didn't turn around, she took a step forward and tried again. Still nothing.

She walked to the side of the chair and leaned directly into Naia's view, but her eyes seemed to look straight through her, like she wasn't there.

Like she was invisible.

In my previous flashbacks, they could see me. Why can't Naia see me?

Emery noticed that on one of the monitors was her picture, on another, lines and lines of text and dates. *My candidate file.* She watched as Naia pulled a highly recognizable item, a small sphere, from her pocket, then released a drawer holding Emery's black training clothes. *That's the device I used to launch the sanaré.*

Naia sifted through the pants and shirt, checking the pockets and turning them inside out. Emery's eyes landed on the combat boots she'd grown to love. She continued to watch Naia closely when a deafening clatter sounded, making both of them jump. With a panicked expression, Naia dropped the device into one of the boots, then quickly stood up and circled the table as Theo strode into the room.

The sight of him made Emery want to gag and cry at the same time. Feelings of betrayal rose up in her throat. She gulped them down as a heavy cloud of guilt took its place. Even though Theo was the enemy, she couldn't deny the fact that she'd had a soft spot for him. In the beginning, he was someone she'd trusted wholeheartedly.

How foolish she'd been.

Theo's sultry tone interrupted her thoughts. "Ready?" he asked, the question directed at Naia.

"Let's go," Naia said ever so calmly.

Within a single blink, the scene before her faded into black. *Okay, well that could have been a fluke. Maybe she just dropped it in my boot because she had nowhere else to put it.*

Surrounded by darkness, Emery fiddled with the pendant. A few seconds passed. Her heart pounded as she remained engulfed in a shadowed world. *Why haven't I been taken back to reality yet?*

Suddenly, black turned to technicolor, which then turned to white, as if she'd just hurtled through space in a time-traveling machine. She blinked a few times, trying to focus on the setting before her. It wasn't even the slightest bit familiar. From the looks of things, it appeared she was still in Dormance in the underground quarters, but in a room she hadn't ventured into.

Naia sat at an oversized desk, murmuring to herself, with her head in her hands. Emery called out her name, just to confirm that she was still in her invisible state. When Naia didn't answer, she hastily approached the desk, her eyes focusing on the monitors. Naia lifted her head from the surface, mumbling to herself as she adjusted the images on the monitor. Swiping left and right, the holographic images appeared, then disappeared. Her search for the right one seemed insurmountable. A deep blue filled the screen, and she could hear Naia muttering under her breath. Something about placement?

Whatever that means.

After five minutes of Naia murmuring and nothing of significance happening, Emery turned to walk to the back of the room. "The capsule isn't enough," Naia said aloud, although no one else was in the room. "It needs to be meaningful or else she won't get it."

Slowly, Emery turned around, her interest piqued. "I won't get what?" Emery asked, even though she knew Naia couldn't hear her. "Show me *something*. Anything." She folded her arms, waiting patiently for whatever it was Naia was about to do.

And then the unexpected happened.

An image of her lifeless mother, underwater, appeared on the screen. Emery's jaw went slack as she witnessed Naia orchestrate the placement of her mother and the capsule. The orange capsule from her first training session.

It was her after all.

Naia was on 7S's side the whole time. But what had she been trying to tell her? And why include her mother? Before Emery could come to a conclusion, the scene in front of her went black.

Her breath caught as the next location came into focus. Brick lined the walls with no doors on either side. A gigantic steel door, the very one Rhea had been standing in front of, loomed before her. Teasing her. Taunting her.

Emery squeezed her eyes shut, as tightly as she could, hoping that the images would fall away. A door creaked. She gave in, her curiosity getting the better of her, and opened her eyes one at a time. She jogged over to the door, shuddering as she walked by the pods within the enormous control room, forcing herself to look up at the ceiling. Kneeling underneath a sign labeled SANARÉ was Naia, her fingers shaking as she fidgeted with the dial to the safe. An orange capsule sat next to her, the contents glowing like a beacon of light.

It really was her. Naia was the one helping me and guiding me all this time.

The realization was enough to make her stumble over her own two feet. Their last connection played over and over again in her head. *I should have just listened to her. Why did I hang up?*

With a heavy heart, Emery closed her eyes, trying to convince herself that it was an honest mistake. And it truly had been. So why did she feel like such a failure?

Upon opening her eyes, she found herself standing in a green haze in the middle of downtown Chicago. She looked down at her now blood-stained hands. A gun clicked into place. She turned around slowly, knowing that she was about to face her worst nightmare. Again.

No. I can't do this again.

Theo's eyes met hers. Bile rose in her throat.

Do something.

"I understand!" she shouted into the universe. "Please take me out of this flashback and back to reality! I understand, I really do!" She dropped to her knees, covering her head with her hands. "Take me back, take me back," she murmured to herself.

Emery wasn't sure how long she remained in her cradle-like position, but when she brought herself upright, she was both surprised and relieved to find herself back in the hotel room, where everything was just as she'd left it. Shaken, she walked over to the bathroom and closed the door softly behind her.

Gripping the edge of the sink, she turned the faucet on, watching the smooth stream of water as it circled down the drain. Her hands dove under the steady flow, cool water splashing onto her face. She reached for a towel and dried her hands, then patted her face dry.

Her gaze met the distraught figure in the mirror. Dirt and ash matted her once rich auburn hair, and the dark circles under her eyes had shifted from a faint purple to a deep violet.

How did I get here?

She sighed, breaking eye contact with the pitiful image before her. Her knees buckled as she collapsed onto the frigid tile, the towel falling to the floor.

How did I let this happen?

Her head fell into her hands, fingers drumming against her temples in rhythm with her accelerating heartbeat. She focused on slowing her breathing.

One Mississippi. Two Mississippi. Three.

With a deep inhale, Emery hoped that she could somehow overcome the feeling of dread that had followed her for weeks. All she wanted was to go home. To see her mom and her sister again. To know that they were safe.

She clasped her right hand over her chest, eyes closing as her heart calmed, the thud low and deep.

That was the thing about shattered hearts. Even in the midst of tragedy, they begin to heal.

13

Mason stirred as a faint vibration sounded throughout the hotel room. With a groan, he sat up and rubbed his eyes, the numbers 5:30 glowing from the holographic clock on the wall in front of him. Emery was fast asleep on the bed, her chest rising and falling with each breath. He groggily stood up, then tiptoed over to the source of the noise and grabbed the buzzing phone from the nightstand.

He wasn't one to snoop, but the name on the screen caught him by surprise. *Why is Naia messaging Emery?* The buzzing stopped as Mason unlocked her phone, then clicked on the message. It read: *You should have mentioned that the portal was closed. I've reopened it—please call me when you can.*

He reread the message, feeling dumbfounded. *Naia doesn't know that the Alpha Drive initiative went down in shambles? Does that mean she thinks Theo is still alive?* He briefly considered sending Naia a message to fill her in on everything that had happened, but then Emery would know he'd invaded her privacy. They'd made so much progress the night before. *I can't risk that.*

Without a second thought, Mason deleted the message and threw a pair of jeans on over his boxer shorts. His eyes searched the room until he spotted the crystal dials gleaming in the dim morning light. He swiped them from the table, dropped them into his pockets, and slipped quietly out of the hotel room.

There was only one person who could help him hack into the Dormance mainframe. *Torin.* Mason shuddered at the thought. Did he really have to befriend the guy that had made his life a living hell the past month?

He shook his head. *That's Warren talking. Get out of my head.*

Still, it was the truth, and there was no denying that the truth stung. Even though he'd been somewhat disoriented when he'd been brought back to Torin's apartment after the lethargum attack, he knew that Torin's apartment was right around the corner from headquarters.

Mason stood outside the hotel under the awning, tilting his head from side to side as he contemplated his choices. Was there any possible way he could do this without Torin? A number of options swirled through his head, but they all ended in failure. Rejection. Humiliation.

He threw his head back as he realized what he had to do. *Let's just hope Torin's awake at this ungodly hour.*

With the crystal dials still in hand, Mason marched past the Chicago Bean and turned down Main Street, eyeing the building numbers that lined the brick walls. Shadows danced to and fro, and there were a few times he wasn't so sure his eyes were playing tricks on him.

In the distance, a rustling sound caught his attention, followed by the soft padding of footsteps. Even though he wasn't doing anything wrong, Mason felt his chest tighten. He briefly considered turning around and running back to the hotel, but what good would that do?

His throat thickened with fear as the footsteps drew nearer. He surveyed the area until his eyes landed on a fire escape, and he quickly recalled how Emery had used it the day she and Torin had left together.

The thought alone was enough to make him cringe.

In his best effort to shove his jealousy aside, he jumped up and grabbed hold of the metal railing, then pulled himself upward until more than half of his body was on the landing. He climbed the rungs one by one until he reached a window that had been slightly cracked, the curtains billowing in the cool morning breeze. He peered inside to make sure he was at the right place.

"Torin?" he called out as he poked his head further into the open window. It was dangerous and downright stupid to intrude and startle someone as tech-savvy as Torin this early in the morning. If he wanted robots and other gadgets attacking him, yelling "Intruder, intruder!"

then sure. Obviously, that was the exact *opposite* of what Mason wanted.

A dark figure emerged from one of the rooms. Something glinted in the figure's hand, and Mason immediately recognized that it was a pistol.

Great.

The figure raised the weapon directly at him, to which Mason quickly reacted by ducking behind the windowsill. "Whoa, man! It's me, Mason." He raised his hands in the air, open-palmed in surrender. "Don't shoot."

"Mason?" Torin whispered. "What the hell are you doing here?"

Mason lifted his head just high enough so that his eyes were the only part of his body visible above the windowsill. "I'll explain in a minute, once you lower your gun." He peered over his shoulder, his forehead taut with tension. "I think someone was following me."

"I highly doubt that. Don't be paranoid," Torin grunted as he placed the weapon onto the chair next to him. He walked over to where Mason was crouching and helped pull him through the window. "Just checking, but you do realize that it's almost six o'clock in the morning, right?"

"I know. I'm sorry," Mason said as he stood up, "but I need your help." He could sense the hesitation just by the way Torin adjusted his stance.

"I'm listening."

Mason gritted his teeth, then forced a half smile. "Emery filled me in on everything and how she thinks she left something valuable behind in Dormance."

Torin eyed him warily. "Like what?"

"The alpha ring."

"Right, the one her mom gave her," Torin confirmed.

Mason's fists clenched at his sides. This was the second thing tonight to catch him off-guard. He hadn't expected Emery to spill *everything* to a complete stranger, which, in his eyes, Torin was, but then again, she'd done a lot of things lately that he never would have expected. He was starting to feel like he didn't know her at all. "That's the one," he stated, trying to hide the contempt in his voice. "Anyway, I think the portal has been reopened somehow. I need you to send me back there so I can find that ring."

Torin narrowed his eyes. "What makes you think the portal's been reopened?"

Mason shrugged. "Just a hunch."

Torin rolled his eyes. "Well, I'm not really into following hunches, especially when there's no basis for said hunch. Not to mention, Emery would probably rather go back and look for it on her own. Have you told her about this?"

Mason pointed to his wrist. "Like you said, it's six o'clock in the morning. This idea came to me just twenty minutes ago."

"Well, maybe we should call her—"

"No," Mason said forcefully. He shook his head. "Please. Let me do this for her. She's already done so much and last night was the first time she's opened up to me in ages." He sighed, his eyes growing heavy. "I just want to show her that I can help—that she can count on me."

Torin stared at him, his harsh gaze fading. "Alright. Let me see what I can do." He pulled out his phone, his fingers flying on the holokeys, as if he hadn't just woken up and rolled out of bed.

Mason waited patiently as a couple of minutes passed. Then five. Then ten. "Any luck?"

Silence filled the space between them as Torin eyed his phone like a madman. A green light shone from the screen, illuminating the crazy, wide-eyed grin spreading across his face. "I can't believe I'm about to say this, but I'm in."

"Really?"

Torin shot him a stern look. "Do you want to do this or not?"

Mason nodded as he rushed to activate the crystal dials, watching as they became one with his skin. Torin handed him an earpiece and instructed him to wear it. Before Mason could ask what it was for, Torin said, "I'm guessing you'll want your hands free while searching for the ring."

Mason hesitated for a moment, and then obliged. He was probably right. Torin typed a few more things into the system, then gave him a thumbs-up. The last words he heard were "Good luck" before a crisp gust of air whisked him away.

Mason landed with a thud in the common room, his knees buckling beneath him. Try as he might to stay upright, gravity worked against him. He collapsed face first onto the ground, his head almost colliding with the edge of a table. "Ow," he groaned as he rolled himself onto his back.

"Graceful," Torin said with a small laugh. "Are you okay?"

Mason's stomach turned as he pulled himself upward. "I hate teleportation," he grumbled as he dusted himself off, then slowly walked over toward the main door.

"Wait," Torin whispered. "See that holographic device on the coffee table? Grab it, otherwise, the minute you step out of the common room, we'll lose connection."

Mason rolled his eyes, but did as he was told. Torin bossing him around wasn't exactly what he'd had in mind when he'd invited him on this rendezvous.

Deep breaths. Don't let him get to you.

Mason made his way down the hallway to the elevator shaft and stepped inside. As the elevator began its ascent to the ground level of Rosemary Hall, Mason could feel his heart pounding in his chest.

"Did you make it okay?" Torin's voice buzzed through the earpiece.

"Yeah. I'm walking through the lobby of Rosemary Hall right now." He paused as a thought occurred to him. "Shouldn't you be able to see me?"

"The connection is less than ideal. I'm sure I'll be able to in a few minutes."

Mason continued to walk through the dilapidated dorm, taking notice of the lobby's complete stillness. The air felt stale, like there hadn't been movement in weeks. There wasn't a soul in sight. It honestly wouldn't have been surprising to see a tumbleweed drift across the ground, save for the fact that he was indoors. *Must be because it's summer*, he thought as he pushed his feelings of unease aside.

Much to his surprise, the door that led to the stairwell was unlocked. He climbed the three flights of stairs, then trudged down the hallway until he reached Emery's old room, number 319. Mason pressed down on the door handle, but it wouldn't budge. "It's locked," he said as he jiggled the handle.

"I got you," Torin's voice assured.

At least he's good for something. Mason waited for his cue, then pressed down on the door handle again, smiling as it opened with ease. "You're like the master hacker of all time," he whispered as he entered the room.

"They don't call me MacPorter for nothing."

"MacPorter? What does that even mean?"

Torin laughed. "You know, like MacGyver, that illustrious computer hacker who was wanted by the FBI five years ago? He basically hacked his identity out of existence. He's like a ghost."

Mason couldn't help but laugh. "I guess I need to update my subscription to Cyberthief Weekly."

Torin snorted. "We're not all bad, you know."

Mason tried to hide his smile. It was in that moment he realized that maybe he'd been wrong about Torin. Maybe Warren had pushed too far into his head. There was no way Torin could be the bad guy. The bad guy wouldn't help Mason do something like this.

Torin interrupted his thoughts. "So, what do you see? Any sign of the alpha ring?"

Mason knew that cleanliness was a huge deal to Emery, and with just one look at the room, he could tell that something wasn't quite right. A picture of her and her sister lay facedown on her desk and random articles of clothing—socks, t-shirts, and undergarments—were strewn about near the closet door. It almost looked like the place had been raided. "I wish you could see this."

"See what?"

"The place looks like it's been ransacked. I think someone was definitely here."

Torin sighed. "Great. Not the news I wanted to hear. You should look anyway though."

"Already one step ahead of you," Mason said as he opened one of Emery's desk drawers. Nothing. He moved onto the next drawer and the next, rifling through the contents with increasing frustration. Still nothing.

His eye caught a jewelry box sitting atop the bathroom sink, but all it contained were earrings and necklaces. No rings. More specifically, no alpha ring.

He tried the closet next, immediately regretting his decision as he dug through countless bins, pulling out shoes, purses, hats, and the like, until he noticed a small silk pouch in the back of one of the drawers. It felt light, but he opened the drawstrings just to be sure.

Crap. It was empty.

"I'm not having much luck over here," he said into the earpiece as he left the closet and walked over to the bed. He slid his hand under the thin, flimsy mattress, hoping that maybe the ring was tucked under it somewhere. "I checked the desk and bathroom drawers and every inch of her closet. I did find this silk pouch, but—"

"That's it," Torin interrupted. "She said she kept it in a silk drawstring pouch. Is it pink?"

Mason's eyes lit up as he examined the pouch again. "Yeah, but it's empty."

Torin let out a long sigh. "I think this is exactly what Emery was afraid of, that someone would take it, and that they'd beat her, and us, to it."

"But who would take it?" Mason asked as he scratched his head. "What is so damn special about this ring?"

"I don't know," Torin contemplated, "but I have a feeling we're about to find out."

14

Later that morning, Torin sat alone in his living room, replaying the conversation with Mason over and over again in his head. They'd both been disappointed when they'd discovered nothing in the silk pouch Mason had found in Emery's room.

His fingers grazed his phone. A hologram of the time appeared, glowing angrily at him. Eight thirty in the morning. *I should call her.*

Mason's plea echoed in his head: *I just want to show her that I can help—that she can count on me.* Torin rolled his eyes at the thought. Although Mason had never given him a reason to dislike him, there seemed to be an unspoken hatred between them. Perhaps it was because of Emery.

Or . . .

Who was he kidding, of course it was because of Emery. She'd invited Torin to go with her back to Arizona on her grand adventure and, in turn, had left Mason behind. Of course he was bitter. Why wouldn't he be?

If he were in Mason's shoes, he'd feel the same way. But Mason had been nicer to him this time around. Perhaps it was just because he'd needed help, but deep down, Torin hoped that it was because Mason might be coming around.

Regardless, Emery needs to know what happened. But what would he say? And how could he tell her without getting Mason involved?

Mason wanted to do all of this on his own, sans any help, yet he'd dragged Torin into his mess without even a second thought. He hated keeping things from Emery, especially when it involved something that could potentially change everything.

And this was *definitely* one of those things.

It was right then and there that he made his decision. He pulled up Emery's contact information and waited for the lines to connect, but she didn't pick up.

Okay, let's try Plan B.

Finding her location was almost easier than making a phone call itself: Hotel Bradbury. Torin glanced over at the T-Port on the other side of the room. He could teleport and get there in a flash. Or he could walk a couple of blocks, get some fresh air, and give Emery more time to wake up. *Decisions, decisions.* He looked back and forth between the T-Port and the door one last time.

Walking it is.

+ + +

The streets were awfully silent for a weekday in downtown Chicago. Torin pulled his hood over his head, his shaggy chestnut hair flaring out at the sides. A crisp breeze swept through the city as the sun began its ascent on the horizon. He made a swift right turn on Main Street, nodding his head at the Chicago Bean as he walked past it. He ran through a couple different variations of what he could say to Emery.

Approach #1: Tell her that *he'd* been the one (liar!) to discover that the portal was now open.

Approach #2: Tell her that someone in 7S had discovered the portal was now open. (Liar! Again.)

Approach #3: Tell her the truth about Mason's hunch and plea for help (in which he'd assisted somewhat against his will) in helping him get back to Dormance to search for the alpha ring.

And then he'd press her to reach out to Naia so they could finally get this show on the road. What could possibly go wrong?

The third option was looking to be the most promising. And if she said no? Or that she wasn't ready to reach out to Naia just yet? Maybe then he'd go with option one or two. And when she saw right through those lies, the truth would finally come out, which left him with approach numero très. *Stop overthinking it.*

As Torin approached Hotel Bradbury, yet another thought occurred to him, this one more unsettling. *Why is Emery staying at a hotel?*

Knots twisted and churned throughout his stomach. He pulled out his phone and scrolled until he landed on the one person he hoped would be far away from the hotel: Mason.

Torin stared at the screen as he waited for Mason's coordinates to appear. He took a deep breath as the dots made their way onto his screen. A blue dot hovered right over his own red one. Torin bowed his head and let out a long exhale. *He's here.*

There was no question about it. Emery and Mason had reconciled their differences and were most likely staying together at Hotel Bradbury. A wave of jealousy washed over him, followed by a surprising sliver of hope. *Maybe I'm jumping to conclusions.*

Torin pulled up Emery's coordinates one last time, just to be sure. Her purple dot hovered over Mason's blue one and his red one. Torin stared at the screen a moment longer, willing the dot to move, to disappear, to be anywhere but here. But it remained.

She was here. With Mason.

With his heart in his throat, Torin turned away from

the hotel, dragging his feet along the pavement as he began the lonely journey back to his apartment.

15

Things sure were easier when Theo had been around. Victor toyed with the remote, watching on the monitor as he made the most powerful man in the world walk in circles around his desk. He chortled, a deep bellow echoing in the empty space around him. Things had gone smoothly—almost too smoothly—up until the point he'd finally met Emery face-to-face.

Victor slid the desk chair over to the control station, his eyes fixed on the alpha and omega symbols that were embedded into the metal. He ran his hand along the dented surface, methodically tracing each symbol with the tip of his finger. He reached into his inner coat pocket, his fingers searching the fabric until he found the alpha ring, then placed it in the shallow curve. Tiny green lights lit up one by one around the ring as the machine acknowledged its presence. With a single beep, it locked into place. The omega indentation sat idly by, dejected and unused.

You'll be next.

As he ejected the alpha ring and stuffed it back into his inner coat pocket, his thoughts momentarily flickered to Dormance. If Emery found her way back, she'd surely get closer to finding out the truth about Alpha One, about Dormance, about *everything*. And that was something he couldn't have happen.

The control station beeped as a holographic image of Naia's contact information appeared before him. The image blinked as the lines tried to connect, but he was met with silence. Frustrated, Victor slammed his fists on the control station, his half-full coffee mug rattling violently. Traitor or not, Naia was the only one who could reopen the portal and, of course, she wasn't answering. If Emery found a way in before he did, his dreams would surely die along with the initiative.

Victor gazed down at his remote. There were millions more microchips at his disposal, however, he couldn't retrieve them unless he found a way back into Dormance. Theo was the one who had advised him to keep the microchips hidden there. Victor scowled at the thought. *I'm an idiot for listening to him.*

If only he'd gone with his original plan, he'd have already deployed the devices by now, seized the pendant, and moved forward with the initiative. But, because of Theo, there were now two things standing in his way instead of just one. Two steps forward, one step back. Seemed to be the way things were going as of late.

Come to think of it, it *had* been a while since Victor had laid eyes on his spectacular creations. Excitement thrummed through his fingertips as he opened a file on the control station monitor. A blueprint appeared before him, shining like the brightest star in the sky.

The blueprint was for a microchip, similar to the ones Emery and her father had, except the mechanism in the blueprint was far more advanced. At first glance, it appeared to be just a microchip, but once activated, tiny legs would protrude from the sides, and a pair of neatly clipped wings would expand. He'd developed it to have the capability to release lethargum into the host's bloodstream, causing them to fall seamlessly into Dormance. The final step was to program the chips, and they'd fly off into the sunset to become one with their hosts. No embedment machine needed. The remainder of mankind, sans those already in Dormance, would slip into unconsciousness and into Victor's control.

Each chip was set to be programmed so that each person would have a proper function in society, and if a certain individual didn't add value, the chip would simply be deactivated, leaving them lifeless and nonexistent. In other words, it was a way to weed out the weak. Free will would be a thing of the past and he'd finally get the society he'd always dreamed of. One where he controlled everything and reaped all of the rewards. Oh, how he'd waited for this day. Ten years of waiting. He was so very close. But, as always, there was something standing in his way. And her name was Emery.

Not this time. This time, I will win. This time, the world is mine.

16

A loud knock on the door stirred Emery from her daydreams. Half dressed, she slid her chair back from the hotel desk, her feet barely touching the cool marble floor. "Just a second!" she yelled as she searched for her jeans and t-shirt.

A robotic voice sounded from outside the door. "Housekeeping!"

"Impatient one, aren't you?" she muttered as she pulled a shirt over her head. On her way to the door, she noticed that the couch was no longer occupied. Odd. Perhaps Mason had gone to grab them breakfast?

She stifled a yawn as she opened the door, but there was no one there. She gazed down the hallway in both directions, but there wasn't a soul in sight.

Empty.

With a shrug, she let go of the door and wandered back into the room, but just as the door was about to shut, something rolled inside. Emery gasped as the object collided with her foot. She bent down to examine the circular device, noticing it resembled a vacuum similar to the one that her family had used in Dormance, except this one had no cords, no wires. And it could *talk*.

"Permission to enter?" the robot-like vacuum requested.

"Well, seeing as you're already here, permission granted," she muttered, watching as the robot housekeeper entered her room and started vacuuming. Situated on top of the robot was a nametag that read "CHI", and underneath that "Clean Hotel Initiative".

She continued to stand by the door until the vacuuming was complete, then watched miraculously as CHI grew arms and legs and transformed into something almost human-like. CHI's arms extended to make the bed, fluffing the pillows just as a normal housekeeper would do.

"Neat," she breathed, mesmerized by the sight. As CHI started on the bathroom, Emery broke out of her trance and walked over to the nightstand. The events from the most recent flashback flooded her mind. *I need to tell Mason. He needs to know that Naia was on our side the whole time.* She grabbed her phone and sent a quick text to ask him where he was.

Another thought entered her mind, but this one wasn't as pleasant. *Torin's a part of 7S and so is Naia. Which means that he knew all along! He knew this whole time that Naia was on our side. And he didn't bother to tell me!*

She hastily typed a message to Torin and pressed send. Not even two seconds later, her phone pinged. It was from Torin: *Meet me at 7S Headquarters.*

She rolled her eyes and quickly typed another message. *Why? And tell me you aren't going to ignore my last text.*

To which he replied: *Hurry!*

As much as Emery wanted to rebel after learning this juicy little bit of information, she knew it probably wasn't in her best interest. There was just too much at stake. "This better be good," she mumbled to herself as she walked out the door and down the hallway to the nearest platform.

Five seconds after speaking her destination to the machine, she found herself standing in the middle of downtown Chicago, right in front of 7S Headquarters. As if on cue, Torin came bursting through the sliding glass doors. From the look on his face, something had him in a tizzy, and she wondered what had gotten him so out of sorts.

Before she could even open her mouth, he grabbed her by the arm and pulled her to the side of the building. "What took you so long?" he panted.

Emery shook her head. "I got here literally two minutes after you sent your text." And then, in a more serious tone, "I have a bone to pick with you."

Worry lines creased his forehead. "What do you mean?"

"How come you never told me about Naia?" she asked as she paced back and forth in front of him. "How could you not tell me that she was on our side this whole time?"

"Emery . . ."

"You knew! You knew the entire time and you didn't tell me." She stopped pacing and crossed her arms with a grunt. "Why would you keep something like that from me? After everything we've been through? I thought you trusted me; that we trusted each other."

Torin heaved a loud sigh. "Look, I wanted to tell you and I'm sorry I didn't. I tried to tell you when Naia called a few weeks ago, but you didn't want to hear what I had to say. You had your plan to go back to your house and search for clues and what not, so I just kept my mouth shut and didn't bring it up again." He looked down at his feet and then back at her. "Wait, how did you find out? Did you talk to Naia? Did she reach out to you again?"

Emery shook her head. "No, although that would be the more believable scenario."

"What do you mean?"

Emery pulled the pendant out from underneath her shirt. "I don't really know how to explain it, but this pendant has abilities. Like, time-traveling abilities."

Torin's jaw dropped. "You've been able to travel back in time? And you didn't think to tell me?"

She knew he was mocking her, so she gave him a pointed stare before rolling her eyes.

"When? How many times?"

"It's hard to explain. It was more like I was in a flashback, seeing things from certain people's point of views." She hesitated, suddenly feeling self-conscious that she sounded like a lunatic.

"And?" he pressed. "Keep going."

"And . . . I don't know. Somehow I was able to see things from Naia's point of view. I saw that she was the one helping me all along, in the trainings, before deployment. Everything."

"Seriously? That's . . . incredible." He ran his fingers along the side of his jaw. "I wonder how it works."

Emery gazed down at the pendant. "I really don't know, but it also flashed me back to some childhood memories. Regardless, it's definitely worth protecting."

"Well, if that isn't enough excitement for one day, there's something I need to tell you, too."

Emery's ears perked up. "Which is?"

He puffed his chest out as if he were about to win an Oscar for best male performance. "The portal to Dormance—it's been reopened."

She looked him square in the eye, trying to discern whether or not he was joking. His voice didn't have its usual "Torin flair", so she could only assume that he was being serious. "Are you sure?" she asked in disbelief. "Where did you hear this?"

He shifted his weight from one foot to the other. "Actually, Mason was the one who called me and told me about it last night. He needed my help to get back there because he wasn't sure how—"

"Wait," she interrupted, "Mason called you last night asking for help to reenter Dormance? Why am I just now hearing about this?"

He sighed. "I was stuck between a rock and a hard place, Em. He told me some sob story about how you'd finally opened up to him and told him about leaving the alpha ring behind, so he wanted to go look for it and help out. He said that it was the closest he's felt to you in weeks . . ." he trailed off, his cheeks flushing a deep shade of burgundy.

His last comment hung thick in the air. She wasn't sure how to feel. Part of her was angry at Mason for revealing the details of their personal relationship to Torin; yet part of her was relieved that he knew and she didn't have to explain herself. It was what it was, and Torin was too polite to press any further.

Emery looked down at her feet, hoping she could find the words to break the uncomfortable silence that now lingered between them. "Okay. So I'm guessing you helped him?"

Torin shrugged. "Of course I helped him. I figured if he could find it, it'd be a win-win for everyone."

"And? Did he?"

He shook his head, his long brown hair covering one of his eyes. "Unfortunately, no. He did find the pink silk pouch that you kept it in, but the ring wasn't in there."

Emery took a few steps forward, her finger tapping her chin. "You're sure it wasn't in there?"

"That's what Mason said."

"You know what this means, right?"

He sighed, already knowing what she was about to say. "You have to go back?"

"As per usual, you hit the nail on the head," she said with a grin as she jogged over to the platform.

"Emery, the ring isn't there. Trust me, we checked. We searched your dorm room inside and out. Not to mention, your room looked like it had been ransacked. Someone must have taken it."

"No, no, I get that," she said, waving a hand dismissively in the air. "I want to go back because maybe, just maybe, there's a clue hiding somewhere in my house. Since there wasn't a clue in this world, maybe there's one waiting for me in Dormance."

A shadow of doubt crossed Torin's face. "Don't you ever feel like giving up on this sometimes? Wouldn't life be easier if we just forgot about it and moved forward?"

Emery stumbled backward and gasped as if she'd just been shoved and had the wind knocked out of her. "You're joking, right?"

His silence told her he was not.

"How can we just 'forget' about all of this? Our livelihood is at stake here. Doesn't that mean anything to you?"

"I mean, of course it does." He cracked his knuckles as he shifted his stance. "I guess I just don't understand why you feel the need to do it all. It's not your responsibility."

His words hit her like a punch in the gut. *Not my responsibility. Is he kidding?* "It may not be an 'official' responsibility, but I have ties to this that you wouldn't even begin to understand."

He raised an eyebrow. "Oh really? Like what?"

"My family," she blurted out without thinking. "I think my family is somehow connected to all of this. And it's my job to figure it out. I *have* to figure this out."

Another heavy silence fell between them.

After a minute of not speaking, Torin finally nodded his head. He pulled out his phone, his fingers tapping away on the holoscreen. "Okay, then, if that's what you want, let's send you back. Ready?"

"Thank you," she said quietly. "And Torin?"

He kept his eyes glued to his phone. "Just go. I'll see you when you get back."

Before she could respond, she found herself standing in the middle of the common room in the Federal Commonwealth's underground headquarters. "I'm here," she said, taking a deep breath as she surveyed the area before her. She half expected to see Naia standing at the door with a tray and a glass of chilled sparkling water.

When she realized that this wasn't the case, she couldn't help but feel a little disheartened. "Okay, I'm heading to my dorm room." She waited a few seconds for Torin to answer. When he didn't, her heart picked up speed. "Torin? Are you there?"

Crackled sounds and broken sentences were the only response. She checked the connection. It was weak, but still there. "I can't hear a word you're saying, but at least we're still connected." More crackling.

Great, looks like I'm on my own.

She tiptoed across the room until she reached the doorway. The door locked in place behind her as she continued her journey along the hallway to the elevator. Up, up, up she climbed. The doors opened to the lobby of Rosemary Hall just like they always had, but she could immediately sense that something wasn't right.

Everything was just as she'd left it.

It wasn't the time on the clock that sent warning bells ringing throughout her head, but the date.

May 12, 2055.

That was the same day she'd found out she'd passed her training. The same day she'd been deployed to the 7S world.

Emery rubbed her eyes, hoping that maybe her contact lenses were blurry, but when she looked back up at the clock, the date remained the same. She pressed a button on her phone, sighing as the current date appeared: June 12, 2055. The clock hadn't changed for an entire month. Thirty whole days. It crossed her mind that perhaps the batteries hadn't been changed, but she knew better.

Instead of heading to her dorm room, Emery rushed out the double doors to the grassy lawn where she and Rhea had bumped into Mason for the very first time. Her heart swelled as an image of Rhea's face drifted across her mind. The image was quickly replaced with a less pleasant one: Rhea lying in her hospital bed, and then, even worse, an image of her fallen roommate just after she'd shot her square in the chest.

Emery blinked back a tear, taking a deep inhale as she tried to refocus. She couldn't help but gasp at the sight before her. People were scattered about the lawn, which was seemingly normal, but they were completely immobile. Not moving.

Cars were stopped in the middle of the street, as if they were still driving, yet they were motionless. She jogged over to one of the cars that had the passenger-side window rolled down and peered in. A man sat in the driver's seat, eyes mid-blink, mouth open, cell phone glued to his ear. It appeared he'd been mid-sentence when, suddenly, everything had stopped.

What in the world?

She walked back to the lawn, over to a group of four girls, two of which were sitting on the grass, cups of coffee in hand, the other two leaning into each other and sharing a pastry. Same phenomenon. One of the girl's mouths was open, as if just when she was about to take a bite, the world stopped on its axis. Lifeless statues of people who once were surrounded her. She stumbled backward, trying to make sense of what her eyes were seeing. *Everything's been frozen in time.*

Without a second thought, she ran back to the lobby and came to a screeching halt at the receptionist's desk. She had to find a way back to her house but, of course, she didn't have the keys to her dorm room or to her car. She rifled through the desk drawers, searching for a spare key labeled 319. It was easier to find than she'd expected.

She grabbed the key from the back drawer and bolted up the three grueling flights of stairs. Stopping only briefly to catch her breath, she jogged down the hallway until she reached her room, hands fumbling to put the key in the lock. The door creaked open. It was clear that someone had been there from the pile of clothing items strewn about on the floor. The pink silk pouch lay in the middle of the pile, looking violated and abandoned. If Torin hadn't told her that Mason had just been there, she definitely would have assumed someone had broken in.

Emery drew open her desk drawers, searching ravenously for her spare car keys. After a few frustrating minutes of probing, her fingertips finally grazed a familiar oval-shaped key ring. Smiling, she pulled the keys out of the drawer and darted back down the stairs to the parking garage, realizing that she had no idea where she last parked her car.

She clicked the panic button, the alarm sounding in the back row about fifteen feet away. She ran toward the flashing tail lights, then slid into the driver's seat and turned on the ignition. Her car had three-quarters of a tank left, which was plenty for the three hour drive to her house.

The great thing about a world frozen in time? No traffic.

She should have known it'd take less than three hours to make it home, seeing as the world was at a complete standstill and all. There had been a few stopped cars on the road, and she'd swerved through them like a crazed racecar driver whose eye was on the checkered flag. There had been long stretches of road where it was a complete ghost town, void of both cars and people. She'd been surrounded by nothingness, like she was the only person who existed.

In a sense, she kind of was.

As she pulled into her neighborhood, Emery did her best to shake off the eerie feeling of being the only living, breathing thing for miles. She passed one of her neighbors who had been walking her dog, the toy poodle mid-prance, just as the world had stopped. She pulled into her driveway and stepped out of the car.

As she approached the door mat, she couldn't help but feel like she was about to commit a crime in her own home. She paused midstep as her eyes landed on the front door. It was slightly ajar. She pressed on the door lightly and entered with caution, her senses on high alert for any abnormal sounds, but it was dead silent.

She switched on the nearest overhead lamp, watching as the area before her illuminated with fluorescent light. Just like Darden, it looked exactly the way she'd left it. She was about to call out for her mom and sister, then realized that they probably wouldn't be there. Or worse, they'd be immobile too. That wasn't exactly something she wanted to witness at the moment.

Emery checked each of the rooms, preparing herself each time for what she might find, but her mother and sister were nowhere in sight. Knowing that she wasn't going to stumble into a lifeless version of her family members eased her mind a little, and she began to relax more as she continued walking through the house.

Don't forget why you came here. Clues. Look for clues.

The kitchen seemed like a good place to start, so she started rifling through drawers full of spoons and spatulas, dishtowels and oven mitts. It was hard to know what to look for, but she had a feeling she'd know when she found it. Ten minutes later, it was clear that the kitchen was a dead end.

Next stop: her mother's bedroom. She searched through the closet, nightstand, and the bathroom, but there was nothing out of the ordinary.

Trying to keep her feelings of defeat at bay, she climbed the staircase to her room, tearing dresser drawers from their hinges, socks and undergarments flying through the air. Nothing, nothing, nothing!

I know I'm not wrong about this. I can't be.

A little over an hour passed and the familiar feeling of failure was nipping at her heels once again. After searching her mother's bedroom twice, she faced no other option than to give up. She fell into an oversized armchair in the living room and laid her head against the cool leather, kicking her feet up on the ottoman. She turned to switch on the lamp when something caught her eye. The one area she hadn't searched.

The coffee table.

Emery bolted upright from the chair and sat down in front of the coffee table. Images of getting ready to leave for Darden and her mother retrieving the metal box from the coffee table flashed through her mind. *This has to be it.*

She closed one eye as she slid the coffee table drawer open. Right there, in all its glory, was a letter marked with her name, in her mother's handwriting. Emery snatched the letter from the drawer and retreated back to her seat, carefully sliding her index finger along the seal. She unfolded the letter, feeling somewhat disappointed when she realized it was only one page long. As much as she wanted to skim the contents for the most important parts, she knew it'd be best to read it all the way through:

My dearest Emery,

I'm sorry I didn't give you this letter the day I gave you your gift, but it was too dangerous. I knew you'd be smart enough to come back looking for it, and that eventually, you'd find it. By now, you're probably aware that the gift I gave you, the alpha ring, is not only special to us as mother and daughter, but also to external parties.

During my sophomore year at Darden, I was recruited by a private company to design a program called Alpha One. This program was responsible for developing chemical technologies for our army base. I was given the directive to create two serums—one to debilitate and one to heal—with the guarantee that these serums would be used to train soldiers for battle in a safe simulation-type environment. Hence, I created what is now known as Dormance. The purpose of lethargum was to render soldiers comatose, while sanaré could bring them back to life with no wounds. This was, by far, my greatest scientific achievement . . .

Until it fell into the wrong hands.

During the laboratory trials, a group of test subjects overthrew the experiment and stole all of the lethargum and sanaré to use for their own agenda—for evil instead of good. I'm sure you've met the members of the Federal Commonwealth by now. I've hidden all of the components and the formulations in an undisclosed location, so the FCW only has a finite amount. It's inevitable that they will run out, and soon.

I'm sure you're wondering what the alpha ring and omega pendant have to do with all of this. There are two mainstations, one in 7S and one in Dormance. In short, the ring and pendant are both keys that I created to completely override the system and destroy Alpha One altogether, in case of an emergency. Both the alpha ring and omega pendant must be secured into either one of the mainstations in order to fully deactivate Dormance.

FCW's leader, Victor Novak, is the one you need to watch out for. Do not let him get his hands on the ring or the pendant. The minute he does, he'll destroy them so that Dormance will continue to exist and remain under his control. In the back of this drawer, you'll find a decoy omega pendant—it doesn't have the special abilities the real one does, but I know you'll find a way to use it to your advantage. Good luck, my sweet angel. I love you.

Love,

Mom

Emery reread the last paragraph, her eyes focusing on one phrase, and one phrase only: *FCW's leader, Victor Novak.* She scanned the letter again, checking to make sure there wasn't a more detailed description. Then again, how much more detail did she need? The *Novak* her mother mentioned had to be Chief Novak, her father's new Secretary of Defense. Surely, her father, the Commander of 7S, had known of the Alpha One program. Maybe this was the secret he'd so urgently wanted to tell her? Until . . .

Until Chief Novak had stepped into the picture.

Emery balled her fists in rage, her grip so intense that her knuckles turned white. Somehow, Victor had found a way to control her father—his actions, his responses, his mind. *Does Novak know that the portal's been reopened?*

She brushed the disheartening thought from her mind, then folded the letter into a small square and swiftly tucked it into the side of her boot. She grabbed her car keys and walked out the front door, feeling even more determined now that she knew the truth. She had to find the alpha ring. And thanks to her mother, she now knew exactly where to find it.

17

The airwaves held nothing but static, and Torin was starting to panic. "Emery, are you there?"

Silence.

Oh god, she's stuck there. I sent her back and now she's stuck there forever. This is all my fault. Why did I listen to her?

Just as his mind started spiraling down the rabbit hole, a faint voice sounded through the lousy connection. He could tell it was Emery's voice, but he had no idea what she was saying.

"Emery, I can't understand you," he said, frantically swiping screens left and right to try and reset the connection. "Just stay where you are."

He could feel it in his gut. *Something isn't right.* He gazed up at the screens, then looked over his shoulder at the T-Port. *What did I miss? The connection has never been this bad before.*

His thoughts shifted to the night before when he'd helped Mason travel back to Dormance. Was it possible that Mason had messed something up without knowing it? There was no way. How could that be possible when he'd gotten him out just fine? Torin groaned and scratched his head as multiple terrifying scenarios entered his head.

Stay calm. Clear your head. Focus.

He steadied his breath before speaking. "Emery? Can you hear me?" More garbled sounds came from the other end of the line. The only solution that came to mind was one that had worked in the past—but it was risky.

Is it too risky?

Torin took another deep inhale before reciting his idea out loud. "Emery, I have no idea if you can hear me or not, but I'm going to talk anyway. I have a plan. You're probably not going to like it, but we're going to have to disconnect." His mouth went dry as the words left his lips. "The connection is awful and there is no way I can get you out of there with it the way it is. I promise though, as soon as the lines click off, we'll reconnect again. There may be a thirty second lag, but it *will* happen."

Something that sounded like an "okay" came over the line. Hopefully, she'd heard him and trusted that his plan would work. *If only I was absolutely sure of it myself.*

"Okay, here we go. About to disconnect." Torin squeezed one eye shut as he ended the call. The screens powered down, leaving him engulfed in darkness that was so pitch black he couldn't even see his own five fingers wiggling an inch from his face. He restarted his phone and turned each monitor back on, one at a time. A bright glow lit up the room again, restoring some of his faith in this ridiculous plan. He located Emery's device and typed in the code to establish a new connection. He waited patiently as the blue lights on the screen blinked steadily in their rhythmic pattern. When they finally stopped blinking and all lit up at once, he let out a huge sigh of relief.

"Emery, are you there?"

There was a short bout of silence before he heard her voice. "I'm here, I'm here." She sounded out of breath. "That was freaky."

"Are you okay?"

"Yeah, I just couldn't hear the majority of what you said," she managed through pants. "Only bits and pieces, so I'll admit, I did panic a little. What happened?"

"The connection was poor, although I'm not sure why." Without warning, his thoughts suddenly whirled back to the night prior with Mason, to the moment right after he'd tumbled through his window. Mason had mentioned something strange, something that Torin had shrugged off as nothing at the time: that he felt like someone had followed him. A shiver ran down Torin's spine. Although it seemed highly unlikely, there *was* always a possibility. *Did someone from 7S follow him? Or someone from the FCW? Do they know that we reentered Dormance?*

"Earth to Torin," Emery cooed.

At the sound of her voice, Torin snapped out of his paranoia. *It's probably best not to freak her out more than I already have.* "Sorry, I'm here. Let's get you out of there. Sound good?"

"Please. Plus, I need to show you what I found at my house." Her voice sounded both tense and excited at the same time.

Torin hit his palm against his forehead. He'd been so worried about getting her out of Dormance safely that he hadn't even thought to ask if she'd had any luck back at her house. "Okay, as much as I want to know right now what you found, we've got to get you out of there. Working on it now."

"While you're working on that, I guess there is one thing I can divulge."

Torin regarded her with an absentminded, "Yeah, go for it." He was not at all prepared for the words that came out of her mouth.

"I'm going to kill Chief Novak."

18

All was well in the world with Emery. Or so Mason had thought. Over the past week, they'd spent a lot of time together (four of the seven days), which was a huge step up from fourteen consecutive days of not seeing her at all. It finally felt like they were connecting again—like they weren't hiding anything from each other.

Even though he felt relieved at the progress they'd made, it was hard not to feel frustrated every time he thought about his failed attempt to find the alpha ring. Finding it would have solidified something for him, albeit he didn't know exactly *what*. All he knew was that finding the ring would have been the icing on the cake. He would have returned victorious, a hero, and all eyes would have been on him.

Mason took a sip of soda that he'd ordered from the SmartMeal machine in the Seventh Sanctum dining hall. Headquarters was actually a fascinating place the more he wandered around. There always seemed to be new places to venture into, places he didn't even know existed before—like the pub in the dining hall. The pub was hidden in a back corner behind a faux-bookshelf door. At the time, he'd questioned what skilled architect would place a bookshelf in a dining hall, but when he'd touched it, the bookshelf had magically turned into a doorway that led to a bar.

Mason frequented the pub as of late, seeing that it was a good place to clear his head—away from the chatter and hustle and bustle that surrounded him on a daily basis. Ice cubes clinked as he downed the rest of his drink. It occurred to him that he hadn't talked to Torin since the night he'd reentered Dormance. As much as he wanted to hate Torin and his close friendship with Emery, it was difficult. All in all, Torin was a pretty decent guy, but that didn't necessarily mean he was trustworthy. He was determined to keep Torin at arm's length and would encourage Emery to do the same. Not surprisingly, the latter had been more challenging than he'd anticipated.

With this in mind, Mason decided it was as good a time as ever to stop by Torin's apartment. Part of keeping the hacker at arm's length was knowing what he was up to. *For Emery's sake.*

Mason strolled out of the dining hall, through the faux-bookshelf, and into the common area. As he made his way toward the sliding glass doors that led outside, he noticed two shadows at the far end of the elevator shaft. He quickly crouched down and pressed himself against the wall, making sure he hadn't been spotted. He deliberately worked his way closer to the shadows until he was close enough to be within earshot. The voices were quiet, but still audible.

"I've wanted to tell you this for a long time . . ."

Mason strained his ears. It sounded like Torin, but it was hard to tell.

"What is it? And why are we hiding in a dark corner?"

Now this voice he knew. It was unmistakable.

Emery's.

"Because I don't feel comfortable saying this out in the open."

She's definitely talking to Torin, Mason deduced. *Who else could it be?*

"Well then, just say it already. Otherwise, people are going to think we're up to no good," she giggled.

"Okay, here it is . . ."

Mason's heart stopped as he listened to the next three words. Anger swelled inside him so quickly that he felt like a balloon that was about to burst. *Love her? How could he love her? He barely even knew her!*

"I've wanted to tell you for so long," Torin continued, his voice shaky, "but I know things have been complicated with your . . . situation."

So now I'm a situation? Gee, thanks, Torin. Even though Mason could only see the back of Emery's head, he could easily imagine her reaction: her lips curling into a sly smile, her cheeks flushing a rosy pink. The image infuriated him even more.

"To be honest," she whispered, "I've noticed a change in my feelings for you, too." She shook her head. "But I can't act on those feelings. It wouldn't be fair. I've made so much progress in my friendship with Mason and I can't risk that. He's important to me, too."

Mason couldn't help but smile as the words danced into his ears. What a nice surprise. He hadn't expected Emery to have him on her mind, but she did.

Torin nodded, a solemn expression clouding his face. "I understand. I just had to tell you. I couldn't keep it a secret any longer." He gulped, then forced a small smile. "So, what is it you wanted to show me?"

Mason had to give it to him—the guy had just been downright rejected, but he was already making the best of the situation. *Good for him.*

"I found it," Emery beamed as she unfolded a piece of paper. "I finally found a clue. It's a letter. From my mom."

A letter? Mason leaned in closer, desperate to hear every word.

"Your hard work has finally paid off," Torin gushed. "Tell me what it says."

"Here, you read it." She gently placed the letter into his hands. "I'd rather not read it out loud."

There was a moment of silence as Torin read through the letter. "Holy smokes." His eyes grew wide. "This is bad. Really bad. We have to find that ring."

"I know," Emery grunted as she retrieved the letter. "But what are we going to do about Chief Novak? He must have found a way to control my father. It's the *only* thing that explains why he's been acting so strange."

Torin furrowed his brows. "I need some time to think. Let's meet at my place tomorrow night and figure this out. We need to come up with a plan or something."

"Works for me," she agreed. "Eight o'clock?"

"Make it a quarter past eight."

Mason watched as Emery handed Torin something, although he couldn't tell what, and just as he made a mental note of their meeting time, his body went slack, eyes closing against their will.

When Mason regained consciousness, he found himself standing in the Commander's Office with . . . Warren? Emery's dad? And an older man who had to be none other than Chief Novak.

"Sit," Victor commanded, motioning toward the chairs. Warren stood next to him, still as a statue.

Mason felt his body move to a sitting position, even though the synapses in his brain hadn't given the rest of his body this command. The Commander sat down at the exact same time he did.

"Very good," Victor purred, his head bobbing in approval. "Well done, Warren."

Mason tried to open his mouth to say something, but his face remained still, as if his lips had been sewn shut. Something told him that he was far away from 7S Headquarters—there had been a shift in elevation, and the temperature was cooler. He was somewhere high up. A mountain range, maybe?

Stand up, he ordered, but his limbs wouldn't respond in the slightest. An unsettling thought drifted through his head. *My mind is not my own. But how can I still think? How do I have the thoughts I'm having right now?* His thoughts were in the here and now, and he was somehow present in the moment, yet he couldn't seem to act on those thoughts. Panic seized his entire body, but to an outsider, he appeared calm and collected.

Victor clapped his hands as he looked at Warren. "I knew that, eventually, I'd find someone who would see my side of the story."

"You made quite a convincing case for the FCW's mission, sir," Warren said with a twisted grin. He turned his attention toward Mason. "You see, after we talked about Torin being in your way, I decided it was best to involve Victor. I eavesdropped on your conversation with Torin the night you reentered Dormance."

The footsteps in the alley, Mason thought grimly. *They were Warren's.*

"I have to admit, I was a little upset when you didn't call *me* first or, come to think of it, at all," Warren scoffed, "but I also reentered Dormance that same night to retrieve these." He pulled a large black bag from behind his back and dumped it onto the floor. Thousands of tiny spider-like microchips sprawled out onto the ground. "I'm sorry I knocked you unconscious, but we had to test these little suckers out. By the looks of it, they're working perfectly."

If Mason could show any sort of emotion, it would be pure disgust. But this new and improved microchip had its hold on him. He was paralyzed. Stuck in his worst nightmare.

"Now it's your turn," Victor grunted, his eyes landing on Mason. "Tell me what you know."

Before he even knew what was happening, words came spewing out of his mouth like a garden hose on full blast, and as much as he tried to stop them, he couldn't. He was helpless. "Emery knows who you are. She and Torin are meeting tomorrow night to strategize ways to defeat you." He immediately regretted those last words.

Victor smirked, his eyes narrowing. "I find that hard to believe. How will they meet when Emery is *there* and Torin is *here*?"

Mason's head turned robotically toward the far end of the room, his eyes landing on a clear capsule with a body in it.

Torin's body—floating freely within the capsule, his eyes shut as if he were in a deep, peaceful sleep.

Mason's head snapped back toward Victor.

"Deploy the first wave of microchips," Victor ordered.

Mason watched in horror as wings grew from the sides of each spider-like microchip laying on the ground. In mere seconds, the devices took flight out of the crack in the enormous glass window.

"By midnight, all 7S employees will have an embedded microchip," Victor declared. "And I will be one step closer to finally creating the society I've always dreamed of."

I have to tell Emery. I have to get out of here!

Mason tried again to stand up, to move even a finger, but it was no use. He attempted to look back over at the capsule that contained Torin's body. *Is he breathing? Is he still alive?* But the chip had its hold on him. He was powerless.

Emery was going to have to face this alone—and even though he had faith that she could do it, that she could defeat Victor all on her own—he was frightened that her faith in herself might just be on the brink of shattering.

19

Where is he? Emery thought as she stood in the middle of Torin's apartment. It was exactly a quarter past eight and Mr. Porter was nowhere in sight. It wasn't like him to be late, or worse, not show up at all.

She wandered into the kitchen, then into his bedroom, looking to see if he'd left a note for her somewhere. She pulled out her phone, hoping to find a message, a voicemail, anything really, that would tell her where he was.

The last time she'd spoken to him was the night before, when she'd shown him her mother's letter and given him the omega pendant. Doubt had flickered across her mind as the pendant transferred ownership, but knowing what Victor was up to, she couldn't risk carrying the real one. She toyed with the decoy pendant that now hung around her neck. The two looked almost identical, except for the miniscule blue dot on the back of the one that was now in her possession.

She continued to examine the replica as she walked back over to the living room. She plopped onto the couch, her thoughts drifting to earlier that day. She'd stayed the night in Mason's hotel room, but when she'd woken, he'd been nowhere in sight. It hadn't concerned her all that much, seeing as Mason was a night owl, but when she'd gone to 7S Headquarters for the day, she'd noticed that most everyone was acting out of the ordinary. Every person she'd laid eyes on had walked with a purpose, like they were on some time-sensitive mission. A mission everyone knew about . . . except for her.

As strange as this had been, the lunch hour had been on a completely different level of disturbing. SmartMeals were ordered, groups of people sat down and started eating, but there had been no small talk. No chatter. Just the sound of teeth grinding against food. *Behaving in the same strange way as my father.*

Emery leaned her head back into the plush leather sofa and closed her eyes. It was clear that Torin either wasn't coming or was held up somewhere. The most likely scenario? He was at 7S Headquarters, working late in his office. *So that's where I'll go.*

With a grunt, she pulled herself up from the couch and walked back into the kitchen. As she was about to order a quick snack from SmartMeal, something unsettling caught her eye in the corner of the kitchen. Specks of red. Her hands and knees trembled as she knelt down to get a closer look. It was blood.

Emery immediately darted over to the window and made her way down the apartment's fire escape. With tears in her eyes, she located the nearest platform and teleported to 7S Headquarters. She couldn't be sure that the blood in the apartment was actually Torin's, but honestly, who else's would it be?

Passing through the security system this time around was easier than expected, meaning that someone had finally done their job and given her access. She waited patiently as the ground quaked beneath her and broke into its usual circular platform. The plexiglass bubble emerged from all around the platform to encapsulate her.

Shortly after, the disc started along the tracks. She'd ridden into headquarters multiple times before, but the journey felt lonely this time. Torin had always been with her when they rode into the core of the building.

As the disc neared the end of the tracks, she pressed the button overhead to disconnect the dome. She hopped out onto the platform and positioned herself in front of the final security checkpoint. The scanner identified her and silent cheers erupted in her head as the wall slid open. For the late hour, it was surprising how many people were still at the office. *They must be preparing for something,* she thought with a glimmer of hope. *Maybe I'm right. Maybe Torin is working late after all.*

But something in her gut told her otherwise.

She'd only been to Torin's office once before, on the eighth floor, but she remembered exactly where it was located. She found the nearest T-Port and made her way to floor eight. The hall was empty. She ran a few feet until she reached Torin's office and peered in through the vertically-paned window. Lights off. Monitors off. Just like the hall, it was also empty.

No sign of Torin.

A wave of uneasiness washed over her as she stepped back onto the platform and, in a rash decision, teleported to the seventh floor. *Maybe Torin's meeting with my dad?*

Emery hurried down the hall to the oak door that led to her father's office. She raised her hand to knock, pausing as another scenario entered her mind. *What if Chief Novak is in there with him? What if this is what he wants and I'm walking right into the lion's den?* Emery lowered her hand and grasped the doorknob, her fingers trembling. *Torin and my dad could be in there with Novak. I have to go in.*

With a deep breath, she turned the knob, feeling surprised when the door opened without a hitch. Complete and total darkness lay before her, stretching on for what seemed like miles. The only source of light, however faint, flickered in the distance. Her view was blocked by a wall at the end of the hallway, so she moved forward cautiously, feeling slightly relieved as more light illuminated the space before her. As she drew closer, her eyes landed on something jutting out from behind her father's desk. *What is that?* She dashed over to the object, the decoy pendant bouncing out from underneath her shirt, her gaze fixed on what lay before her.

It took everything in her to stifle a bloodcurdling scream.

20

Victor watched Emery fall to the ground at the sight of her father's slain body. He stood at the other end of the desk, waiting for her to glare at him, yell at him, charge at him—but there was none of that. It was almost as if he didn't exist. Instead, she'd positioned her body over her father's, as if she could protect him and keep him out of harm's way. *A little too late for that, isn't it?*

He cleared his throat to announce his presence, adjusting his posture as Emery raised her head. He tried to suppress a shiver as her steel grey eyes met his. Her face was already swollen and puffy from crying and, for a fleeting moment, he felt a pang of guilt, but it quickly subsided as a familiar darkness told hold.

"You . . . coward," she sneered through gritted teeth. "I didn't take the leader of the Federal Commonwealth to be such a damn fool, but you proved me wrong."

It didn't take much to ignore her insult. Frankly, he'd heard worse. "You have something I need." His gaze dropped to her neck where the omega pendant was shining in the faux moonlight.

Emery scowled and turned back toward her father, stroking his blood-matted hair. "You didn't have to kill him," she whispered, the rage in her voice growing. "You don't have to kill anyone. No one needs to die."

Victor chortled, a low bellow sounding from deep within his chest. "Alas, you may be right. Unfortunately, that isn't how we do things around here."

Hands shaking, Emery slowly pulled herself up from the ground. Before he could register what was happening, the girl snatched an electrified dagger from her father's desk and lunged, flinging the pulsing blade at him with all of her strength.

Although taken aback, Victor crouched and swerved to the left, the blue currents buzzing past his ear, the blade piercing the wall behind him. He collapsed as his foot caught the side of the desk and landed with a thud on the floor. As he propped himself upright, he could see Emery tugging at the handle to no avail, unable to pry the dagger loose.

Before she could attack again, Victor swiftly extended his right leg so that his foot struck the side of her knee. She yelped in pain as her body crumpled to the ground. Blue currents traveled along the wall, getting dangerously close to the floor. Sheer agony covered her face as she attempted to stand again, but failed.

With a smug look, Victor managed to bring himself to a standing position. He pulled the remote from his pocket and commanded Warren and Mason to enter the room. They emerged from the shadows on the wall, their eyes focused on their master.

Emery's eyes grew wide. "Warren? Mason? What the hell is this?"

"Take her," he spat as he pulled the dagger from the wall with ease. He leaned down so he was eye to eye with Emery. For once she actually looked fearful.

Good.

He snatched the pendant from around her neck, her head jolting forward from the force. "Thank you, Ms. Parker, for your cooperation."

"No!" she yelled. "No, I'm not leaving my dad!" She thrashed in her captors' arms. Curses filled the room as Mason and Warren carried her out of the office. When it was finally silent, Victor closed his eyes and smiled, his hand closing around the final piece of the puzzle.

21

Mason narrowed his eyes as he followed Warren, who had Emery thrown over his shoulder, her arms swaying lifelessly to the rhythm of his footsteps. Much to his dismay, she'd been knocked out cold and there was nothing he could do to help her.

A rage churned inside of him as he continued to follow his friend-turned-enemy down the hall. It was hard to believe that Warren, of all people, would succumb to the dark side and join forces with Novak.

What was he thinking? Why would he do something like this?

Warren was someone he'd grown so close with over the last year, someone who had earned his trust—but now, he seemed like a complete stranger, someone he didn't know at all. Even worse, he was a traitor.

The Warren he knew wouldn't have switched sides. The Warren he knew was steadfast and loyal to his core. *Which is what makes this whole situation so infuriating.* It was almost as if they'd time-warped or entered some parallel universe where everyone said and did the opposite of the things they believed in. And that was a world Mason did *not* care to live in.

Warren stopped abruptly in front of him, jolting him from his thoughts. Somehow, his body knew to stop just before running into him, even though his mind hadn't given the command. He'd come to terms with the fact that his mind and actions were being controlled, but Mason had to wonder whether or not Victor realized that he still had his own thoughts and feelings. He could still *generate* his own opinions and was consciously aware of them. Even though he couldn't act on them, they were there. He was still himself, trapped inside of a robot soldier, obeying any and every command he was given.

Earlier, when he'd walked into the Commander's office and laid eyes on Emery, he'd wished more than anything that he could have gone to her, to comfort her. Witnessing the grief written all over her face had been almost too much to bear. It'd taken a moment for him to understand why she was so upset—and that's when he'd seen it: her father lying motionless behind his desk, blood dripping from the corners of his mouth.

Dead.

He'd almost hurled at the sight, but the commands inside his head had forced him to do otherwise. So, in a decision that wasn't his own, he'd helped Warren pick Emery up and carry her out of the office.

His thoughts returned to the present as they reached a platform. "Well, go on then," Warren said as he gestured to the machine.

In his mind, Mason shifted uncomfortably from one foot to the other as he stepped onto the platform. *What's going to happen to her?* It was the one question he so desperately wanted to ask, but couldn't.

Warren and an unconcscious Emery joined him. "President Novak's Chamber," Warren instructed the machine.

"Access code required," a female voice ordered.

Warren pressed a seven-digit code into the machine's holographic interface and waited for confirmation. A few seconds and frigid gust of air later, they found themselves inside what could only be Novak's command station—it was the same place Mason had been brought to when he'd been captured.

Glass windows lined the perimeter, but the rest of the structure was made of stone—the floors, the walls, the ceiling—like a dungeon from back in medieval times. It honestly wouldn't have been surprising if knights in full suits of armor suddenly appeared to take them prisoner and throw them into some twisted torture chamber.

"This way," Warren ordered as he took a few steps down a narrow hallway. Mason did as he was told, his eyes following the endless mountainous terrain until stone walls terminated his view. As he walked along the corridor, bright circles lit up the ceiling. He turned to look behind him, noticing that as they left each section, the lights turned off, one by one.

The corridor finally came to an end. An enormous steel door was the only thing separating them from whatever was on the other side. Warren scanned his hand, then typed in the same seven-digit code he'd used on their way there. The steel door creaked and clacked as it lifted upward into the ceiling.

On the other side of the door was yet another hallway. In his mind, he let out a disgruntled sigh and continued to follow Warren. This hallway looked exactly like the others, except for the multiple rooms lining each side. Warren stopped at one numbered 082, Emery's arms still swinging over his shoulder with each motion.

Warren crouched down so that he was eye-level with yet another scanner. A green light flashed across his retina and the door popped open. "This will do," he said without a hint of remorse in his voice. He transferred Emery from his shoulder to Mason's, then rolled his hand in a sarcastic gesture.

Mason walked into the cell, then knelt down to the ground and carefully rolled Emery from his shoulder onto the damp stone floor.

Still unconscious. Still unmoving.

Don't leave her here, his mind warned. But as much as he wanted to stay, he found himself moving out of the cell and back into the hallway. The door locked loudly behind him.

Do not leave her.

His pleas were pointless. With one foot in front of the other, Mason submissively followed Warren back down the hallway, glaring at the back of his head the entire way.

22

It could have been days. Weeks. Months. It was difficult to tell exactly how much time had passed.

Emery sat in the corner of her damp cell, arms crossed, teeth chattering. Drops of water splashed onto the stone floor at various intervals, each one making a larger plopping sound than the last. They seemed to be growing larger. She rubbed her fingers over her eyelids, cursing her contact lenses for making her eyes so dry. If she took them out, she'd be blinder than a bat. But if she left them in, she'd probably still end up blind from an infection, or worse.

Hopelessness was starting to cave in. Having faith wasn't easy when it'd been *days* since she'd seen the outside world. She may as well be dead. Nonexistent.

Does anyone even know I'm here?

She banged the back of her head into the stone wall, wanting to feel something . . . anything. Pain coursed through her body, her head stinging from the impact. Sadly, that pain was the only thing telling her she was still alive. That this wasn't all a terrible nightmare. It was real. *Terrifying and real.*

She squeezed her eyes shut, mustering all her strength to pull some kind of memory from the depths of her mind as to what had happened and how she'd gotten here. She'd tried this tactic a few times before to no avail; but this time, as her head throbbed and pounded, memories started to resurface. Sparse at first, and then all at once.

Her father's body.

Her failed attempt to kill Victor.

The awful blow to her knee.

The people who had taken her here . . .

The memories began to fade. Emery hit her head against the wall again. Dots blurred her vision, but it worked. She was remembering.

Two people had taken her here. Two people she knew.

The realization came swiftly like a slap in the face.

Mason and Warren. Victor's already gotten to them.

And then, another heartbreaking realization dawned on her.

My father is dead.

She fell forward into her hands, eyes burning as tears threatened to fall. She squeezed them shut and bit down hard on her lower lip.

You are not defeated. You are not defeated.

But her positive mantra only made things worse. Sobs erupted low and deep from within her stomach and crept up her throat. She let out a faint whimper, not wanting whoever was on the other side of the door to hear her. She pulled her shirt up over her mouth to muffle the sound.

With her knees tight against her chest, Emery rocked back and forth, slowly, as if she were in a rocking chair. It had a calming effect, like an ocean breeze ruffling the fronds of palm trees. She sat in silence for a few minutes, willing herself to stop heaving. When her chest finally halted its sporadic rhythm, she somehow found the strength to pull herself up from the floor. Though blurry, she spotted a small rectangular window at the top of the cell wall.

Standing on her good leg, she raised herself up onto her tiptoes, even though it was obvious she'd be too short to see out. She attempted to jump, immediately realizing what a terrible idea that was. Her bad knee popped as it hyperextended. She cried out, falling to the ground in immense pain, clutching her knee and praying for the pain to go away. *I just want to know where I am. How long I've been here. If I'll ever find a way out. If there even **is** a way out.*

Then, as if someone up there *was* looking out for her after all, the door began to creak open. Her fingers grasped for the pendant out of habit, but she was grabbing at air. Her heart picked up pace, thumping loudly in her ears. *Where's the pendant?*

Panic coursed through her veins, until she remembered Victor snatching the decoy pendant from her neck. She'd given the real omega pendant to Torin. *But where is Torin? Is he trapped in one of these cells, too?*

The door continued its long, steady creak. *Play dead or make a run for it?* She shook her head at the thought. She'd never make it out. Not with her bum knee that was now even less functional due to her delusional thoughts of reaching a window three times her height. She grimaced as the door opened.

In walked Victor with his usual smug demeanor. "Looks like you've settled in quite well," he snarled.

"A blanket would have been nice," she shot back as she stood up. Pain exploded through her leg like fireworks on the fourth of July.

Novak narrowed his eyes, clearly unnerved by her sarcastic remark. He pulled an oval-shaped device out of his jacket pocket. The surface was covered with small dials and knobs. A smirk lined his face as he pressed one of the buttons.

Emery's eyes widened as a pair of holographic cuffs, buzzing with multiple electric currents, wrapped around her wrists. Shortly after, another pair of cuffs appeared around her ankles and a plexiglass dome formed around her. She placed her bound hands against the dome, banging them loudly in an effort to shatter the surface.

Novak grinned as he watched her pitiful attempt to break free. "Testing, testing," he mocked, the sound of his voice filling the dome.

It took everything in her not to cringe. Her disgust toward him was growing deeper and deeper with each passing second.

He slithered over to her and placed a blinking orange device on the outside of the dome. "If you'd be so kind to follow me," he instructed as he walked out of the cell door.

Without warning, the dome jolted forward. It was a strange feeling—almost like she was encapsulated in a gravity-free zone but somehow, she stayed upright instead of spinning in circles like she'd seen in every space astronaut film. She looked down at the holographic cuffs that bound her wrists and ankles. As she tried to lift her hands through the cuffs, something zapped her as if she were a dog trying to escape through an invisible fence.

She floated out the door right behind Novak and, although she was a prisoner being held against her will, couldn't help but feel astounded at the advancement of technology in the 7S world. Her anger dissipated, while only briefly, as she continued to float along an invisible track.

Without warning, Novak came to a stop. She leaned to the left to peer around him. They'd reached the end of the hallway. She looked around, expecting to see a door of some sort, but there wasn't one. Instead, the walls seemed to be getting longer and longer, further and further away.

She shifted her gaze downward as the floor they were standing on lowered into the ground. *Whoa.*

The ever-expanding walls seemed to stretch on for miles, making it difficult to bring her gaze back to the man in front of her. Novak didn't make a sound, his eyes focused straight ahead, as the walls stopped moving.

And then everything was still.

She squinted in the darkness, trying to make sense of where he'd just taken her. Her vision was already limited, and if it weren't for the glowing light from within her pod-like structure, her sight would be nonexistent.

Novak pressed another button on his remote. The end of it extended into a glowing silver orb. With this new guiding light, he walked forward into the darkness. Seeing as she had no choice in the matter, her pod moved along behind him at the same pace.

Her eyes drifted upward and she gawked at the enormous steel walls surrounding them. The area was so spacious and secure that it felt as though they'd entered some underground storage area. *Storage for what? Machines? Robots? A lifetime supply of lethargum?*

But the truth as to what was actually stored there was far more grotesque than anything she ever could have imagined.

Novak came to a stop in front of one of the walls, her pod halting in sync with his movements. With the touch of one button, hundreds of pod-like structures, just like the one she was currently occupying, came jutting out of the walls, one appearing after the other, as if they were on some sort of rotating device. It reminded her of when her mother would take her to go pick up her dry cleaning and the attendant would cycle through the racks to find her clothes.

What is this place?

As her own pod inched closer to the others, a disturbing realization hit her. Her stomach turned as her eyes landed on the contents of each pod.

Human beings.

Bile crept up her throat. Emery yanked her hands in an upward motion to cover her mouth, but the holographic cuffs wouldn't budge. She closed her eyes and took a deep inhale through her nose.

Keep it together.

Novak cycled through ten of the pods, grunting out of frustration, until he found the one he was looking for. He turned to face Emery, his mouth curling into a sickening grin as he brought her closer. She closed her eyes, not wanting to look at whatever he was about to show her.

His tone was harsh. "Open your eyes," he commanded.

Unwillingly, Emery did as she was told, gasping at the sight before her. There lay her mother, surrounded by tiny, but visible, buzzing blue currents. She was completely clothed and her hair was done up like she was heading off to work. She hadn't aged a day.

In that moment, all Emery could see was red. "What the hell is this place?" she managed through gritted teeth.

Novak rolled his eyes as if the answer were obvious. "It's where we store the bodies of all those living in Dormance."

Memories of the Dormance control room surfaced, specifically the one where she'd sliced the wires to Theo's pod and the pods of the eleven other members of the FCW. When she'd shot them in the 7S world, they hadn't survived. It made even more sense now.

I disconnected their pods. They had no life source to feed off of.

She'd figured that all of the dormants' bodies had to be stored somewhere, but she never would have imagined it would be a place like this—a dark, dreary underworld that never saw the light of day with hundreds of thousands of human beings left to be preserved. And when their DNA was no longer useful, they'd be killed off. The value of a human life reduced to nothing.

It was appalling.

"Get me out of here," she snapped. "You are a sick, sick man."

"On the contrary," Novak drawled, "it's quite remarkable. We were able to preserve every single human being that we've rendered comatose. When we need DNA for testing, it's readily available. The advancements we've made in stem cell research and biochemistry are truly astonishing. I would show you yours . . ."

Emery's eyes widened at his comment and she feared she might be sick. "Show me *my what?*"

"The pod containing your body." He paused. "But unfortunately, this isn't possible. Those that participated in the Alpha Drive don't have bodies here. Not anymore, at least." He sighed.

As disgusted as she was with Novak, the FCW, and the entire concept of Dormance, Emery felt a visceral desire to know more. To understand. "What do you mean, *not anymore?*"

"Let's see, how can I explain this?" He tapped his chin with his index and middle fingers. "When you were deployed to the real world, your dormant body merged with your real body."

Emery shook her head in disbelief. "How?"

"For the sake of time and avoiding an unnecessary technical conversation, I'll give you the condensed version."

What Emery wanted was the full unadulterated explanation, but she kept her mouth shut. She didn't want

Novak to suddenly change his mind. A little information was better than no information.

"Your real body, along with the other Alpha Drive participants, was preprogrammed to be extracted from the pod to immerse as one with your dormant body during the teleportation process."

She took a moment to digest the information. "So you're saying that everything that happened to me in Dormance also happened to me in the 7S world? And vice versa?"

He raised an eyebrow and nodded, clearly impressed by her quick understanding.

She blinked, unsure how to respond.

"I digress," Victor continued. "The real news here is that you've finally provided me with both of the keys." He held up his left hand, her long-lost alpha ring dangling from his pinky finger, then pulled the omega pendant from his jacket pocket. The pendant spun through the air like a ballerina making her debut performance.

Emery refused to break her gaze from the pendant. She waited patiently for the horseshoe to slow its rotation, until the back of it finally faced her. She tried to hide her smile as the tiny blue dot revealed itself.

Hello, my friend.

Hope resurfaced. Not all was lost. Victor hadn't uncovered the real pendant yet.

23

After the introduction to the underworld storage system, Victor had hurriedly guided Emery back to her cell. With a grunt, he'd dismantled the pod and holocuffs, then threw her back into her cell with only a thin, measly blanket to boot.

Days later (or at least what she *thought* was days later), Emery sat wrapped up in that same measly blanket in her usual corner, trying to calculate how long it'd been since she'd last seen Novak. The window at the top of her cell had proven to be helpful in determining the time of day. Even though she couldn't see the exact position of the sun, she at least knew when it rose and when it set. Cloudy days were the most difficult. They felt endless.

But today was a bright and sunny day. The sun had just risen, making it approximately four days since she'd last seen the chief.

She crawled toward the door, waiting patiently for her meal, which was normally a stale piece of bread, a slice of questionable meat, and a vegetable medley slopped in some sort of salty broth. At least the water was ice cold—it was hard for anything to stay warm in this altitude.

The tray of food appeared in front of her, first as a hologram, before it transformed into physical food. Although the meals were redundant and her taste buds were bored, she devoured every bite, only stopping to wash the food down with the chilled water. When she finished her bland meal, she pushed the tray toward the edge of the door, watching as it disappeared into thin air. It made her wonder where all of the trays went. Perhaps into an abyss somewhere?

She pulled herself up to her feet and walked back toward her designated corner with the blanket draped around her shoulders. She gazed up at the window, realizing it wasn't as small as she'd originally thought. Actually, it was close to the size of the tray she'd just eaten from. Maybe there was even a possibility that she could find a way to slip out . . . if she conjured up the right tools.

A light bulb switched on in her head.

Lunch time came and went. As the tray appeared with the second round of food, Emery called out to request another blanket. She wasn't sure if anyone had heard her, or if there was even anyone on the other side, but it was worth a shot. She called out again. No response.

After finishing her meal, she pushed her tray to the edge of the door, watching as it vanished. She waited hopefully, but no blanket appeared. She curled up into a ball and secured the thin piece of fabric around her. Her teeth chattered as she leaned her head against the wall. Although she was cold and the food was bland, a full belly was enough to satiate her and allow her to doze off into a semi-restful sleep.

Dinner time. The final meal of the day. Her knee was starting to feel better as the days wore on. Every time she awoke, she'd do her best to elevate it and try to keep the blood from swelling around her knee. It was working so far.

The sun was just starting to set, meaning her dinner should arrive at any minute. With less of a limp, she moved toward the door, her breath catching as a tray appeared with a dinner roll, pork chops, and a whole potato. *An actual meal.* She knew she should be grateful, but there was something she wanted just a little bit more. She lowered her head and closed her eyes. *Please give me a blanket.*

To her delight, a neatly folded blanket appeared next to the dinner tray. She almost jumped out of her own skin as she grabbed the blanket first, then the tray, and brought them over to the corner of the cell. Her fingers gathered the edges of the new blanket. It was just like the one she had. Thin and measly. But both blankets were thin enough to fasten together. The only question was, would it hold?

Emery began to tie knots throughout the blankets, feeling like a young child making an escape ladder for play. She took a quick bite of her meal before dumping the rest of the food onto the ground and worked the tray into a knot in her rope-blanket. She triple knotted the blanket in two areas—where the two blankets met and where she'd fastened the tray horizontally at the end. This plan would either be a complete success or a total failure. Either way, she was about to find out.

Standing a few feet back from the window, she turned the tray so that it was vertical and upright, her fingers grasping onto a couple feet of the makeshift rope. She focused on the center of the window and took a deep breath. The tray catapulted upward, hitting the edge of the window before clattering back to the ground. She grimaced and ran over to pick it up, hoping that no one had heard the noise.

When she was sure there was nothing but silence in the hallways, she tried again. She turned the tray vertical again, but this time, laid it flat against her palms. She took another deep breath and launched the tray into the air, watching as it slid seamlessly through the window over onto the wall outside. *Yes!* She tugged on the blanket, the tray catching on the outside perimeter of the window. She yanked on it one more time to be sure it was secure, then started her climb upward.

She placed her right foot on the wall and leaned back, tugging on the rope again to make sure it would hold her. She wasn't entirely convinced, but there wasn't much time—the food trays normally disappeared from her cell after thirty minutes, whether she'd finished her meal or not. (Unfortunately, she'd learned this the hard way.) If the tray disappeared while she was climbing up the wall, it'd be bad news for her. She'd either face-plant or back-plant, depending on the fall. And that stone floor wasn't very forgiving.

The divots in the wall made it easier to climb than she'd expected. Imaginary sounds of the blanket ripping filled her ears, and she had to stop a few times to make sure it was all in her head and not actually happening. When she finally reached the window, she grasped at an indentation on the outside wall. With her right hand, she pushed the tray away from the window, holding firmly onto the blanket. She pulled her head and shoulders through the window, the blanket secure underneath the weight of her body, and peered over the edge.

A roof covered in conifer branches and pinecones lay beneath her, about ten feet away. There was no other choice than to push her entire body through the window and hope that the leaves and branches would miraculously catch her fall. She held on for as long as she could, thinking skinny thoughts as she wiggled her hips out the window, until finally succumbing to freefall. She pushed off the window with enough momentum to change her position in the air so that she'd land butt-first instead of head-first. The blanket whooshed behind her as her rear landed on the hard metal surface.

"Oww." Emery opened her eyes and wiggled all ten fingers and toes to test her mobility. After they responded like they were supposed to, she stood up. She wobbled over the pinecones that had broken her fall and carefully ventured to the edge of the roof to gaze out into the distance. *I'm definitely on a mountaintop.*

For miles and miles, all she could see were trees and mountainous terrain, branches swaying violently as harsh gusts of wind made their way through the wilderness. She sat on the edge of the roof, contemplating a safe way to scale down the mountain. There weren't many options. Her eyes landed on a hefty pine tree standing just a few feet away from her. With a running start, she could probably jump and grab hold of one of the thicker branches, then work her way down to the ground. She observed the area in its entirety before deciding it was the best course of action.

She glanced back up at the window she'd just climbed through. No alarms were sounding. No voices were yelling. *I'm still safe.*

She took a few steps backward to allow enough room for a running start, but paused as a rustling noise made itself known on the west side of the building. Her first instinct was to hide, but seeing as she was on a roof, completely out in the open, that wasn't an option.

Her ears on high alert, she mustered up the courage to walk toward the noise, squinting as something came into view. At the far end of the building was an entrance to what looked like a cave. A shadowed figure stood in the middle of the cave's entrance, beckoning her to approach.

It could be a trap. What if it's Novak? Or one of his soldiers? This is it, the gig is up.

As much as she wanted to turn and run the other way, her gut told her not to. With caution, she drew closer. An outline of a female formed, one that was wearing a headset and holding a tablet.

Emery could hardly believe her eyes.

It was Naia.

24

The joy Emery felt as soon as she laid eyes on Naia was unlike anything she'd ever experienced. She held her arms out for a hug and wrapped Naia in a tight embrace. "It was you all along," Emery whispered into her ear. Tears pricked her eyes, threatening to fall. "You helped me the whole time. You saved me. You saved us."

Naia gave her another squeeze before letting go. Her hair was even shorter than last time and was styled into an angled bob. Her face was chapped from the cold weather and Emery wondered how long she'd been on the mountainside. *Does Novak know she's here?*

"Come on, we'll talk about all that later. It's freezing out here. Let's get you inside," Naia said as she pulled Emery inside.

She kept close to Naia, following her into the darkness for what felt like an hour. In reality, it was probably only five minutes. It was shocking just how far back the cave went. They finally reached an area that looked like a living room, bedroom, and kitchen, all in one, like a studio apartment. *Or in this case, a studio cave.* A wall at the end of the cave separated the main area from whatever was behind it.

"Have a seat," Naia said, gesturing toward a makeshift chair made of pine branches and needles. "I am so relieved to see that you're okay. I'm guessing you put the pieces together and figured out it was me helping you all along." Naia's face lit up as Emery nodded. "I knew you would."

Emery sat down, wincing as pine needles poked her in the back. "I had a hunch, but it was actually the omega pendant that confirmed everything."

Naia tilted her head, eyes blazing with questions. "Do tell."

Before answering, Emery's eyes swept the cave. She noticed that the only source of light came from a few tablets that were meticulously set up in each corner of the cave. "Before I do, I have to ask—how are those able to hold a charge?"

Naia shifted her gaze, quickly picking up on the items in question. "Oh, the tablets are charged wirelessly from the signal given off by President Novak's Chamber," she explained as she swatted a gnat from her face.

Emery froze. "You're using the signal from the chamber?" Her cheeks burned crimson. "What if Novak finds out? What if he knows you're here?"

Naia laughed. "Calm down. Everything here is encrypted. We're completely off the grid."

Emery bit her lower lip and shook her head slowly. "I wouldn't be so sure."

"Trust me. You're talking to the person who manipulated your training without Novak or anyone else in the FCW knowing. I'd say that gives me loads of credibility." Naia gave a reassuring smile. "So, as much as I want to learn more about what happened with the omega pendant, I'll be a good host and ask the question: are you hungry?" She nodded toward a SmartMeal machine that sat adjacent to her. "The signal isn't as strong as I'd like it to be, so it takes awhile for the food to get here, but it's well worth the wait." She grinned, the corners of her eyes crinkling. "You look hungry."

Emery smiled back. At first, she'd thought Naia had been roughing it on the mountainside. Fortunately for her and her grumbling stomach, this wasn't the case. "I'll take whatever will get here the fastest."

"I've had a lot of luck with pizza. How does that sound?"

Emery nodded graciously as Naia placed the order with SmartMeal.

"It should be here in about ten minutes," she said as she turned back around. "I hope that's okay."

"Better than being locked in a prison cell for god knows how long," she muttered, shivering at the thought.

"You poor thing," Naia cooed. "I hate that you were taken captive. If I could have prevented it, I would have."

"It's okay, you've done more than enough and I am forever grateful." She gave Naia a warm smile.

"Okay, so start from the beginning. I want to make sure I understand everything."

Emery paused for a minute to gather her thoughts and reflect on everything that had happened since she'd last spoken to Naia. All she wanted to do was believe everything the omega pendant had revealed to her in her flashbacks, but what if they were wrong, or worse, been tampered with somehow? What if Naia couldn't be trusted?

Emery could feel Naia sensing the apprehension in her eyes. "How about I start? Right out of the gate, you need to know that I was never one of them, Emery. I've worked for the Seventh Sanctum all along. The Commander—your father—sent me to watch over you. It wasn't an easy feat getting in with the Federal Commonwealth, but I managed." She shrugged. "I didn't have a choice. I *had* to."

"So this whole time . . . you've really been one of us? On the 7S side?"

She nodded. "I was the one who coordinated with Torin to have him reach out to you. I couldn't leave Dormance to show you the real world myself—it was too risky. We would have been caught. But I was able to travel back and forth to retrieve the pendant and put it somewhere you would find it. I also knew Torin would lead you to the right conclusion and that you'd switch sides to fight for the right team."

Emery smiled at the thought. "That was probably the most confusing time of my life, but you were right because he did. If it weren't for him . . ." Her words caught in her throat. She lowered her eyes to the floor as a fountain of sadness welled inside of her. *Where is Torin?*

"What exactly did the omega pendant reveal to you?"

Emery welcomed the question—anything to keep her from thinking about Torin. She snapped her eyes up from the floor. "In the flashback, I saw that you were the one who dropped the spherical device into my boot, and that you meticulously placed the capsules and my mother in the training, and that you put the very last capsule of sanaré into the vault for me to find. I watched it all from your point of view," Emery explained. "It was almost as if I were there, experiencing everything in real time with you. If it weren't for you, we'd all probably be dead."

Naia beamed at the recognition. "Everything the pendant revealed to you is the truth. I'm so happy it chose to reveal my actions."

"How does it work? I mean, how was I able to go back in time and see everything from your point of view?"

"Your mother is a brilliant woman." A fleeting look of sorrow passed over Naia's face. "What you experienced is something called the Order of Omega. When you activate the Order, the pendant pulls you back in time and reveals whatever information will benefit you most."

Emery thought back to the day of her first flashback. She'd been distressed over Torin and Mason, and her conflicting feelings for the two, but when she really thought about it, there *had* been an underlying issue— something she hadn't wanted to face at the time, but it was the one thing constantly eating away at her. The one thing that kept her up every single night: *Who can I trust?*

"You didn't know who to trust," Naia said, as if reading her mind.

Emery nodded. "Now I do."

"I'm happy that you know now. I really am." Her smile slowly started to fade. "But what I'm still trying to figure out is what happened after deployment. There was a glitch in the system and my monitors went blank, causing me to lose connection with the 7S world."

Emery brushed a stray hair from her face. "Well, it was all a blur, really. Theo unleashed the lethargum bomb, so I countered with the sanaré, that I now know you hid in the control room. I sliced the wire connecting Theo's pod to the mainstation, as well as the eleven other pods, before deactivating Dormance, but I guess it was only a temporary deactivation." She hesitated for a moment, contemplating how to word the next part of her story. "I, uh, pulled a gun on Theo and the others."

"You shot them?" Naia gasped, a look of bewilderment in her eyes.

"You have to understand," Emery added hurriedly, "they had a gun to Mason's head. What was I supposed to do?"

Naia considered this, then sighed. "Go on."

"Well, since I disconnected their pods, the sanaré didn't save them. Theo and his soldiers are dead."

Her last words hung in the air, thick and heavy.

Naia nodded, a solemn look in her eyes. "Theo was my friend, but he was also working for the enemy. You did what you had to do—for the greater good. I wouldn't have expected anything less from you." She reached over and patted her on the shoulder. "So what happened after that?"

Emery sighed. "I found out that my mom was in charge of creating Alpha One."

"Ah, yes, the simulation program used to train soldiers in a safe environment," she recalled, a twinkle in her eye. "I remember it well. Very impressive."

"Obviously it fell into the wrong hands. Do you know about the keys?"

Naia nodded. "I know them well. I also know that President Novak needs to destroy both the alpha ring and the omega pendant so he can remain in power and control the world as he wishes. Where are these keys now?"

"Novak has the alpha ring." A coy smile crossed her face. "And he *thinks* he has the pendant . . ."

Naia chuckled. "You clever girl. What did you do?"

"I gave the real pendant to Torin." She grinned, wider this time. "My mother left me a decoy pendant and that's the one Novak has."

"Bravo," Naia commended. "I'm impressed with not only your mother, but also with you. But, like I said before, I wouldn't expect anything less from the Parkers." She abruptly turned her attention to the cave's entrance. "Did you happen to get a grand tour of President Novak's chamber and if so, what exactly does he keep in that monstrosity of a fortress?"

Emery shuddered, thinking back to her mother's pod. "The bodies," she whispered. "All of them."

Naia's eyes grew wide. "The dormants' bodies?"

Emery nodded.

"But how?"

"They're in an underground lair—it's like a storage center for human beings and all the bodies are preserved with these strange electric currents. It's disgusting." She shook her head, trying to clear the image from her mind when a shuffling noise from behind the cave wall interrupted their conversation. "What was that?"

"I was so wrapped up in your story that I almost forgot to tell you . . ." Before Naia could finish, a burly man emerged from behind the cave wall. His face was scruffy and he had dark circles under his eyes, dried blood caked across his chin, but there was no mistaking who he was.

"Dad!" Emery cried out in astonishment as she ran toward him.

He looked surprised to see her. "Em?" He wrapped her up in a bear hug and squeezed her tight. "Thank god you're alright," he breathed, his voice full of relief.

Emery turned her gaze from him to Naia, then back to him again. "But how? I saw you . . . lying there . . . in all that blood . . ."

"Sanaré," Naia stated simply. "I had an emergency syringe hidden in Theo's desk. I brought it with me, just in case." She stood up from where she was sitting and walked over toward them. "I must have left Dormance just in time, right before you temporarily deactivated it. I teleported to the 7S world and stayed at a hotel, fully undercover, but I had no idea what was going on. Eventually, I found an opportunity to go visit your father, but when I walked into his office, he wasn't breathing." Her eyes dropped to the floor. "I actually took him for dead. But I used the last syringe on him, hoping that it hadn't been over twenty-four hours since the incident—"

"—otherwise he'd really be dead," Emery finished. She looked up at her father, eyes brimming with tears. "I thought I'd lost you again." She leaned in for another hug, his brawny arms covering hers.

"That bastard," her father reproached. "I don't know how Novak did it, but he found a way to control me. I was a prisoner in my own body." He lifted his arms as his eyes locked with hers. "You never have to worry about losing me again. I'm not going anywhere."

Emery hugged him again, the scent of pine and ash filling her senses. It reminded her of home, of a happier time, so she took another deep inhale.

"Any word from your mother? Your sister?"

Emery dropped her arms. The question was unexpected and immediately made her stomach turn. "They're inside," she whispered, nodding her head in the direction of the chambers. "Novak has them trapped in pods like the others."

Byron furrowed his brow, looking determined. "Not for long. Novak better prepare himself. This storm is one he'll never see coming."

Emery trained her eyes on her father, trying to absorb the confidence that was radiating from his entire being. For the first time in a long time, she felt like maybe there was a chance, and that maybe, just maybe, they would come out on top after all.

25

Mason trudged along the stone floor, trapped in movements that weren't his own. It was tiring, willing his body day after day to listen to his mind but never receiving a response.

He made his way toward Emery's cell, 082, completing the necessary security measures before attempting to open the door. At first, he felt a jolt of panic as his eyes searched the empty cell, but then his heart warmed at the realization. She wasn't there. She'd escaped.

The first thought that came to his mind was how long he'd be able to keep this information to himself. If there was ever a time he could gain some control of his mind, this was it. Mason walked further into the empty cell, examining the area before him. How had she gotten out? No trace of escape tools existed. It was like she'd vanished into thin air.

Just as he turned to leave, the window at the top of the cell caught his eye. He smiled. That had to be it. *But where did she go after that?*

What was on the outside of President Novak's Chamber was a mystery, but he was certain it wasn't all daffodils and daisies. He commanded his body to move closer to the window, but instead, found himself turning away from the cell and walking out the door. He marched down the long hallway and made a swift right turn at the end.

No, no, no.

He knew exactly where he was headed and it wasn't good. If only he knew exactly how long ago Emery had escaped. He wished he could give her as much time as possible to get away, but as he approached President Novak's office, he knew this wouldn't be the case.

He commanded his body to stop moving—to turn around and go back to his chambers. But, of course, his body and mind wouldn't sync up. He stepped into the President's office, his gaze fixed on the back of the evil dictator's head.

Novak spun around in his chair, his eyes landing on Mason. "What is it, boy?" he huffed. "Can't you see I'm busy?"

Fury ignited in Mason's stomach. *Don't say it. Keep quiet.* "Cell 082 is empty." It pained him to hear the words come out of his mouth, to rat out Emery like this, but the choice wasn't his to make.

Novak narrowed his eyes. "Warren!" he bellowed.

Warren appeared, running full-speed into the office, as if he had a pit bull nipping at his heels. "Sir?"

"I've just been informed that Cell 082 is empty," Novak snarled. The glare in his eyes was borderline lethal as he drummed his fingers on the desk.

"Th-that's impossible," Warren stuttered as he searched for his handheld monitor. He flipped through a number of screens on the tablet until he landed on Emery's cell. His eyes grew wide as he realized that the cell *was* indeed empty. No movement. No sounds. No Emery.

"When did you discover this?" Novak snapped.

Mason tried to keep his mouth shut, but it was no use. "Just now, sir."

Novak snapped his eyes from Mason back to Warren. "Set up a perimeter," he demanded through clenched teeth, "and enable a search team. Find her and bring her back to me." He paused, his brows furrowing. "We'll discuss your punishment later."

Warren gulped, his face as pale as a ghost's, then darted out of the room in a tizzy.

Novak's steely gaze shifted. "Good work, soldier. I had my doubts, but you're starting to become one of us."

Mason nodded robotically, then turned on his heel to walk toward his chambers. *Over my dead body.*

26

Emery bit into her slice of pizza, smiling as the cheese oozed from the corners of her mouth. After being locked away and fed food that resembled cardboard in both appearance and taste, she'd almost forgotten how good *real* food tasted. She licked her lips, wanting to savor every single bite. Her father and Naia sat across from her, legs crossed indian-style, so that together they formed a circle.

"So Dad, now that you're here and *not* under Novak's control," Emery managed between mouthfuls, "I have so many questions."

Byron leaned back in the makeshift chair. "I'm sure you do. And I want to answer them in whatever way I can."

Emery's brows drew together as she contemplated where to begin. "When we first saw each other again, at 7S Headquarters, it seemed like there was something really urgent you wanted to tell me. What was it?"

Byron set down his plate and reached for a water bottle. "Before I answer, did you find the letter? The one your mother left for you?"

She nodded as more cheese spilled onto her plate.

"I'm sure that helped explain some of it," he said after taking a swig of water. "Did the letter explain what the alpha ring and omega pendant stand for?"

Emery tilted her head sideways, trying to recall the contents of the letter. "Actually . . . no, I don't remember it being mentioned."

Byron smiled. "Sandra loves biochemistry, but she is also fascinated by the Latin and Greek cultures. Alpha is the first letter in the Greek alphabet, Omega is the last."

Emery leaned forward as the pieces came together. "Alpha and Omega. The beginning and the end."

"Exactly. Both the ring and pendant are keys that will fully deactivate Dormance." A tear caught in the corner of his eye, but he quickly blinked it away.

Emery couldn't understand why he was getting so emotional. "What's wrong?"

"The irony of it all. Your mother is the creator of Alpha One, yet also the destroyer." Sadness washed over his face like waves crashing onto a deserted beach.

It was starting to make sense, but she still had so many questions. "Did you know about Alpha One when you married mom?" Emery whispered.

Byron lowered his eyes and let out a long sigh. "I didn't want you to find out this way. Truth be told, I didn't want you to *ever* find out; you nor your sister." He shifted in his seat uncomfortably. "But yes, I knew about Alpha One when I married your mother. She was so young when she designed it, right around your age. We lived in the 7S world, the real world, as a happy family for a while, but then they took her . . . and you. And your sister." Tears filled his eyes. "I never left you, Alexis, or your mother, Em. They *took* you from me and forced you into Dormance."

Emery could feel the pain pulsing from her father as if she were experiencing it herself. As much as she didn't want to cause her father more pain, there were too many questions that needed answering. "When did that happen? When did they take us?"

"Do you remember when I was permanently deployed?"

Emery remembered that day *almost* perfectly, but there had been a brief period of time that she couldn't quite piece together . . . almost as though time had frozen, just temporarily, and then started again.

And then it came to her.

She gasped as the realization hit her. "That same day, the day you were deployed—I was six and Alexis was four. That's when it happened?"

Her father nodded, a solemn look in his eyes. "The FCW was stationed just outside our house as I was getting ready to leave. I was going to visit the sponsor of the project to see if we could get more funding. Your mother had come down with something and asked if I could go in her place." He drew in a shaky breath. "The minute I stepped outside, the FCW attacked and held me captive. They administered the lethargum on you, your sister, and your mother. They made me watch as they carried your lifeless bodies from the house." His last words were barely above a whisper.

Tears burned her eyes. "Where did they take you?"

"I was held prisoner for a while. For years, they'd tried to get information out of your mother, but she never budged. Their tactics were impressive, but they weren't clever enough. Your mom saw through their schemes every time." His face lifted from the darkness for a brief moment. "Strong woman."

"What happened after that?" Emery whispered.

"Seeing as your mother, the sponsor of the program, and I were the only ones who knew the intimate details of Alpha One, they went for the next best alternative: to try to break me to the point where I would tell them what they needed to know, while holding my family as collateral."

Emery's jaw tensed at the thought. "And that's how you got the . . ." She hesitated, then pointed to her cheek to clarify that she was asking about his scar.

Byron averted his gaze to the ground, then nodded. "Just one of Novak's many tactics for getting information."

"I'm so sorry, dad," Emery said, her voice shaking. "I had no idea."

Byron lifted his gaze. "For what, sweetheart? You didn't do anything wrong. And there was nothing you could have done to stop them. You were just a little girl."

"I know. It's just hard to hear." She cleared her throat, hoping that her father would continue this uncanny streak of openness with her. All the questions she'd had about Dormance were finally being answered. Things were finally becoming clear. "It's hard to think that mom would create something that could have such dire consequences. She created Alpha One for the right reasons," she pressed, her cheeks flushing. "Didn't she?"

Byron sighed. "That's a difficult question to answer. Yes and no. At the time, I understood the premise—train our soldiers in a simulated environment where they would be safe and free from harm. But my biggest concern was what would happen if the technology fell into the wrong hands." He paused. "Unfortunately, that concern became a reality."

Emery fidgeted with the edge of her napkin, tearing off small pieces bit by bit. "Mom didn't know it was going to fall into the wrong hands . . ."

Suddenly, as if she'd flipped a switch, her father's eyes blazed with rage. "Regardless, it should have been part of the protocol. That was the one major flaw in the Alpha One initiative. No one, not even your mother, took the time to put measures in place to ensure that it could never fall into the wrong hands." He grunted. "The naivety of the whole thing still baffles me to this day."

Emery sat back, in shock at her father's sudden outburst. "I'm sure she would have—"

"No. It's not that simple. If Alpha One had never been created in the first place, none of this would have happened. You have to understand, Emery. I didn't know if I'd ever see my family again. I've lived with that uncertainty for most of my life." He shook his head. "Alpha One went from your mother's pride and joy to my worst nightmare."

Now it was Emery's turn to be angry. "Mom didn't know that this was going to happen, and I'm sure if she did, she would have halted any and all progress on Alpha One. You need to stop blaming her. This isn't *all* her fault!"

"That's enough, Emery," her father scolded. "What's done is done. It's in the past. There's no use rehashing what could and should have happened. We're here now, so let's focus on the present." He picked up his slice of pizza, dismissing the conversation entirely.

All Emery could do was sigh. She'd pushed him too far.

After fifteen awkward minutes of complete and utter silence, Naia spoke up. "So," she said cautiously, "since we're focusing on the present, we should probably discuss the plan from this point forward. By now, I'm sure Novak and the others have realized that you've gone missing."

Emery drew her lower lip between her teeth. "There's something else. Mason and Warren are under Novak's control. Torin seems to be missing and, although I have no idea where he is, I'm guessing that Novak has something to do with his disappearance. He has to be here. Somewhere."

"What makes you say that?" Naia asked.

"Well, the night I was captured and brought here was the same night I was supposed to meet with Torin to strategize. I'd just filled him in on everything in my mom's letter." She paused to look at her father, hoping he wouldn't lash out again. When he remained still, she continued, "But that night, I felt something strange. It felt almost as if someone were watching us." She sighed. "I just hope he's okay."

Naia lifted an eyebrow. "Victor wouldn't hurt him. He'll come to find that Torin is too valuable."

"Too valuable?" Emery looked at her questioningly. "In what way?"

"He hasn't built the disintegration module yet," her father interjected.

Emery looked back and forth between Naia and her father. Obviously, she'd missed something important. "Disintegration *what?*"

"A ticking time bomb." Byron shook his head. "It's the only way to completely destroy both the alpha and omega keys. And, seeing as Torin is one of the most tech-savvy people in the world, President Novak will need him to build it. This could end very badly."

"It could," Emery said as she looked from her father to Naia, "unless we get to Torin first."

27

The search team had been on the ground for exactly four hours and thirty minutes since discovering Emery's empty cell. Victor sat at the control station, his patience wearing thin. *Why haven't they found her yet?*

He gazed up at the holomonitors. One showed a dozen soldiers that had been deployed to downtown Chicago to check Seventh Sanctum Headquarters. Another monitor showed six soldiers in Arizona, who were currently searching Emery's house, neighborhood, and the surrounding area. Victor had sent both Mason and Warren back into Dormance to check the Darden campus, as well as her house. In the meantime, all he could do was sit and wait for their return.

Victor skulked over to Torin's pod, watching as the boy floated amongst the electric blue currents, his eyes sealed shut. He pulled the ring and pendant out of his pocket, scrutinizing each of the keys. They were made of carbon steel, one of the toughest metals known to mankind. About a year back, he'd started working on a schematic to destroy them, realizing early on that the task was much more complex than he'd originally thought. He'd considered using fire to melt the metals and mold them to take a different shape, but after a few rounds of failed testing, he discovered that heat only made the metal stronger. It was then that he realized one of Mother Nature's forces wouldn't be powerful enough. He needed the effects to be completely irreparable.

That's where Torin came in.

And, it just so happened that Emery's feelings for Torin were strong and only growing stronger. As an outsider looking in, it seemed that she was head-over-heels for the guy. Even if his squadrons didn't locate her, he knew Emery would come back. If she hadn't already, she'd realize that Torin was missing and she'd come looking for him—which meant that his time with Torin was limited.

Victor typed a seven-digit access code into the holoscreen on the outside of Torin's pod, watching as the dome-like glass slid upward. The minute oxygen entered the inside of the pod, the boy's eyes flew open. His expression was one of pure confusion as he looked at his surroundings. Confusion quickly transformed into fear.

"I'm sure you feel well rested," Victor chirped, "and if you don't, I really couldn't care less. It's time for you to get to work."

Torin's feeble attempt to escape from the pod was enough to make Victor bellow with laughter.

The holocuffs held him in place. "Where the hell am I?" he snapped.

"In my chamber, where all the magic happens," Victor replied, already reveling in his upcoming victory. "I've heard you're quite the young man—gifted when it comes to technology and, shall we say, hacking?"

"You heard right," he shot back, "but if you think I'm helping you, you're out of your goddamn mind."

Victor chortled, a low rumble sounding from his belly. "Let me put this into terms you'll understand. If you don't help me, the girl dies."

Torin clenched his teeth. "Don't you dare lay a hand on her."

"Or what?" Victor teased. "You should feel lucky. Normally, you'd already have a chip embedded and I'd be controlling your every thought, your every move." He walked around Torin and the pod like a lion stalking its prey. "There's just one problem with this, however," he coughed as he took a seat back at his desk. "It pains me to say that I don't have the knowledge to build the machine I've designed in my blueprints. I need your knowledge, skills, and expertise." He sighed. "And, in order for me to utilize those, you must be free to think on your own. My microchips are no good in this particular situation."

Torin glared at him, his mouth pressing into a firm line.

Victor continued on. "Let's move forward then, shall we?" He whirled his chair around to face the control station. After typing in a bunch of codes, a holoimage of a blueprint appeared before him. "This is my schematic for the disintegration machine. Now, I'm sure you're familiar with these?" He pulled out the alpha ring and omega pendant, dangling them in front of Torin's face.

"How did you—?"

"How I got them is irrelevant," Victor cut in. "You see, these little babies are made of carbon steel."

A know-it-all-expression crossed Torin's face. "The toughest metal known to mankind."

Victor smirked. "Very good. I knew I picked the right protégé. I built a machine a few months back, but unfortunately, it had the wrong, shall we say, *components*. Originally, I wanted to use fire to force the keys to take a different shape. They'd be unusable . . . but I quickly discovered that heat actually makes carbon steel stronger."

"Everyone knows that," Torin muttered.

"Watch yourself, boy," Victor warned as he stood up from his chair. "Don't think for a second that I won't make your life a living hell after this is all over. Show me respect and we won't have an issue. Understood?"

Besides narrowing his eyes, Torin remained still, not saying a word.

"I know that you're well-versed in the science of teleportation. I'm thinking we can use the crystal dials to our advantage. Essentially, the crystals have the power to dissolve the human body, then rebuild them into the same DNA structure in a new location. My thoughts are to cut out that last step, and use only the dissolving properties of those dials."

The lines in Torin's forehead creased as he considered this proposal.

"Well?" Victor pressed.

Torin furrowed his brows. "How do you expect me to work when I'm bound to this . . . thing?" He gazed up at the structure he was standing in.

"It's a captivity pod," Victor replied. "Now, I *will* release you, but only under certain circumstances."

Torin gave him an exasperated look. "Which are?"

"I can't let you have free rein of the chamber, given recent events." He bit his tongue, not wanting to mention the debacle surrounding Emery's untimely escape. Best for him to think that Emery was still under his watch, even though she wasn't. "You can use the laboratory, but you'll be supervised by one of my soldiers at all times."

Torin grunted. "Fair enough."

"We've wasted enough time. If you'll follow me . . ."

The pod's glass dome resurfaced, closing Torin in as it had before. He floated along behind Victor until they reached a glass-paned double door, to which he scanned his retina, grinning as the doors opened to welcome him.

"Ready?"

+ + +

As Torin entered the lab, he could hardly believe his eyes. The equipment was unlike anything he'd ever seen before. The latest and greatest teptrometer stood at one end of the room, which was used for testing the long-term effects of teleportation on the human brain. The REGAL 5000 stood in another corner, a testing device for decreasing the time element in international teleportation. The only other machine he recognized was the ARC-G2, which was used to test physical and internal properties and compatibilities of any substance in the world. There were at least a dozen others that were completely foreign to him.

Victor came into Torin's line of sight, stopping at one of the white lab tables to press a button. A giant holoscreen illuminated above the table. "For your reference, the work we do in here is all holobased. Just search for the materials you need here," he pointed at the top left of the screen, "then fashion it into the optimal shape, preferably along the same lines as the blueprint."

Torin nodded, his eyes wide with amazement. He didn't want to appear too excited since Victor was technically the enemy, but this lab was top-of-the-line. Actually, it was *far above* top-of-the-line. This was his forte.

On the inside, he was fully and completely geeking out. Novak's facility was a dream come true.

"You can adjust the properties here," Victor continued, pointing to the lower right corner of the screen. "Obviously, we need the proper weights assigned to each object to ensure it doesn't self-destruct. I assume you know how to code?"

"Learned it when I was eight years old."

Victor turned toward him. "I see." He gazed at the dome Torin was standing in. A shadow of doubt flickered across his eyes but, he appeared to have made up his mind because he moved closer to the pod and slowly released Torin from its confines.

The holocuffs disappeared as if they'd never been there to begin with. Torin rubbed his wrists, the skin slightly pink in color, tender to the touch from the electric currents.

"Get to work," Victor instructed as he headed toward the door. "Oh, and that gentleman you see just outside the door?"

Torin's gaze landed on a large, burly man standing outside of the glass walls. He was half human, half machine. He gulped, waiting for Victor to continue.

"That's Von. Try to escape and you'll be down for the count before you know it." He smirked, then strolled through the sliding glass doors.

Torin looked down at the screen in front of him, then at Von, then back at the screen. He eyed the holographic schematic. *This is going to take a while.*

28

Four days had passed since Emery's escape from Novak's chamber. Four days, and she was still free. She'd stayed safely tucked away in the cave with Naia and her father, spending every waking moment brainstorming ways to defeat Victor. Needless to say, their brains were fried.

Unable to process another thought, Emery picked up a tablet from a nearby table and loaded a mindless game that required her to guide a cartoon bunny through a maze of hunters. Her objective, of course, was to keep it alive. *Story of my life.*

Naia emerged from the back of the cave, her hair tousled and unkempt. Clearly, she'd just woken up from a nap. "Come up with any bright ideas?" she yawned.

"I don't know how you sleep back there on that 'bed' of pine needles and leaves," Emery responded, dodging the question.

"I'm going to take that as a no," Naia murmured as she walked over to the SmartMeal machine. "On a different note, if you happen to have an idea as to how to make my coffee arrive faster, let me know."

"Har-har," Emery joked. "While speeding up the delivery time of your coffee is super important, there are other things topping my list at the present moment."

Naia smiled. "I still think that turning yourself—"

"Don't even say it," Emery interrupted, knowing exactly what she was about to propose. "I just escaped. I can't go back there. Novak will just throw me in a cell again and leave me to wither and die." She shuddered at the thought.

Naia rolled her eyes. "Don't be so dramatic." She smiled as a cup of coffee slowly materialized underneath the SmartMeal machine. "Three minutes. That has to be a new record." She picked up the mug and blew on the steaming liquid before taking a sip.

"Impressive," Emery mumbled, distracted by the game on the tablet. She directed the bunny to crawl and hide under a hedge as a hunter tiptoed by with his spear raised and ready to strike. The feet stopped where her little creature was hiding. After what felt like an eternity, the hunter finally walked away. Without realizing it, she let out the breath she'd been holding in. *Not so mindless after all.*

Naia marched over and grabbed the tablet right out of her hands. With indignation, she pressed the "off" button.

Emery pouted as the screen went black. "I almost won, you know."

"Oh, come on, you didn't stand a chance. That hunter was going to find you one way or another."

An awkward silence filled the room.

"You mean like Novak's going to find me? One way or another?" Emery asked, her voice barely above a whisper. The thought was truly terrifying. How had he not found her yet? He was one of the most powerful people in the world and she was right underneath his nose.

Naia waved away her insecurity. "That's not what I meant, and you know it. Come on, we need to focus," she scolded as she sat down across from her. "What if you turn yourself in and—?"

Emery folded her arms. "I already told you to not even mention that. You need to wipe the idea from your mind."

"Just hear me out," she pleaded. "Draw us a diagram of what you remember from President Novak's Chamber. That way, after you turn yourself in, your father and I can work our way in and kill the rat bastard." Her eyes gleamed with devious intent.

"There's just one problem with your plan," Emery pointed out. "I don't remember anything from the chamber. I was completely unconscious and when I woke up, I was in a prison cell."

"But you said he took you underground. To see the bodies . . ."

Without warning, an image from that day resurfaced. With wide eyes, Emery moved forward to the edge of her seat. "I'm remembering something. A long hallway. I thought there'd be a door at the end of it, but there wasn't. Just a giant wall." She scrunched her face, trying to recall what else she'd seen. "The floor suddenly began to lower while we were on it until we reached a basement. It was pitch black."

Naia scratched her chin. "Did you notice any exits or entrances while you were down there?"

Emery shook her head. "Honestly, no. It was so dark and I was so disturbed when I saw the bodies . . . that was all I could focus on."

Naia sighed, taking another sip of her coffee. "Well, it isn't much, but it's a start." She powered on one of the tablets and handed it to her. "Can you try to draw it?"

Emery nodded, taking the tablet into her hands. "I can't promise it'll be pretty, but I'll do my best."

Naia sat back in her chair and closed her eyes while Emery tapped away on the tablet, moving her finger back and forth and up and down on the screen.

Five minutes later, she nudged Naia's shoulder and handed her the child-like illustration. She could feel the heat rising in her cheeks. "Art was never my strong suit."

Naia laughed. "Like I said, it's a start. Hey, Byron!"

In a split second, Emery's father appeared from the back of the cave, looking disgruntled and tired. "Based on this drawing, do you think we can pinpoint where the entrances to the chamber are?"

Byron rubbed his eyes as he walked over to where they were sitting. "I was trying to sleep, you know," he grunted.

"Well excuse me, but I think we have more important things to be doing than sleeping," Naia teased as she extended the tablet to him. "Here, look."

Byron examined the drawing, zooming in and out a few times before speaking. "If I'm being completely honest, I'm not sure there's enough information here." He shot an apologetic glance at his daughter. "It's good, just not enough. We need more."

Emery shot Naia a knowing look. "I tried."

"When you say we need more," Naia began, "what exactly do you mean?"

Byron ran a hand through his grey-flecked hair. "Ideally, we need someone who's on the inside."

Their silent unison confirmed what they were all thinking.

Emery sighed. "If only we had Torin." She stood up, offering to take the tablet back from her father. "He's our inside-man."

"Keep your chin up," Naia reassured. "We'll figure this out somehow. We always do."

As badly as Emery wanted to believe those words, she knew it was a long shot. Without Torin, everything felt hopeless. She'd gone from being an insider to an outsider in the blink of an eye. Torin was the one person they needed most, and he wasn't here.

Emery turned away from her father and Naia, hoping to hide the bleak expression that was clouding her face. She reloaded the game on her tablet, watching hopelessly as her rabbit was brutally decimated by a hoard of angry hunters.

29

What am I doing? Torin thought as he threw a piece of carbon steel to the side of the desk. He'd been working in the lab for seventy-two hours straight with no sleep and very little food. In that time, he'd managed to create two prototypes of machines that he truly thought would destroy the carbon steel, but during the testing phase, the samples had remained unharmed and untouched.

Not to mention, all he could seem to think about was Emery. She'd know what to do. As strange as it sounded, she was always the one coming up with ideas and strategizing her way through the muddiest of waters. Sure, he had the knowledge, but Emery had the drive. *She probably would have figured out a way out of here by now.* His heart sank as he realized that he had no idea where she was. If she was safe. If she was even alive.

Of course she's alive. No more negative thoughts. He focused his attention back on the task at hand. There was only so much coding he could do before everything started to blur together. Victor had entered the lab that morning, asking him for an update on his progress. Torin had lied, saying that he was close to having the final prototype ready, even though he was far from it. Victor had reminded him that it needed to be completed by day five.

It was day three.

Torin spun his chair around, noticing that Von wasn't in his usual spot. His eyes searched the outside of the glass, looking for some sign of the half-robot bodyguard, but he was nowhere to be found. Ideas of freedom flourished in his mind, if only for a brief moment. In his heart, he knew it was too risky to try to escape on a whim—there were guards everywhere and cameras documenting his every move. He needed a plan, and a good one at that.

This is where having master hacking skills came in handy.

His side project, in addition to building Novak's disintegration machine, was Project Contact-Anyone-In-The-Outside-World-And-Soon. He needed a better name, but for now, it'd have to do.

He'd decoded the lab's main phone line, allowing him to discreetly make a call or send a message. Now he just had to make sure that no calls nor messages were tracked or registered on any of Novak's communication logs.

He looked over his shoulder, checking once more to confirm Von hadn't returned. The hallway was still empty.

This might be my one and only shot.

He whirled back around in his chair, quickly typing the slew of codes into the control station. A green box appeared with the words: DIRECT COMMUNICATION TO. He leaned forward in his chair, licking his lips as adrenaline coursed through his veins. This was it.

He tried to recall Emery's phone number from the top of his head, but the numbers were a giant jumbled mess, like everything else he was working on. Victor had confiscated his phone before he'd entered the lab, so that wasn't an option. He banged his head on the desk in front of him, his aggravation climbing. When he lifted his head, another box appeared at the bottom right corner of the screen. This one said: SEARCH SIGNAL.

Memories of years past flooded his mind. He'd been the one to program all of 7S's tablets and electronics when he'd first started working there, before he'd gotten promoted to Junior Head of Technology. Every device had been programmed with the same four-digit code, 7STC followed by a dash and a number to differentiate between the different devices. He typed in the letters, waiting impatiently as the database searched for a signal.

Two minutes went by slower than a tortoise making its way to water.

He was about to give up hope when the screen lit up.

Available Network: 7STC-14N.

Torin almost fell out of his seat. He touched the holoscreen, watching as the system attempted to establish a connection with 7STC-14N. His fingers flew as he typed a message, then pressed send. The message icon hovered in the air. It pulsed slowly at first, then grew more rapid.

Come on. Send.

The icon was hardly recognizable, like a mirage in the desert heat, as the pulsing grew quicker. Torin blinked and when he opened his eyes, the icon was gone. He breathed a sigh of relief as a new icon, a green light, blinked in its place to indicate the message had been sent.

Success!

He made some ludicrous hand motions in the air, air-fives and the like, feeling proud of his nearly impossible accomplishment. And then it dawned on him. He wouldn't get an answer right away. He'd have to wait.

He brought his hand to his mouth, biting on what was left of a hangnail. Torin had no idea who would receive the message, or who was even on the other side, but he could only hope that whoever it was would be the ticket to his freedom.

30

"This isn't possible!" Naia shouted from the back of the cave. In a flash, she appeared from behind the back wall, tablet in hand. She ran over, waving it in the air frantically.

"What isn't possible?" Emery asked in a disinterested tone. She was starting to get cabin fever, or in this case cave fever, which made it hard to feel energized or even the slightest bit hopeful.

"It's a message," Naia huffed, trying to catch her breath. "Just . . . here, you read it."

Suddenly interested, Emery jumped up from her seat and grabbed the tablet from Naia. She scanned the words on the screen: *Sergeant Torin Porter here. Anybody out there?*

Her heart swelled like a dozen balloons that had just been released into the air. He'd found them. He'd found a way through.

"Quick! Write something back before we lose the connection," Naia urged, peering over her shoulder.

Emery here. With Naia and my father. She pressed send, waiting anxiously for him to respond. After only a few seconds, the screen lit up again.

Thank god. Where are you? Are you safe?

Emery tapped the letters onto the screen as quickly as she could manage. *We're safe. We're in a cave on the mountains, west of President Novak's Chamber. Where are you?*

It took longer this time for the response to come through. Emery ran her fingers through her hair, hoping that it hadn't been lost somewhere in holospace. Two minutes passed before the screen lit up again.

In Novak's Chamber, in the lab. Has me building a disintegration machine to destroy the ring and the pendant. SOS.

"The connection's getting weaker by the minute," Naia warned, pointing to the signal strength.

Emery nodded as her fingers picked up pace. *Can you send us a schematic of the chamber? We need to find a way in.*

They waited anxiously behind the screen—their beacon of hope, their guiding light.

Thirty minutes passed without a response. Emery continued to stare at the screen, trying to keep what little hope she had left alive.

"We lost the connection," Naia said with a sigh as the last bar on the signal disappeared.

For some reason, Emery just couldn't accept that the connection had been lost. "We need to try to reconnect. He *will* reach out to us again. I know he will."

With a sad smile, Naia shrugged and patted her shoulder. "I sure hope so, but Torin's the guy for that, remember?" She gestured to herself and her father. "If anyone can fix the signal and reconnect, it'll be Torin, not us."

Emery's shoulders slumped. She knew Naia was right, but didn't dare admit it.

"Hey, look on the bright side," Naia added quickly. "At least we know where he is and that he's safe."

"Safe?" Emery retorted. "No one is safe in there."

Naia sighed. "There's not much we can do about it right now, so we may as well order dinner and get some rest," she suggested as she walked over to SmartMeal. "We'll need our strength once the schematic is in our hands. Agreed?"

Again, Naia was right, but Emery didn't say a word.

Naia ignored her pouting. "Does anything in particular sound good?"

Emery wasn't hungry. She couldn't even think of eating nor sleeping at a time like this. Naia's question went unanswered as she powered on a nearby tablet. *Poor Torin. Stuck in the chamber all alone.* She could only hope that Novak was treating him better than he'd treated her. Albeit a prisoner, it sounded like Novak needed him sharp and

226

focused, which meant he probably wasn't being thrown into a cell to rot every night. *And* he was probably being fed better food than she'd had the luxury of tasting; but even if this wasn't the case, she had to pretend it was, for her own sanity.

Tablet in hand, Emery sulked to the back of the cave, away from her father and Naia who were conversing quietly over a makeshift table. She knew she should join in, but the thought of discussing Novak and his plans, Torin's potential plans, plus their *own* plans was exhausting. Enough already.

All she wanted at that moment was to be alone to process everything, to feel everything she was feeling. Anger, hurt, worry. What if they failed? What if Novak won, forcing all of humankind to live in a world where their every action, their every move, was controlled? Never to speak an original thought or feel a true feeling ever again?

These feelings of doubt were familiar. The last time she'd felt like this was a few months ago. And who had been there to guide her through it all and help keep her head high when all she wanted to do was let it fall?

Torin.

With a loud sigh, Emery laid down on the makeshift bed. She fluffed some pine needles underneath her neck for support, but they didn't do much in the way of comfort. Her eyes focused intently on the tablet's black screen. *Come on, light up.*

She prayed for a message to come, but after an hour had gone by, it was clear there wasn't one coming. Not tonight. Her eyes didn't leave the screen until finally, her mind forced her eyes shut, and she drifted away into a restless sleep.

31

Von was back.

Torin moved quickly to shut down the system as fast as possible without looking hurried or panicked. Von entered the laboratory, followed by an irate Victor. Torin hastily grabbed one of the prototypes and started messing with it, pretending to be hard at work.

Victor approached his work station, his mouth pressed in a firm line. "Is this the one?"

Torin looked up from the prototype. "Almost. Just a few more kinks to work out and we should be all set." He was sure the chief could hear the guilt lining his voice.

Victor swiped the prototype from his hands and examined it in great detail. "This looks exactly like the last one," he snarled as he tossed it onto the desk. "I'm moving your deadline up. Have the machine completed by tomorrow at noon."

Torin's eyes grew wide. "I can't promise—"

"You'll do it," Victor commanded. "Or you'll be of no use to me. And do you know what I do to things that are of no use to me?" He glanced over at Von who was busy reloading his AK-47.

Torin nodded, catching his drift. "Tomorrow then."

"Tomorrow *at noon*," he corrected, his fingers sliding across the smooth surface as he strode toward the door.

"With all honesty, I'll probably need close to the whole day." Torin gave him his best puppy-dog eyes. Victor stopped in his tracks and turned to give him a menacing look, to which Torin shrugged and simply replied, "You can't rush genius."

The chief took a few steps back in his direction. "Wipe that smug look off of your face. And actually, I *can* rush genius. My house, my rules," he hissed. "Get it done."

Torin didn't say another word as he watched the chief walk out the doors. The room was dead silent. He spun his chair back around to face his work station, his mind jumbled with all the items on his to-do list. *First things first.* If he ever hoped to escape, he had to get the schematic to Emery. The disintegration machine would have to wait.

By the time he looked up at the clock, it was well into early morning, around two o'clock. Before getting started, he'd sat patiently, waiting for Von to leave, but after thirty minutes of no movement, he'd given up on that thought.

He couldn't afford to waste another minute. He'd managed to work on the schematic without Von even noticing—at least, he didn't *think* Von had seen him.

Using the rotation feature on the holoscreen, he examined his latest and greatest schematic of Novak's chambers to make sure it was up to par. One area was missing information—Novak had never taken him there, so he didn't want to draw anything that could be misleading. Instead, he'd applied shading, graying it out, so as to not confuse Emery, Naia, or the Commander. He glanced at the clock again. His comrades were probably fast asleep, but he decided to send it anyway, seeing as time was of the essence.

Hacking into the mainframe was easier this time around, and so was connecting to the signal. He attached the file containing the schematic to his message and wrote: *Deadline moved to today at noon – help!*

A wave of relief washed over him as he pressed the send button. Even in such a technologically-advanced world, the large message still took time to make its way across the server. He looked at the progress bar underneath the message icon. Twenty minutes.

In twenty minutes, they'd have everything they needed to get him out of there.

As inconspicuously as he could, Torin turned his head to steal another look at Von who was still standing with his eyes forward, not moving.

Good. He didn't see me.

His nerves began to settle. He switched his focus from the schematic of Novak's chambers to the blueprint for the disintegration machine. He picked up the most recent prototype, scrutinizing every last detail. An idea came to him—an utterly stupid, yet brilliant idea. Novak would probably have his head if he went through with it, but what did he really have to lose? Sure, he'd make the disintegration machine, just as Novak had requested.

But ease of use? Now, *that* was the one thing he had complete control over.

32

Ping.

Emery's eyes fluttered open, her head subconsciously turning toward the source of the noise. A soft white light emanated from one of the tablets across the room. She pulled herself upward, her back aching from sleeping on the cave floor all week. She tiptoed over to the tablet and lifted it to eye level.

A new message.

She tapped on the file greedily, watching as the schematic downloaded. Ten minutes loading time. *Really? Even in the 7S world?*

With a grunt, she set the tablet down, trying to figure out what to do to pass the time. She decided to order a coffee from SmartMeal. *Three minutes gone.*

She drank said coffee, sipping it as slowly as she could manage. *Four minutes gone.*

She walked over to where Naia was sleeping and woke her. *One minute gone.*

She hurried over to her father and woke him. *One minute gone.*

With only sixty seconds remaining, Emery, Byron, and Naia all huddled over the tablet, anxiously awaiting the schematic's arrival.

3 . . . 2 . . . 1.

And there it was. Right before her very eyes. It was the most detailed drawing she'd ever seen. The straight lines, the sharp edges, and the defined corners all came to life as Naia pushed a button on the tablet. The schematic floated before them in holographic fashion. Emery swiped her hand across the image, watching as the 3D blueprint of the chamber made a 180-degree turn. If she hadn't known any better, she would have sworn a professional architect had created it. Torin had even labeled certain areas with an X to indicate where the guards were stationed.

"This is quite impressive," Byron exhaled, unable to take his eyes off of it.

When Emery finally broke her eyes from the image, she noticed that there was a message accompanying the file. She quickly opened it and read the text, biting her lip so hard that she drew blood.

"We have a slight problem," Emery announced as she looked up from the tablet.

Byron and Naia turned toward her with weary expressions. "What is it?" they both asked in unison.

"Torin's deadline," Emery groaned. "It's been moved up. To today at noon."

Byron nodded, completely unfazed. Seeing as he was the Commander of the Seventh Sanctum, sleep was a mere luxury. Always on the go, always fighting new battles, no matter what time of day it was. With complete focus, he pointed to one of the side entrances on the east side of the building. "We could enter here."

"Even though Torin didn't draw any Xs, I'm guessing the outside entrances are probably heavily guarded with armed soldiers," Naia thought aloud, her finger grazing her chin. "What about here?" She pointed to an area with a large glass window.

Emery shook her head. "That glass is probably triple-paned and will be impossible to break without making too much noise and drawing unwanted attention to ourselves." She knelt down to observe the schematic in more detail, her eyes flitting back and forth between the two entrance points. "From what I know about Novak, he'll expect us to try to sneak through a window or side door. Those will be the most heavily armed."

"Perhaps there's another cell window that we can get through," Byron chimed in. "One that's not holding a prisoner captive? The door wouldn't be locked."

Emery shook her head again. "That's risky. I highly doubt Novak keeps those cell doors unlocked." She gave the schematic another once-over, then sighed. "I can't believe I'm about to admit this, Naia, but I think you were right all along."

Naia looked up from the hologram, her face beaming. "About the glass window?"

"No, about . . ." She hesitated, not wanting to say the words. "Turning myself in."

A giant grin stretched across Naia's face. She beamed with satisfaction. "I knew you'd come around."

Emery folded her arms. "But only as a distraction. See this area right here?" She motioned toward the front door and the side door, an X stationed in the middle of the hallway. "It's the only area where there's just one guard, but two entrances. If I enter through the front, both the guard and Novak will be preoccupied with taking me back to my cell." She shivered at the thought, the scent of the damp, musty stone coming back to her. "Then, the two of you can enter through the side door."

"What do you propose if, by some stroke of misfortune, Torin got the placement of the guards wrong?" Naia asked.

"Naia has a point," Byron pointed out. "The guards could be on a rotational shift every thirty minutes or hour."

Emery pondered this for a moment. "That's just a risk we'll have to take. Even if there's a guard at that side door, it's still two against one. I have no doubt that you and my father would be able to take him out."

"Speaking of taking people out," Naia said as she walked over to the opposite side of the cave. "We'll probably need these." She brushed her hands across the ground, removing a layer of pine needles, leaves, and branches to reveal a small collection of artillery. She pulled out one M60, one AK-47, and one electrified dagger.

A pang of guilt hit Emery square in the stomach. It was the same dagger that Rhea had thrown at her. Right before she'd . . .

Emery eyed the dagger, trying to keep the image of Rhea's lifeless body at bay. "I'll take that," she said, reaching for it. "These were hidden here the whole time?"

"It was all I could manage to bring with me," Naia explained as she handed the M60 to the Commander. "We searched for more at 7S Headquarters after I found your father, but the place had been raided."

"Meaning that the guards in the chamber have a nice collection of weaponry to choose from," Byron added.

Emery nodded as she tucked the dagger into the back waistband of her pants, then pulled her shirt over the handle.

For the remainder of the morning, the trio discussed their plan in greater detail, playing the what-if game to prepare for worst-case scenarios. Her father was the best at coming up with these, albeit some of his ideas were a little out there. Only when it felt like they'd beaten a dead horse did they decide it'd be wise to get some rest. Emery looked at the tablet, realizing that it was 6:30 in the morning. A little shut-eye couldn't hurt. "We've been at this all morning. Time to give it a rest."

Naia and Byron looked up from where they were seated, scribbled holotext floating in waves around them. Yes, their plan was a mess. Yes, it was slightly unorganized. But at least they had *something*.

"I'm not sure we're ready yet," Byron said firmly. "We need at least another hour."

The bags underneath his eyes and permanent crease in his forehead said otherwise. Emery looked at Naia. Her hair was tousled and her eyelids had started to droop. "We'll have an hour or so to prepare *after* we get some sleep," Emery responded. It sounded more like an order than a suggestion. "Otherwise we're bound to fail."

"I thought our plan was to strike tonight?" Naia asked as she continued to scribble text into the air.

Emery walked over to where they were sitting. She held her hand out, waiting for them to fork over the tablet. Naia rolled her eyes, but obliged. Emery shut it down, watching as their plan faded from the air. "We'll make adjustments once we wake up."

"And what adjustments are those?" Byron asked.

Emery tilted her head. "Something they'll never expect."

Byron and Naia regarded her with confused expressions.

"A morning raid," Emery clarified with a coy smile. "We sleep for two hours. And then we strike at 0900. Today."

33

It was early morning and Torin awoke to someone shaking his shoulder. It was Von. "No sleep. Machine incomplete."

Torin yawned, stretching his arms overhead, wishing that the giant lug would leave him be. "Okay, okay. I'll get right on that."

Von turned on his heel and walked back outside the glass doors, positioning himself in the same usual spot, as if the coordinates were permanently mapped in his brain. Who was he kidding? They probably were.

Torin turned his attention to the most recent version of the disintegration machine. After sending the schematic of Novak's chambers to Emery, he'd immediately started working on his original project. He hoped he'd get some sort of response from her explaining what their game plan was, but there'd only been crickets.

Nothing but silence.

He'd double-checked to make sure the message had been delivered and opened. And it had. He'd just have to trust that they'd received it in time and had been able to come up with some semblance of a plan. And that they'd come for him sooner rather than later.

Torin's thoughts scattered as he looked down at the current prototype. In its current state, it was easier to use than a toaster-oven: place the item on the platform, press the black button, and *poof!* What was once metal would turn to dust. He placed a sample of carbon steel on the small platform, lining it up just right, then pressed the button. Just as he'd predicted, the sample disintegrated right before his very eyes; what was once indestructible metal turned to tiny specks of dust and ash. He sat back in his chair, rubbing the stubble on the side of his cheek.

It's too easy.

It didn't happen often, but he was stumped. Making his masterpiece more difficult to use wasn't as simple as he'd originally thought. A few ideas sprang to mind, but none of them seemed feasible given the time restriction he was currently under.

He tapped his fingers on the table, waiting for another brilliant idea to come to him. He pulled the omega pendant from the inside pocket of his shirt and stared at it, hoping that it would suddenly shout an idea at him, or at least guide him in the right direction.

"Come on," he whispered as he turned the omega pendant over in his hands, trying to remember what Emery had told him. "You worked for Emery."

He closed his eyes, squeezing them shut as he held the pendant tightly in his grip. After a few seconds, he opened one eye, dismayed to see the pendant still staring back at him. "Give me something. Anything." He glanced around him, hoping that maybe his surroundings would change. He had no idea how the pendant worked, but he was determined to find out.

"Omega!" he barked, then squeezed his eyes shut. Upon opening them once again, nothing had changed. He was still in Novak's lab.

He looked at the pendant more closely. "Omega, omega. Your counterpart is Alpha." A thought occurred to him. "Alpha and Omega," he said softly, hoping it would work.

And it did.

When he opened his eyes, he was no longer in the lab, but instead, standing in the middle of FCW's underground quarters. In Dormance.

I did it! I'm in a flashback.

His heartbeat thrummed in his ears with disbelief and he tried to neutralize his sudden adrenaline rush by taking slow, deep inhales. With each exhale, his heart calmed, but his anxiety only grew. His eyes traveled up a nearby wall and he couldn't help but gape at the intricate detailing of the room. Sure, he'd seen the underground quarters through a holoscreen when he'd reached out to Emery, but actually being there, in person, was entirely different. The walls were covered in a crisp gold paint with maroon and black embellishments dashed every here and there. He gazed at the marble crown molding, swirls of black, grey, and white intersecting at various points to create breathtaking designs. Two oversized leather chairs sat across from one another, separated only by a coffee table. Torin recognized it all. Images of Emery in that very room flashed through his mind.

He jumped as a door creaked open.

Behind door number one is . . .

Light on his feet, Torin made his way over to the door, peering around the edge to see where it led. A sigh of relief escaped his lips. It was just another hallway of seemingly little significance, but he noticed that, just a few feet away, another door was slightly cracked as well. With his body flattened against the wall, he snuck over to door number two and carefully poked his head around the frame. The first thing his eyes settled on was a blonde head of hair.

"Naia! Oh, thank god," Torin said as he made his way into the room. "I was starting to get a little nervous there." He waited for her to turn around, to respond, but she remained still. "Are you ignoring me?" His eyes shifted from the back of her head to the monitors.

Wait a second. This is familiar. Too familiar.

Emery's file was splayed out on the holomonitor for all the world to see. Line after line of text and picture after picture filled the screen. It was the same scene he'd witnessed after first hacking into the FCW's mainframe, right before Naia had reached out to him for help. Before he'd found out that *she* was one of them, one of the good guys. Before he'd ever met Emery.

And he was about to relive it.

He moved closer to Naia, waving his hand in front of her face. "Naia, hello?"

She continued to stare at the screen, scrutinizing every last word.

She can't see me. His eyes flickered to the screen. Now that he thought about it, he'd never actually had the chance to uncover what was in Emery's file. His eyes scanned the numerous lines of text, searching for something of significance. And that's when he saw it.

Emery Rae Parker. Candidate number 082. Eleven-digit microchip identification number: 00000005694. Fingerprint archive.

He watched as Naia pulled a small sphere from her pocket, then released a drawer holding Emery's black training clothes. *And this is where she drops it into Emery's boot,* he recalled, watching as that exact action took place. Torin noticed the scene floating further and further away from him, like he was on a slow train moving backward through time. He clasped the pendant tight, squeezing it in the palm of his hand as everything around him went dark.

When the light returned, Torin found himself back in the brightly lit laboratory, just as he'd left it. The prototype was still on the table and Von was still guarding his post.

He gazed at the omega pendant, feeling amazed by what had just happened. He quickly tucked the necklace back into the inside pocket of his shirt and logged onto the database. He had no choice. He had to hack into the same system he'd just seen in the flashback, the one that stored all participant information for the Alpha Drive initiative. He typed in Emery's name, tapping his foot impatiently as the system searched through hundreds of files. Finally, it landed on the one he was looking for.

Emery Rae Parker.

The same girl he'd been swooning over for months. The same girl who had stood there, frozen in time, when he'd told her he loved her. She *had* said that her feelings had grown. Their chemistry was undeniable. She had to feel the same way he did . . .

Right?

Torin pushed the thought from his mind and focused on the task at hand. He located her participant number, 082, as well as her eleven-digit microchip ID, 00000005694. He looked at the number more closely. Did that number mean she was the 5,694th person to have a microchip implanted into her body? How many others had Novak gotten to?

Perplexed by this discovery, he diverted from his current mission to research the global population at the close of the last calendar year, 2054: 10.6 billion.

Interesting.

He reopened Novak's database and began searching for the number of people with implanted microchips. After doing some digging, he finally found what he was looking for: 10,599,999,997. He sat back from his chair, baffled by this number. There were 10,600,000,000 people in the world and 10,599,999,997 people had microchips. Which meant that, currently, there were only three people in the entire world that didn't have one. His eyes widened as he realized who those people were.

Warren. Novak. And me.

That meant Novak had already deployed all of the microchips and that they should be fully activated. It also meant that the chief could allegedly control whomever he pleased. But in taking a closer look, he realized that only half of the microchips were in use.

Why haven't the rest been activated?

As long as Novak had the disintegration machine, there wasn't even a slight chance he could be stopped. He would rule without consequence. And eventually, Torin would be forced to get his microchip and finally succumb to the chief's control. He shook his head. Sadly for the chief, the plan he'd worked so tirelessly for was about to blow up right in his face.

Torin had a new plan. And boy, was it a good one.

He opened the programming module for the disintegration machine and keyed in Emery's candidate number and microchip identification number. He saved the programming, then rebooted the machine (which he'd so aptly named the Porter 8000). He placed another sample on the platform of the machine, crossing his fingers that the programming would work. He brought his finger to the button and pressed it, watching as the scanner tried to identify his fingerprints.

Invalid ID.

His grin stretched from ear to ear. "It worked," he whispered, breathing a sigh of relief. He rolled his chair away, feeling proud of what he'd just created. Novak could destroy the keys . . .

But he'd need Emery's fingerprint to do so.

34

A nightmare visited Emery during her nap. It was one that would haunt her for years to come.

She was at home with her mother and sister in Arizona, enjoying a hot, dry evening splashing around in the pool. As her mother got out of the water to check on the barbecue, Emery noticed she was moving much slower than usual. Her body looked frail, almost skeleton-like, as she slinked toward the grill.

Emery got out after her, realizing that her own body was moving just as slow. She looked down at her feet. Her anklebones were protruding and her toes were starting to shrivel up underneath her, making it difficult to maintain her balance. She stood in place, afraid that if she took another step, she'd crumble to the ground in pieces.

"Mom," she called out, "are you okay?"

Her mother turned to face her, tongs in hand. There were patches on her skull where her hair had fallen out, her hairline receding further and further back from her forehead. Her deep grey eyes were sunken in along with her cheekbones, accentuating her jawline in an unhealthy way.

Emery staggered back at the unexpected change in her mother's appearance, feeling both terrified and concerned for her well-being.

"We all have to die at some point," her mother said, her voice empty as it echoed through the desert. "It's unnatural to live forever."

"What are you talking about?" Emery whirled around to face her sister, who was still floating in the pool. "What is she talking about?"

But her sister wasn't her sister anymore. She was now a pile of bones, laid out perfectly on a pool raft, as if someone had excavated her grave and pulled her out piece by piece only to be scorched by the unforgiving Arizona sun. The bones began to disintegrate. A gust of wind swept them away.

Emery reeled back toward her mother, her eyes wide with fear as a single drop of crimson bled from her mother's nose. "We all have to die at some point," she said again.

Emery tried to take a step toward her, but her feet wouldn't move. They were stuck to the ground in a blue gel-like substance. She began to cry, reaching her arms out to her mother, wanting more than anything to help her.

Her sobbing grew louder as she watched her mother's skin melt away from her face, her arms, her legs—until there was nothing left but a pile of bones on the ground. Another gust of wind ruffled Emery's hair as it picked up her mother's remains and scurried them away into the desert heat.

She fell to her knees, chest heaving, unable to control her sobbing. As she lifted a hand to wipe her face, she screamed. The skin around her hands had turned a sickly grey, and was rapidly disappearing. She watched in horror as the wind began to sweep away her greyed flesh, working its way down her legs and up her arms. She continued to scream until the wind reached her throat, the noise ceasing, until it took all that was left of her and scattered her around the earth.

Emery shot up from her makeshift bed of pine needles and leaves, her heart pounding, sweat trickling from her forehead. She brought her hands to her face and turned them over, scrutinizing them in the dim cave light, then patted her arms and legs. Her skin was still intact. The wind hadn't taken her away.

She was still here.

Feeling shaken, Emery stood up and walked over to SmartMeal to get some water, gulping down two glasses with ease before walking back to bed. She swiped the screen on the tablet to check the time. Seven o'clock in the morning. She covered herself with a blanket of leaves and tried to fall back asleep, but every time she closed her eyes, images of her mother and sister's skeletons appeared. She lay awake for a full hour, her mother's voice haunting her.

We all have to die at some point.

35

Mason searched through Emery's bedroom in Dormance, looking for any clues that might indicate she'd been there recently. Warren was downstairs in the kitchen doing what he assumed was the exact same thing. An eruption of glass echoed throughout the house as dishes and silverware collided with the floor. The search for Emery seemed to really be testing Warren's patience.

"Mason!" he called from downstairs.

What now? Mason willed his body to stay where it was, but his feet did otherwise. Being able to think his own thoughts without being able to act on them was growing really old really fast. He sighed as his feet marched down the stairs toward the kitchen, until he stood in front of a pile of broken dishes.

"What did you find?" Warren asked.

"Nothing," he responded. The voice was his own, but he had no idea how he was forming the words without thinking them. "We should move to the next site."

Warren looked around the house one last time. "I agree, but we've already checked the entire Darden campus or, at least, the places Emery used to frequent." He came around the kitchen island, stomping through the broken glass as if it didn't exist. "We can't show up empty-handed. Disappointing President Novak isn't exactly an option."

But betraying one of your closest friends is?

In that moment, all Mason wanted to do was punch Warren square in the face. He was still reeling with animosity toward him. How was he okay with turning on them like this? In what world was joining the enemy's side the answer? He tried to gain control of his actions for the umpteenth time, ordering his fist to curl, his arm to lift and then to strike like a king cobra. But his arm remained at his side. Lifeless and unresponsive.

A phone rang, snapping Mason out of the imaginary fight scene he'd fabricated in his head. He watched as Warren answered, then turned his back, as if that would muffle the conversation.

"No, sir. We haven't had any luck. I don't think she's in Dormance."

There was silence as the other end of the line prattled away.

"We've run out of places to search. I'm telling you, sir, she's not here."

More prattling.

"Understood. We're on our way."

Warren clicked the phone off and shoved it back into his jacket pocket. "Come on. We're needed back at Novak's chambers."

Mason couldn't help but feel relieved that they hadn't found Emery. Wherever she was, he hoped she'd stay there. It was a damn good hiding spot when the most technologically-capable "chief" couldn't find you.

He followed Warren out the door, one foot in front of the other, until they reached the car. He glared at the back of his head, wishing more than anything that he could stop his now-enemy and talk some sense into him. This wasn't the Warren he knew. Why had he switched sides? Why had he betrayed them?

Warren drove them the full three hours back to Alpha Drive on the Darden campus, dodging through hundreds of statues of people who once were. Just the thought, let alone the sight of everything, was enough to give Mason chills, but it didn't seem to faze Warren. In fact, nothing seemed to faze him.

He parked the car in front of the Sychem building and burst through the front doors.

Mason unwillingly followed close behind him.

"Ladies first," Warren mocked, gesturing toward the portal.

He was lucky Mason didn't have ownership over his actions. Because if he did, Warren would be facedown on the ground with his skull bashed in.

36

Today's the day.

Victor stretched his arms overhead, yawning as he brought himself to a sitting position. Falling asleep had been difficult, seeing as Torin had made very little progress on the disintegration machine. But once he'd succumbed to the night, he'd been out like a light, and he'd stayed out. Contrary to yesterday, he felt refreshed, rejuvenated, and ready to take on the day. It was time to see what the boy-genius had come up with. *He better have something and it better be good.*

Victor changed into his usual attire—black combat boots, black dress pants, and a black oxford button-down—and grabbed a starched white lab coat from its hanger. He buttoned the coat from top to bottom so that it covered his clothing. Depending on Torin's progress, things could get messy and he didn't want to ruin his clothes.

The hallways were unusually quiet as he walked from his bed chambers to the laboratory. Warren and Mason were due back last night, but he hadn't waited up to hear their reports. If they'd found something, he would have known. Their silence had spoken volumes.

Failures.

He nodded to Von as he entered through the laboratory doors, fixing his eyes on the back of Torin's head. "What do you have for me?" he asked as he walked over to the desk. It wasn't so much a question as it was a demand.

Torin swiveled in his desk chair, looking startled by the sudden entrance. In his hands was a small black and silver machine, no more than one foot high and six inches wide.

Victor snatched the machine from his hands, lifting it up to the light so he could examine it more closely. "Spectacular," he breathed. "I assume you've tested it?"

Torin nodded, his eyes flitting from Victor to the door. "It works."

"How?"

Torin swallowed, and Victor noticed faint beads of sweat forming across his hairline.

"Just press the button."

It was obvious something was bothering him. Victor tilted his head, eyeing him dubiously. "Come to think of it, I'd rather you show me instead."

With trembling fingers, Torin reached for a sample of carbon steel and handed it to him. He licked his lips, then wiped his hands on his pants. "Put it on the platform, then press the black button."

Victor did as he was told, his heart racing in his chest. This was it. This was the moment he'd been waiting for. The moment he'd finally have the means to destroy the alpha and omega keys.

He lifted his finger and brought it closer to the button, feeling empowered as he pressed it. A little screen above the button blinked red. *Invalid ID.*

He shot a look at Torin, who was trying to hide his smile and failing miserably. Victor's eyes blazed with fury. "What is this?" he spat.

"Your disintegration machine," Torin answered with an intentional smirk on his face.

Victor stepped forward and, without the slightest hesitation, backhanded him. Hard. "This isn't what I asked for. Fix it!" he boomed.

The impact was enough to make Torin fly from his seat. Blood pooled at the corner of his mouth as his back collided with the leg of the desk. "I . . . c-can't," Torin sputtered as he held his cheek. "Emery's fingerprint is hard-coded into the machine. She's the only one who can unlock it."

Victor stared at him with wild eyes, furious. His anger only grew as the corners of the boy's crimson lips turned upward. "You little bastard. You created it to be this way, and now you're going to fix it."

Torin shook his head and grabbed the edge of the desk. Wobbling, his knuckles turning a ghostly white, he pulled himself up. The difficulty of maintaining his balance was written all over his face. He met the President's harsh gaze. "It's unfixable. In order to destroy the keys, you need Emery. Plain and simple."

That was it. He'd had it with this little shit. Victor didn't give second chances, let alone third or fourth chances. He threw the machine onto the desk, the dials and springs clanging against the metal surface.

"I said I would build it for you," Torin reminded him. "I never said I'd make it easy to use."

Victor glared at him, then motioned to Von to enter the laboratory. "Take him out of my sight," he hissed.

Von grabbed Torin by the arm and lugged him out of the laboratory. Victor followed the trail of blood droplets to the common room, watching as Von hoisted the boy-genius into his pod. With the press of a button, a dome emerged and clicked into place. Von marched out the door as Victor walked over to the pod, remote in hand. "You know what's interesting about these encapsulated pods?"

Torin turned his head and coughed. A spray of blood flew from his mouth, covering the opposite side of the pod in misshapen polka dots. He gazed down as holocuffs formed around his wrists and ankles.

Victor's question was met with hostile silence. He cocked his head. "I'll tell you," he continued, circling the pod like a spider entangling its prey. "These pods can either save you or severely harm you, depending on the circumstance." His eyes narrowed. "Unfortunately, you've disappointed me, so there's no point in saving you."

He pointed the remote at Torin's pod and prepared to unleash hell.

37

At first there was nothing. But then there was a pinch. And another. And another.

Torin looked down at his legs, realizing that the pinching was coming from tiny holographic insects.

Holoants.

Although only holograms, the pinching felt like it was coming from real insects. He watched in horror as the holoants seeped through the fibers in his pants, one by one, to feast on his skin. He could feel their tiny little movements as they crawled up his shins, over his knees, onto his thighs. He cringed as they continued to crawl up to his stomach, multiplying by the hundreds. It only took seconds for them to reach his chest and neck.

Pinch, pinch, pinch.

His entire body felt like it was on fire, like it had been thrown into hell's pit of fury.

His eyes met Victor's. He opened his mouth to scream, but no sound came out. The holoants crawled into his throat, latching onto his uvula, his esophagus burning like he'd just swallowed bleach. He squeezed his eyes shut to keep them from creeping in, but they did anyway. He couldn't breathe. He couldn't see. He couldn't think.

There was only pain.

Torin tried to imagine a happier time, like the first time he'd met Emery and the late nights they'd spent together preparing to take down the Federal Commonwealth. If he was going to die, he wanted her face be the last one he saw.

A burning sensation lit up his entire body, growing more intense by the minute. He clenched his teeth in order to stifle a scream, but the pain was unbearable. With every inch of his body throbbing, he let out a low guttural sound that eventually turned into a full-fledged wail. It felt like an eternity, like it was never going to end.

Finally, just when he thought he couldn't take anymore, the pain began to subside. The holoants started to dissipate. The weight lifted from his eyes, the pressure from his throat and neck. He fell to his knees and took a deep breath, rubbing his eyes to clear his vision. He looked down at his arms, expecting there to be dozens of swollen ant bites, but there were none. It was like they'd never existed. Like nothing had even happened.

With clenched teeth, Torin took another deep inhale,

then lifted his gaze to the sinister man standing before him.

"Are you ready to fix the machine?" Victor shouted from the other side.

Torin knew this wasn't the time to be snarky, but he couldn't help it. He crossed his arms. "It's called the Porter 8000. And, like I already said, it's unfixable."

Victor clicked his tongue against the roof of his mouth. He shook his head. "So be it," he growled as he pressed another button on his remote.

Torin braced himself, not sure what to expect next. How could anything be worse than being eaten alive by ants?

Hold that thought.

He immediately knew what he was in for as the sound of rushing water filled the dome. He looked down with wide eyes as water shot out from the sides of the pod, rising slowly at first, then faster and faster. Within mere seconds, the water had reached his midsection and completely saturated his pants, weighing him down like an anchor in the glass dome.

This is not good.

Amidst it all, he knew he absolutely could not panic. He waited until the water rose to chin level, which didn't take long, before taking a deep breath and going under. He had to admit, the water felt good on his burning skin, but his lungs weren't equipped to hold much air after the ant brigade that had just attacked them.

He opened his eyes. It took a second to adjust to his now-blurry vision, the scenery outside the pod rocking and swaying with the movement of the water. Struggling against the heavy weight of his pants, he swam to the top of the pod, hoping that he'd be able to find an air pocket, but there wasn't one. He was completely entrapped in this stupid death-defying fish bowl.

His lungs constricted, desperate for air. Panic set in. Small air bubbles floated up from his nose. Dots began to fill his vision. He did everything he could to keep himself from inhaling, to keep as much air in his lungs as humanly possible, but his mind wasn't strong enough. The floodgates opened as his nose filled with water, his mouth opening in a scream. Liquid waterfalled into his lungs.

This is it. I'm a goner.

Torin closed his eyes as a choking sensation took hold. He could feel his body convulsing, trying to rid itself of water while being surrounded by even more of it. Before all of the oxygen depleted from his brain, he tried to convince himself that it was okay, that he was prepared to die. He could let go.

I'm sorry, Emery. I tried.

Just as another huge wave of water entered his lungs, Torin felt himself float slightly upward. The water level was lowering. With what little strength he had left, Torin catapulted his body up to the top of the pod and came into a small pocket of air. He kicked his feet as hard as he could to remain in the small air bubble, coughing incessantly as the water drained out the sides of the pod into an imaginary sewer channel.

When all of the water had disappeared, he fell to the ground, sputtering and gasping for air. The noises coming from his mouth were what he imagined a dying cow would sound like, but he didn't care. He swallowed large mouthfuls of oxygen, desperate for more. Slowly, the pain in his lungs waned.

For a few minutes he sat, unsure as to whether or not his body would ever feel strong enough to move. Out of the corner of his eye, he could still see Victor standing there. The man didn't flinch.

Torin raised his head to make eye contact with the chief once again. The smug look on his face only made him more determined. He pulled himself upright, his legs wobbling. With his chin held high, he stood up straight with his shoulders back, chest out.

Victor chuckled under his breath. "I'm going to ask you one last time and I'd advise you to *really* think before you respond." He shifted the remote from one hand to the other. "Will you fix the machine?"

Torin kept his gaze on the chief. His body ached. His mind felt jumbled. His psyche was begging him, "No more!" All he wanted to do was give in and fix the machine.

Victor would leave him alone and hopefully let him go in peace. But he couldn't.

This was bigger than he was.

He stood a little straighter before answering. "No."

"Is that your final answer?"

Torin took a deep inhale. "It is."

Victor took a few steps closer, the heat from his breath fogging up the outside of the pod. "I sure hope you enjoyed that last breath," he snarled, "because it's the last one you're ever going to have."

Torin closed his eyes. *Stay calm.* He took another inhale to soothe his sore lungs, but was met with opposition. He tried again, but was met with the same resistance. *Oh god.*

As if his lungs hadn't been through enough after being stung repeatedly and essentially drowning, depleting oxygen really was the icing on the cake.

His breaths became shorter and shorter, shallower and shallower, until he was pressed up against the glass, gasping for air. Oxygen was leaving the pod at an alarming rate. *I can't breathe. I'm suffocating.*

Torin sank to the ground, his body spasming uncontrollably. He could hear Victor's menacing laugh on the other side. His hands met his throat and he wished more than anything that he had the strength required to squeeze it tight enough for it to be over with. His brain started to shut down, his sight overwhelmed with little black dots. Just as he was about to surrender to the other side, something came into his view. A waterfall of long crimson hair. Olive complexion. Piercing grey eyes.

Emery had come for him.

38

The sight was almost too much to bear.

Torin, on his hands and knees, locked in the same glass pod that she'd been trapped in when Victor had decided to take her on a tour of the chamber's underbelly. She didn't know why he was on his hands and knees, but one look at her friend's face told her that he was close to succumbing to unconsciousness. To death.

The look on Torin's face was enough to make Victor spin around. "Well, well, well. What a delightful surprise." He turned back toward his prisoner, who was still kneeling on the floor of the pod, gasping for air. "Lucky for you, it looks like the tables have turned."

Emery rushed over to the pod and pressed her hands against the glass. She pounded on it as hard as she could, hoping it would be enough to break it, but deep down, she knew better. And she was right. Not a single crack formed from the impact. "Let him go," she demanded.

Victor chortled. "Now, I could do that, seeing as I have everything I need right here." He held up a black and silver machine, his eyes gleaming with malicious intent. "But where's the fun in that?"

Emery's eyes widened as she looked at the machine, then back at Torin. Fear was written all over his face. For a moment, she wanted to succumb to her panic, to let it take over, but then her eyes landed on something underneath his shirt. She squinted to get a closer look. It was a faint shadow of a horseshoe, barely visible beneath the cotton. *The real omega pendant. He still has it. Victor hasn't gotten to it yet.*

"Guards!" the President yelled, his voice echoing throughout the laboratory. "Seize her!"

Emery put her arms in the air to surrender as Mason and Warren haphazardly approached her. Warren grabbed one of her wrists while Mason grabbed the other. They cuffed her hands behind her back, then shoved her in Victor's direction.

"This way," he ordered as he walked out the doors.

She turned her head, her confidence fading as Torin's pod remained in its place. If she'd just thrown her dagger at Victor the minute she'd laid eyes on him, none of this would be happening. But the look on Torin's face, his crumpled body lying on the floor of the pod, had distracted her. How could it not? Her concern for him had clouded her judgment.

A potentially lethal mistake.

She shifted her gaze to Mason. His hand was on her left shoulder as he guided her down the hallway. He looked at her, and while there was something different in his expression, underneath it all, she could still *see* Mason. He didn't look the way her father had when he'd been under the control of the microchip. His eyes were pleading and full of emotion, unlike her father's, whose had been empty and dark. She looked again just to be sure, but it was hard to tell. It was like Mason was still in there, somewhere, but trapped and looking for a way out. She nodded at him, trying to communicate that she'd find a way to free him.

They reached the common area and Warren shoved her with so much force that she fell abruptly to her knees. She grunted as she swung her head to the side and blew a stray hair from her face.

"So," Victor said as he sat the small machine down on his desk, "you came back. I find it odd that someone who escaped would come back to the very place they were taken captive. Unless of course, you missed us. Care to tell me why?"

Emery licked her lips, her voice cracking as she spoke. "I guess you could say we have some unfinished business." Her eyes darted to the main entrance. Her father and Naia should have barged in by now. *Where the hell are they?*

Victor noticed her shift in attention. "Expecting someone?" He whistled and one of the guards emerged with a lifeless body over his shoulder. He grumbled as he dropped it to the floor with a sickening thud.

Emery gasped. She'd know that blonde pixie cut anywhere. Her stomach turned not once, but twice.

They'd gotten Naia.

She looked back up at Victor with the most expressionless face she could muster. "I don't know who that is," she lied. Playing dumb could possibly work in her favor, but more likely than not, he'd see right through it. Either way, it was worth a shot.

"I'm sure you remember Naia," Victor said with a sadistic laugh. He walked over to the motionless body and kicked it lightly in the side. "I was surprised to see her after such an extended period of time. She showed up with this." He pulled the AK-47 from behind the wall. "I found this a little disturbing, given that she's just a sweet, innocent girl." His eyes locked on hers, then narrowed, his pupils slitting like a snake's. "Tell me, Emery, why would Naia have a gun, and an assault rifle at that?"

She blinked, doing her best to keep her emotions in check. "How would I know? Maybe for protection?"

Victor considered this for a moment, then shook his head. "You want to know what I think?"

Not really, she thought, her mind reeling in fifteen different directions. Where was her father? Had he been captured, too? Had she dug herself into a hole there was no escaping?

"I think you two are on a team," he continued, his voice steady. "I think you escaped, contacted Naia, and planned how you would take me down. But what you didn't realize is that I'm the master of cliché strategies. Having been a part of them myself many, many times over, I can sense them from a mile away. I know how to recognize them." He placed the gun back against the wall and walked over to where Emery was kneeling. He placed his finger under her chin, tilting her face upward. "So much wasted potential," he murmured to himself.

The sight of him made her want to vomit. The bags under his eyes had shifted from a slight purple to a dark grey. Crow's feet extended at the corners in all directions. His touch was rough on her chin's delicate underside, his face and hands more wrinkled and leathery than the last time they'd met. She wanted to spit in his face, remove her dagger, and penetrate the blade so deeply into his eye that it protruded into his skull and sliced right through his brain. A man with such malicious intentions should not have the freedom to think and act on his beliefs. *I could do it now and end it. It could all be over with.*

"So?" Victor purred, interrupting her thoughts. "Am I hot or cold? From the look on your face, I'd say I was getting warmer."

She twisted her neck to break the contact between his fingertips and her chin. There would be no use lying to him. She wasn't very good at it anyway. "You're right," she admitted. "I found Naia after I escaped and she agreed to help me." She eyed her partner's immobile body. "Apparently, our strategy had some holes that we didn't plan for."

"You see, that's where I'm having trouble. It's quite unlike you to ignore something so blatantly obvious. So you can understand why I'm hesitant to believe a single word that comes out of your mouth." He walked back over to the desk and picked up the machine Torin had created. "No matter. I have what I need now, thanks to your friend."

Emery looked back in the direction of the laboratory. When she'd walked in, there was no doubt in her mind that Victor had been torturing Torin. For how long, she hadn't a clue. It'd almost seemed as though she'd arrived right as Victor was about to take Torin's life. She shuddered at the thought, forcing down the bile that was rising in her throat. "Let him go," she muttered under her breath.

"Who? Little boy-genius?" Victor laughed. "What good would that do me?"

"Your machine," she interjected, "what if something goes wrong? What if it malfunctions? Who are you going to call on to fix it if not him?"

"Oh, you naïve girl. I won't need this machine for long. I only need it to destroy this." He held up the decoy omega pendant. "And this." He pulled the alpha ring from out of his pocket. The ring glimmered brightly, even in the dim chamber lighting.

Emery drew in a sharp breath. Conflicting feelings overwhelmed her as she laid eyes on the ring: sentiment because it had been a gift from her mother, and terror because of the immense power that it held. She had to think fast. Buy time. Distract him.

"But if there are more keys . . ." she trailed off, hoping she could lead him to a pot of gold that didn't exist.

"Don't be crass. These are the only two keys out there. These two are all I need."

She cocked her head to the side, eyes challenging his answer. "Are you sure about that?"

Victor furrowed his brows as he studied the two keys. He contemplated her statement and, after a few minutes, turned his attention back to her. "I'll decide what to do with boy-genius later. But right now, we have more pressing matters that need tending to."

He marched over and seized her by the neck of her shirt, dragging her bound body to the table. With one swift movement, he grabbed a triangular sample of carbon steel from his desk, then delicately placed it on the platform of the machine. He pressed the button.

Emery closed her eyes halfway, trying to shield her face from whatever the machine was about to do. She waited. And waited. But nothing happened.

"Just as I thought. Your turn," he ordered.

She regarded the machine with great clarity as she realized what Torin had done. In order to activate the built-in disintegration mechanism, Victor needed her identification, her fingerprints. Without them, the omega pendant and alpha ring couldn't be destroyed. She smiled. Without even knowing it, she'd been right about there being more than two keys. Maybe she and Torin were still on the same wavelength after all.

He had made *her* the final key.

39

Torin's eyes fluttered open as he regained consciousness. He was slumped against the glass wall of the pod, arms and ankles still bound by holographic cuffs. His eyes scanned his surroundings as he tried to remember where he was and what had happened. He took a deep inhale, coughing as a bounty of oxygen entered his lungs. It hurt.

Everything hurt.

Using the walls of the pod for support, he pushed himself up off the ground, his entire body resisting the upward motion. His shallow breaths fogged up the dome as he gazed out the fingerprinted glass. His mind traveled back to right before he'd lost consciousness. Had he really seen Emery? If so, was she still here? Or had it all been a hallucination, a side effect of Victor's torture tactics?

She's here. She has to be.

Torin brought his hands to his face and rubbed his eyes, the holocuffs zinging his skin. He'd seen Emery, but neither Naia nor the Commander had been with her. If only he knew what their strategy was; at the very least, it would put his mind at ease and prepare him for whatever might happen next.

He looked around the pod, searching for a way to escape. *There's always a loophole.* Novak was only human and was bound to make mistakes—there had to be another way out. He knelt back down onto his hands and knees, examining the crevices along the floor. Nothing. He stood up and slid his hands along the glass, feeling for a crack or a seal. Nothing. His hands made his way to the top of the pod, feeling around for an escape door. Still nothing.

This pod is literally more secure than 7S Headquarters.

Torin leaned against the glass, suddenly remembering something. He brought his hands to his chest, his fingertips grazing the outline of a horseshoe. He breathed a sigh of relief. He still had the pendant.

His ears perked up as a loud *thump* sounded from just outside the laboratory doors. He looked to his left, his eyes landing on Von. His oversized body suddenly jolted forward like he'd been punched in the stomach, then disappeared from sight as it slunk down the glass onto the floor.

What the hell?

Torin pressed his body against the back wall of the pod, not sure who or what to expect. The laboratory doors opened and in walked the Commander, half of his face beaten and bloody, the other half clean-shaven and polished. His knuckles were white from gripping an M60 assault rifle, the butt of the weapon covered in crimson.

Byron raced over to the pod, limping a little along the way. "Are you okay?" he asked as he came closer.

"I should ask you the same thing." Torin shook his head from one side to the other. "I've been better."

The Commander examined him closely. "You don't look so good. What happened?"

Torin kept his eyes glued to the laboratory doors and windows, praying that no one would notice Von's sudden disappearance and the Commander's timely entrance. "When Novak found out that he needed Emery's fingerprints to operate the disintegration machine I'd built for him, he was anything but pleased." He broke his stare from the door and looked at the Commander, who happened to be grinning back at him, a rare moment for Torin. Definitely one for the books. "He demanded that I fix it, but I refused. And so the torture began."

"Keep talking," Byron instructed as he circled the pod. "I'm going to look for a way to get you out of this thing. It seems to be a similar technology we use at Seventh Sanctum Headquarters, for different purposes of course."

He blushed. "It shouldn't be that difficult to figure out." He looked up at Torin. "How bad was it?"

"The torture?" Torin considered this for a moment. "It was probably the worst thing I've ever experienced in my life." He lolled his head back against the wall of the pod. "First, there were thousands of tiny ants seeping into my skin, my mouth, my eyes. My whole body stung and I couldn't breathe or see."

"That sounds pleasant," the Commander retorted as he continued to examine the outside of the pod.

"I can assure you it wasn't. The second treatment," he continued, "was worse. This pod was filled to the top with rushing water. A perfect remedy for lungs that had just been stung repeatedly," he said sardonically. "I had to hold my breath underwater."

"How refreshing."

Torin rolled his eyes, catching onto the sarcasm. "It was, at first, until I couldn't breathe and my lungs overflowed with water. But then it drained, and I was left sputtering like a fool. The final treatment was the worst." He shifted from one foot to the other, his lower lip trembling from the thought.

"What could be worse than almost drowning?"

"Suffocating," he whispered. "I was stuck in here as the oxygen was slowly depleted from the pod."

Byron made a disgusted face. "You're right, that is worse. Novak really didn't want you to breathe, did he?"

"I guess not. During that last one, I really thought I was going to die. I swear, I was about to see the white light and venture to the other side. But your daughter's face . . ." he cut himself off, cheeks flushing.

Byron stopped what he was doing and smiled. "What's that about my daughter's face?"

"Just, uh . . . I-I thought about what the plan was," Torin rushed. "I knew that she'd come for me—"

"Found it," Byron confirmed. There was something below the pod he seemed to be working on that Torin couldn't see. "I should have you out in just a few minutes."

"Thank you," Torin said, feeling humiliated.

But Byron wasn't letting him off that easy. "Now what were you saying about my daughter?"

Torin groaned, wishing that he'd just kept his big mouth shut. "I just meant that I saw her in the laboratory, right before I passed out from the lack of oxygen."

"And Naia?"

He shook his head. "I didn't see her—just Emery." The dome began to slide down around him as it locked back into the underside of the platform, the holocuffs disappearing. Torin stepped off of the platform, his legs shaking underneath him. Not the best time to be weak.

"They must have gotten Naia," the Commander said as he helped Torin down from the platform. "Emery too. That means it's just you and me, Sergeant."

Torin shook his arms and legs, then rolled his neck around in a circular motion. He drew in a shaky breath and tried to steady his legs. "Let's just hope we're not too late."

Byron nodded as he handed Torin the pistol he'd stolen after taking out Von. The Commander's steely gaze met his own. "When are you ever going to learn? It's never too late."

40

I will not press that button.

Emery stared at the carbon steel sample as it waited patiently for its inevitable demise.

I will not let him win.

She shifted her gaze toward the ceiling wishing that, more than anything else, they hadn't gone with Naia's plan. They'd been short on time, so they'd gone with the quickest, dirtiest option—but that same option had left Naia unconscious and her father missing. She lowered her gaze to President Novak. She clenched her teeth, her stomach twisting with disgust.

"Remove her cuffs," Victor instructed.

Mason and Warren walked over to where she was kneeling and obeyed his command.

"Thanks," she murmured, more to Mason than to Warren. As she brought herself to a standing position, Warren stomped his boot over her calf muscle, the cleats digging deep into her skin. Emery bit her lower lip, eyes watering from the pain as she was forced to lower back to the ground.

"Press the damn button," Novak commanded.

She glared at him, not saying a word. *I will not let him win.*

The chief laughed. It was more than obvious that his patience was wearing thin. "Well, boys, it looks like we have another resister." He walked over to her and grabbed a fistful of hair, then smashed her cheek against the surface of a nearby desk. "Trust me, this will be much easier on you if you just do what I say."

Emery looked up at him, the world sideways from where her cheek was firmly pressed against the metal. "No," she managed, the nerves in her face quivering in pain.

He pressed down even harder on her head so that her nose and mouth were completely smashed against the desk, making it almost impossible to breathe normally. "You're in no position to refuse my demands." With one hand planted firmly on her head, he used his free hand to grab her arm and pulled her index finger from her clenched fist.

Emery gritted her teeth, doing everything in her power to keep her finger away from that machine, away from that stupid button, but he was too strong.

She lifted her head slightly, watching as her finger was forced onto the button. A scanner identified her print, then flashed green. The machine hummed as it fired up and, within seconds, there was a flash of bright white light followed by a faint puff and a cloud of smoke. When the smoke cleared, all that remained of the carbon steel sample were specks of dust.

"Magnificent," Victor breathed, tapping his hand against the table in applause. "Now that I've seen it with my own eyes, I'm done wasting time." He pulled out the alpha ring and omega pendant. "Don't worry, I won't need your assistance this time around. Once the keys are inserted into my mainstation, the connection with Dormance will be reestablished and I'll have full control over you and your actions." A sly grin crept across his face. "And everyone else's."

"So that's your big plan?" she spat. "What next?"

Novak didn't seem to catch on to her blatant sarcasm. "Afterward, the keys can finally be destroyed, and you're going to be the one to do it. You'll be the one to destroy the very thing your mother created."

Emery's mind flurried with confusion. She thought back to her mother's note. *Both the alpha ring and omega pendant must be secured into either one of the mainstations in order to fully deactivate Dormance.* If that were the case, then why was Victor willingly going to place the keys into his mainstation? It would do the exact *opposite* of what he wanted, but it would do *exactly* what she'd been trying to achieve all along. For a brief moment, she felt elated, but her heart quickly sank as her eyes landed on the pendant.

The *decoy* pendant.

It's not going to work.

She watched in despair as Victor approached the mainstation with both keys in hand. He seated himself at the massive desk, outlining the indentations with his fingertips. "Finally," he murmured. He carefully placed the alpha ring in position, followed by the decoy omega pendant.

Emery shook her head. *This could have been it. It all could have been over with.* The realization was more agonizing than any punch or blow she'd ever taken.

A minute passed and with it, Victor's smile. Nothing happened. Nothing changed. Everything remained exactly the same. He fidgeted with the control panel, checking the mainstation for any potential system errors. "It's not working," he huffed, his fingers frantically searching for an answer that didn't exist. "These keys aren't working!" he shouted at a decibel high enough to shatter even the densest glass.

Without warning, he shot up from the desk and strode toward her, pulling out his remote and directing it straight at her face. She froze, unsure how to react. The man was acting like a full-fledged maniac. "You're not doing what

I'm telling you to do!" he boomed. "You're not under my control. It's not working! What did you do?"

His pointed stare made her cringe. "What are you talking about? I didn't do anything. How could I have? I've been sitting here the entire time."

"Then why," he said through clenched teeth as he came closer, "aren't the keys working?"

This is my chance. I have to play along. Emery sighed. "Because you don't have the right one."

Victor took her face in his hands, lifting her chin to an uncomfortable height. "What do you mean," he hissed, "I don't have the right one?"

Emery struggled to free herself from his grip, but it was no use. "It's a decoy pendant," she managed through ragged breaths.

"A decoy?" Victor let go of her face and hurried back to the mainstation. He ejected the pendant from its slot. Realization swept over his face as he turned it over in his hands. He marched back over to her and thrust the pendant so that it was just inches from her face. "Is this some sort of joke? Tell me where the real one is. Now."

Emery hesitated, spitting blood from the corner of her mouth. She was sure her teeth were covered in crimson, blood caked at the corners, and yet, a wicked smile managed to stretch across her face. If she told him, he'd grab the pendant from Torin and unknowingly deactivate Dormance himself. It was the perfect Plan B, one that she hadn't even thought was in the realm of possibility until now. "Your little boy-genius has it," she taunted.

The decoy pendant clattered as Victor threw it onto the ground. It landed on its side before falling over completely. The alpha ring remained locked into the mainstation. *You're so close*, she reassured herself. *Don't give up yet.*

She tried to hide her grin as Victor stormed through the double doors in a frenzy of frustration. And then a thought she hadn't even considered emerged. Maybe she hadn't quite thought this through. Fear struck every inch of her heart.

The Order of Omega.

What would the omega pendant reveal to Victor?

41

Victor rushed over to the laboratory, his determined expression falling as he approached the entrance. His eyes followed a trail of blood that was smeared along the glass until they landed on one of his own.

Von's corpse lay motionless on the ground.

With a grimace, Victor pushed himself through the lab doors, his eyes locked straight ahead on Torin's now-empty pod. Stifling a scream, he entered the lab, erratically kicking chairs and swiping everything off of the counters. He'd been too consumed by what he'd thought was the *real* pendant to even consider the fact that maybe it wasn't. Emery was a smart girl—he knew that. So why hadn't he seen this coming?

Footsteps echoed from just outside the lab. He rushed over to one of his armory cabinets, waiting impatiently for the retinal scanner to grant him access. He equipped himself with a pistol, then pulled out a dagger and tucked it in the back of his pants for good measure. The cabinet slammed shut as he popped up from his crouching position. He made his way back over to the laboratory doors, wishing that he could somehow revive Von, but there wasn't enough time. He had to move fast.

With his back pressed against the jagged stone, he crept down the elongated hallway. A gust of wind swept through the chambers, causing his lab coat to flutter in the breeze. He halted as he reached the end and peered around the edge.

There stood boy-genius, in the middle of the hall, looking left and right at one of the many forks-in-the-road Victor had purposely designed his chambers to have. Torin's head was turned, and Victor could see that his mouth was moving up and down. Obviously he was talking to someone, but to who, Victor didn't know. All he could see was a shadow.

He darted from behind the wall and sprinted down the hallway, opening fire on Torin. The boy whirled around, his face twisted with fear as a bullet grazed his elbow. He turned and bolted toward the left fork as the shadow ran to the right. Victor veered left and followed Torin down the hall. Barred windows blurred past him. After thirty seconds of full-out sprinting, the boy began to slow as he reached yet another fork in the road. This time he turned right.

Victor smiled to himself as he copied Torin's actions, just mere seconds behind him. His sinister smile grew wider as he imagined the look on Torin's face when he discovered that this hallway led to a dead-end; and sure enough, it was exactly as he'd pictured.

Desperate. Frightened. Hopeless.

Victor chortled as he approached the boy with the gun aimed directly at his heart. "You have something I need," he said as he took another step closer. The outline of the pendant was clear as day through his cotton t-shirt, making him feel even more stupid for not realizing it sooner.

Torin pressed himself against the wall, his chest pumping up and down from exhaustion. "I built you your machine," he panted. "What more could you possibly need from me?"

"I'm aiming at it."

Torin gazed down at his chest, then back up at him. "Well, I'm sorry to break it to you, but you can't have it."

Victor inched one step closer. "Give me the omega pendant," he snarled, his jaw clenching harder with each word. "Now."

As Torin went to draw something from his pocket, Victor slammed the butt of his pistol down on the boy's temple. Torin moaned as his eyes rolled into the back of his head, his body crumpling to the ground. Victor tucked the pistol into the back of his pants, right next to the dagger. He knelt down and reached into the front of

Torin's shirt, searching frantically for the pendant. He let out a sigh of relief as his fingers curled around the familiar shape.

It was about damn time. The omega pendant, the *real* omega pendant, was finally his. There would be no stopping him this time.

42

Emery's heart pounded in her chest, her eyes trained on the door Victor had exited just ten minutes prior. As much as she tried to think happy thoughts, images of Torin being beaten senseless flooded her mind. *Maybe I shouldn't have told Victor that Torin had the real pendant. Maybe I made a mistake. It wouldn't be the first.*

Her back stiffened as footsteps approached the door. It swung open with gusto, rustling her matted hair in the breeze. In walked Victor with his usual smug look and, behind him, two hefty guards. As they came closer, Emery realized that one of the guards had something slung over his shoulder. A body.

Torin.

Emery bit down on her tongue to keep from screaming. *Definitely a mistake.*

The guard dropped Torin's body next to Naia's.

Emery's gaze shifted between both of her friends' bodies. Although impossible, she hoped her determined stare would be strong enough to wake them up—for them to show a sign of life, a flicker of hope. *Anything*.

But neither of them moved.

Her father was nowhere to be seen, and she could only imagine that he'd suffered a fate just as terrible as her friends, if not worse. It was all her fault. She was completely alone with this lunatic, but, given the circumstances, maybe she deserved to be.

Novak walked over to her and crouched down to her level, but remained high enough to continue looking down on her. It was a power-play, one that was supposed to get into her head, but she couldn't let it. Her mind was all she had right now. She couldn't lose that, too.

"Thank you for your honesty," he snarled. The pendant rose in front of her face. It dangled from his fingers, swaying back and forth in a grandfather-clock-like motion.

Tick-tock. Tick-tock.

If only time were on her side.

Novak straightened, then turned on his heel to make his way toward the mainstation. He held the pendant in both hands, admiring it on the stroll over. Emery could hear him muttering to himself, although she had no idea what he was saying.

Please keep going. Please don't pause.

But Victor stopped in his tracks, just inches from the mainstation. He looked at her, then back at the pendant.

She could tell by the look in his eyes that, somehow, he knew. Either Torin had cracked or he'd known all along. But no matter what had happened, one thing was for certain.

They were completely and utterly screwed.

She closed her eyes as those three fateful words left Victor's lips. "Alpha and Omega."

There was no stopping it. Victor was about to discover a startling truth.

43

Where am I?

Victor sat at a round table in a place he'd never wanted to visit again. Seventh Sanctum Headquarters. On either side of him were two people he also didn't care to ever see again. The Commander and Naia.

He jumped up from his seat, hands flying to the back waistband of his pants, frantically searching for his weapons. When he realized they weren't there, he scanned the area for an escape route of some sort, but there wasn't one.

"Unbelievable," he muttered to himself. He remained standing, fists curled and ready for battle. He expected both the Commander and Naia to be staring at him with their full attention, but instead they were looking at each other and whispering.

Victor gazed down at the pendant, wondering why he wasn't back in his chambers. He'd been just about to lock the pendant into place on the mainframe and finally get the very thing he'd worked so hard for. Instead, he found himself here, in a very confusing and less preferable situation.

He looked from the Commander to Naia, noticing that her hair was shoulder length, much longer than when he'd first employed her. With a sinking feeling, he realized that something was off. *Very* off.

"Sir, we're all set to initiate Project Viper. On your call."

"Project Viper?" Victor questioned. "What is that? And where am I?"

His questions went ignored.

The Commander continued to look at Naia as he nodded his head. "You're sure? Everything's in place?"

Naia cleared her throat. "Affirmative," she responded in a shaky voice, one that was very unlike her.

"Hello?" Victor said as he walked over to the Commander and waved his hands in front of his face. "I don't appreciate being ignored."

The Commander continued to stare straight ahead at Naia. He arched an eyebrow. "What's wrong? If there's something I should know, you need to tell me."

Novak waved his hands again to no avail. *They can't see me. I'm invisible.* He clenched his fists, his frustration climbing.

Naia took a deep breath. "It's Novak, sir. I'm just worried that he'll see right through this. Right through me." She cast her eyes down at the table.

Victor's eyes widened as he watched the scene play out before him. *See right through her?*

The Commander placed his hand on top of hers and gave it a light squeeze. "He won't. And you want to know why? Because you're the best I've got. You can do this."

Naia squeezed her eyes shut, then nodded. "Okay. I can do this."

"For Emery."

A faint smile touched her lips. "For Emery."

"You have got to be shitting me!" Victor shouted as the realization of what was going on hit him square in the eyes. He slammed his fists on the table. "You," he declared, pointing his finger at Naia, "I knew I never should have trusted you."

He knew they couldn't hear him. He knew that no matter how loud he shouted nothing would change. The damage was done.

"I need to tell you about the keys," the Commander said quietly.

Victor froze in his rage, then gazed down at the omega pendant in his hand. *The keys.*

"I know that we need them in order to deactivate Dormance," Naia replied, "but how?"

The Commander ran a hand through his hair. "Sandra created the keys as a failsafe so that, if anything ever went south, we could destroy Dormance forever. There are indentations of alpha and omega symbols on our mainstation and the one in Dormance. If the keys are locked into place on either one of the stations, the entire system will shut down and Dormance will no longer exist."

Victor shuffled backward, almost losing his balance. He gripped the omega pendant harder, his knuckles turning white, as the words sunk in. All this time, he'd been chasing after the ring and the pendant, the so-called "keys"—keys that would do the very thing he'd been fighting his whole life to keep from happening. The keys were the *destroyer*, not the activator. Which meant . . .

I've had the ability to control the microchips this whole time.

He balled his hands into fists, his nostrils flaring. He could feel his face burning as his body temperature rose.

"Traitor!" he roared as he lunged across the table at Naia, reaching for her head so he could crack her skull on the marble table and finally give her what she deserved. Just as his fingers were about to wrap around her head, she suddenly vanished. Wisps of cloudy air took her place.

In an instant, the scene before him faded, and Victor found himself back in the 7S world, back in his chambers. He gazed down at his hands and balled them into fists, closing his eyes as his entire body shook with rage. When he opened them, he caught Emery gaping at him, her eyes stricken with fear. He cast his eyes toward the immobile bodies on the ground. *Torin. And Naia.* He stormed over to where Naia lay, his eyes blazing with fury.

"Don't touch them! Please!" Emery screamed, her voice cracking. "Leave them alone!"

But Victor wasn't listening. With a multitude of kill tactics swirling in his head, he approached the blonde head of hair. *She needs to be awake for this.* He swung his leg back and kicked her in the ribcage with his steel-toed boots. Her bones cracked from the impact. "Wake up, traitor!"

Tears streamed down Emery's face. "Stop! Please!"

He ignored Emery's continuous pleas in the background as he waited for Naia's body to shudder—but she was still.

Just as he was gearing up to kick her again, a single gunshot sounded. As if in slow motion, Victor watched as a bullet sailed toward him. He wailed as it tore through his left knee, causing him to collapse face-first onto the cold, damp floor.

Emery jolted forward, her ears ringing from the deafening sound. She opened and closed her mouth a few times, hoping that her hearing would return to normal. A thick haze of smoke floated around her. She narrowed her eyes, trying to bring the obscure figure in front of her into focus. A shadow rushed toward her, and she realized immediately who it belonged to.

Her father.

She smiled so wide that the edges of her mouth threatened to crack, but it abruptly faded as two more figures emerged from the left, running straight for her father. Warren and Mason.

No, no, no.

Although her faith in her father was strong, it was never good to be outnumbered, especially at a time like this. She hurriedly brought herself upright and immediately focused on Victor, who was across the room, propped up on his elbows, falling in and out of consciousness as blood gushed from his leg. His pants were completely shredded around his kneecap, and she could see fragments of bone protruding from the skin's broken surface.

She turned her attention back to her father, who was now surrounded by a calm Mason and an irate Warren. Mason had positioned himself behind her father, his forearms tightening around his neck to secure him in a chokehold, while Warren was facing Byron, throwing fierce punches at his face and stomach. It was already becoming difficult to distinguish his eyes from the rest of his face as the skin around his cheeks puffed up from hit after hit. She grimaced as Warren struck him right in the temple, her father's head lolling to the side, eyes rolling backward. For a moment he didn't move, and it took everything in her to convince herself that he wasn't dead (again). Only unconscious.

Her eyes darted over to Naia. Still facedown on the ground. Still unmoving. Emery took a deep breath as a harsh realization hit her. *It's up to me. I have to do this.*

Without a single second to spare, she pushed herself up off the ground and dashed into the middle of the chaos, trying to ignore the immense pain shooting up her leg. Her body felt weak, her mind blurry, but she forged on, knowing that if she didn't stop Warren soon, it really could be too late for her father.

Warren must have sensed her coming because just as he was about to lay another punch into her father's face, he whirled around and prepared to backhand her. Emery ducked underneath his arm just in time, using her momentum to reverse-lunge and drive her elbow into his lower spine. Warren cried out in pain as his back cracked and arched from the impact.

Stunned by her sudden strength, she took the opportunity to kick the backside of his knee, forcing him to collapse. He crumpled to the ground, the surprise of the attack written all over his face.

When she looked back up, she was glad to see that her father was no longer in a chokehold, but concern clouded her mind as she realized that Mason was nowhere in sight. *Where did he go?*

She rushed over to her father to help him to his feet when the sound of heavy footsteps filled the room. She looked over her right shoulder, her gaze landing on the many soldiers that had just arrived. Her heart sank as she counted in her head. *They outnumber us twofold.*

Although his eye was swollen and his vision was impaired, Byron charged forward to take on the guards. Emery's nerves buzzed as she watched her father attack the burly men one by one. Her father was a large man himself, but so were the guards, *and* there were more of them.

A lot more of them.

She looked to her left, eyes darting back and forth as she searched for Torin's body. Naia's hadn't moved an inch, but Torin's had disappeared altogether.

"Emery!"

She whirled around at the familiar voice, her eyes locking on Torin's. Somehow, he'd managed to move himself over near Victor and the mainstation, all while being surrounded by daunting men clad in heavy-duty armor. "Catch!" he yelled.

Emery gaped as the real omega pendant left his fingertips and spiraled through the air toward her. She took a step forward and jumped, wincing as her leg went numb. She reached her arm as far as it would go, fingers cupped in the shape of a shrunken baseball glove to ensure she'd catch the pendant.

It felt as though she were watching the pendant in slow motion as it flew toward her. She continued to stretch her arm out as far as it would possibly go and, after what felt like an eternity, the chain finally looped itself around her index and middle fingers. A sigh of relief escaped her lips as she closed her fingers to secure the pendant in her grip. She turned toward the mainstation, immediately focusing on the empty indentation. It was time to put an end to this . . . to all of this. But her relief quickly turned to angst as she locked eyes with the one person standing in her way.

Mason.

44

Let her pass.

Mason stood like a stone wall in front of the control station. He eyed the omega pendant that was dangling from Emery's index finger, the horseshoe spinning counterclockwise.

Don't hurt her.

Unfortunately, his body seemed to be listening to an imaginary voice that wasn't his. He took a few steps forward, arms raised for combat, a gun in one and a baton in the other.

"Mason," she pleaded, "I need to get to the mainstation. You have to let me pass."

I know who you are, Mason thought to himself, *but this blasted microchip doesn't.*

"We have one shot at this," she continued, eyes begging. "I need you to let me pass. I need to fully deactivate Dormance once and for all."

A chuckle reverberated throughout the room. Mason watched as Emery's head turned toward the source of the noise. Even with a shredded knee, Victor had somehow found a way to stand. "You can talk to him all you want, but there's no one in there. He's dead inside."

Mason's eyes stayed on Emery. *He's wrong! I'm still here!* He wanted to scream the words, but his mouth wouldn't move, no matter how hard he tried.

"What are you waiting for?" Victor yelled. "Attack her!"

Don't listen to him. Don't do it. But it was no use. Mason raised his baton in the air and lunged forward, striking it down toward her shoulder.

"Mason, please!" she yelled as she dodged the attack and rolled to the other side of the room. She pulled the electrified dagger from her waistband as she popped back up into a fighting stance, holding it at the ready. "Please don't make me do this," she whispered. "I can't go through this again."

He willed his body not to move. To drop the weapons. To surrender to her. *Just stop,* his mind begged. *It will all be over if I just stop.*

To his dismay, he found himself lunging forward again, this time with the gun pointed directly at her head. Emery's eyes widened as she crouched quickly to the right, her dagger clattering to the floor. He stumbled over it and lost his footing along the way.

Emery took the opportunity to charge at him, weaponless. She grabbed the top of the baton and yanked it from his hand, then grabbed both of his wrists. She sank into a low fighting stance and twisted his wrists away from each other, somehow using the motion to disarm him of his gun. She stumbled backward with the gun in hand and pointed it directly at his chest. Her hands were shaking, eyes wide with terror. The chamber loaded as she cocked the pistol. "Please, Mason! Back off!"

Listen to her. But neither his nor her pleas mattered. He was a machine. One of Novak's robots.

He side-stepped to try to divert her attention, knowing very well that she might pull the trigger, then swung his arm and landed a haymaker punch right across her cheek. A series of *cracks* erupted as her jaw loosened from its socket and her neck flew backward. Her body thrashed to the side from the impact and the gun flew from her fingers, scattering across the room.

He watched in horror as blood spewed from her mouth like a geyser, wanting to catch her before she hit the ground with a deafening thud. Her hands flew up to her face and she groaned as she rolled onto her side.

As if he hadn't done enough already, he approached her, slowly, and geared up to kick her in the side not once, but twice. *You're hurting her!* A voice screamed inside of his head. *You moron! You're going to kill her!*

A dark purple bruise had already started to form where he'd struck her, just below her temple. Blood continued to spurt from her mouth as she coughed again and again, unable to catch her breath.

Go to her. Help her. Do something! But his pleas were useless. He walked over to where the gun had scattered during their scuffle and picked it up, the cool metal soothing his stinging hand. He looked around at the other soldiers who were still in full-fledged battle with Emery's father and Torin. Mason lifted the gun and aimed it right at her forehead.

She finally caught her breath as she stared down the barrel. A single tear fell down her cheek. "It's okay," she whispered. "This isn't you doing this. It's okay."

Drop the gun, drop the gun, drop the gun. Those three words repeated in his head over and over again. He hoped that, somehow, amidst all of the chaos, he'd finally find a way to control his actions. His finger hovered over the trigger. *Don't shoot, don't shoot, don't shoot.*

He wished that there was something, anything, that could stop him from what he was about to do. *I can't kill her. Don't kill her.*

But the microchip Novak had created was too powerful. It had its hold on him, and there was no breaking free from it. His chip had been preprogrammed to complete one mission and one mission only: destroy the enemy. It chose who lived, and it chose who died. There was nothing he could do about it.

I'm sorry Emery. Please forgive me.

Just as he began to put pressure on the trigger, a gunshot sounded, but it wasn't from his gun.

The deep grey eyes in front of him morphed into a pained expression as he collapsed onto the floor. Mason let out one final breath.

Emery was the last thing he saw.

45

Emery wailed as a bullet tore straight through Mason's skull, his body thumping to the ground.

Oh my god. Oh my god.

She couldn't move. She couldn't breathe. It felt as though her mind were in a state of complete paralysis.

With shaking hands, she turned her head in the direction the bullet had come from. Naia still lay on the ground, motionless. Her father was in the middle of fighting off the last remaining soldier. And then there was Torin.

With a smoking pistol dangling from his hand.

He was still for a moment, his eyes trained on Emery. As his gaze shifted to Mason, Torin fell to his knees as the impact of what he'd just done began to sink in.

Emery's eyes brimmed with tears as she watched the agony on his face grow with each passing second. As much as it pained her, she looked again at Mason's lifeless body.

Memories of downtown Chicago came flooding back to her.

Theo. The gun. Mason.

As heart wrenching as that experience had been, she'd found a way to save him. The sanaré had brought Mason back to life. *She* had brought Mason back to life.

She frantically searched her pockets, knowing full well that there was no more sanaré. That this time was different. There was no saving him. He was really gone.

There's no bringing him back.

Despite her shock, it dawned on her that Torin had just saved her life. Mason had been under Novak's control, so there was nothing stopping him from shooting her. He would have done it. Mason would have killed her. He *almost* had. But Torin had stopped him.

Watching someone die for the second time is incomprehensible.

She fell to her knees and crawled over to Mason's body, throwing her arms over him. She squeezed, tighter and tighter, rocking back and forth. "I'm so sorry," she whispered. "You didn't deserve this." She lay there for a few minutes, holding him, wishing more than anything that she could feel his heart beat one last time.

The room was silent. The world was still. For once, she could finally see clearly. For once, she finally *understood*. With one last look at Mason's face, she pulled herself up off the ground and wiped a tear from her eye. Boiling anger replaced her sadness. She was done with death. She was done with Novak. This all ended.

Right. Now.

She wiped her eyes with the back of her hand and, even through all the physical and mental pain, began to limp toward the control station.

Byron had just finished taking out the last soldier and was now standing over Victor, who'd taken advantage of the current situation and had been trying to crawl over to the mainstation.

With blazing eyes and an angry shout, Byron lifted Victor up by the collar of his shirt and reamed one of his fists into the chief's stomach. Victor doubled over in pain and started to wheeze uncontrollably, unable to catch his breath.

When his breathing finally returned to normal, he spat, "Is that all you've got?"

Without answering, Byron tightened his grip and kneed the chief square in the stomach. Blood spurted from his nose and mouth, spraying the grey stone with specks of red. "Is that enough? Or do you want more?"

Victor held up a reluctant hand, palm open, signaling his surrender, but it didn't matter. Byron walked behind him and secured his arm across his chest. He grabbed a fistful of white hair and tugged backward, forcing the chief to watch whatever was about to take place.

Albeit on unsteady legs, Emery finally arrived at the mainstation, the pendant still dangling from her fingertips. She glanced over at Torin, who was still on the floor, completely grief-stricken. She took a deep breath. "I need you, Torin," she called out to him. Her voice sounded calm from the outside, but on the inside, she was violently thrashing.

"I-I . . . di-didn't mean to . . ." Torin sputtered.

"It's okay," she reassured, even though her heart had just been shattered into a thousand tiny pieces. "It's time for this to finally be over. So let's finish it. For good." She forced a smile. "You and me."

Torin remained still for a moment. His breathing was labored and he looked as though he were about to vomit.

"Come on, Torin," Emery said boldly, even though she wanted nothing more than to curl up and die. "I need you."

He nodded as he slowly pulled himself up. He sulked over to the control station with his head down, stepping over limb after limb of Novak's fallen army.

When he finally made it over to her, Emery held out the omega pendant. She waited for him to extend his hand, then dropped it into his open palm. "You should be the one to do this."

He looked up at her. His voice shook. "Are you sure?"

Emery nodded. "I'm sure."

Torin squeezed his eyes shut as he wrapped his fingers around the key. Emery carefully led him to the mainstation, one step at a time, as if they both might crack at any second.

When he was facing the open indentation, she stepped behind him, watching intently as he hacked into the system and typed in the Latin word for disarm, *exarmet,* just as he had the last time they'd attempted this elaborate scheme. The words *Disarmament Initiated* flashed across the screen and a familiar voice began to count down from thirty seconds.

She looked down at the embedded symbols in the mainstation, the alpha ring nice and cozy in its place. She drew her gaze upward until it met his. "Ready?"

Torin's chest rose as he took a deep breath. He nodded slowly. "Ready."

He placed the omega pendant into the open slot. A soft green glow illuminated from underneath the keys.

10 . . . 9 . . . 8 . . .

The room was quiet as the voice continued to count down.

7 . . . 6 . . . 5 . . .

Emery clenched her fists at her side as she took a deep breath.

4 . . . 3 . . . 2 . . .

Out of nowhere, she felt Torin's hand grab her own.

1 . . .

She continued to hold her breath as the last number was counted.

0.

The control station powered down, the screens going black. Emery let out her breath, waiting for some sort of sign to indicate that the deactivation was complete. When nothing happened, a flurry of panic swirled in her stomach. *Please work. Please let it be over.*

Finally, white letters flashed across the screen. *Disarmament Finalized. Deactivation Complete.*

They watched in astonishment as the ring and pendant suddenly dissolved into the station, filling the embedded areas to make the shapes whole again. In mere seconds, the keys were gone, having become one with the machine. In that moment, all Emery wanted to do was scream and celebrate and yell and curse for all the things she'd been through over the past year.

Torin turned toward her and pulled her in for a hug. "It's done," he whispered. "I'm so sorry."

As angry, sad, and disgusted as she was with his actions, she met his embrace. They sat there for a moment, arms intertwined, rocking back and forth in victory.

"We did it," she whispered.

A sputtering fool interrupted their moment. "You think this is over? You imbeciles," Victor coughed as Byron tightened his grip. "This is far from over. There's always another way."

Emery released herself from Torin's embrace, then slowly made her way toward where her father had the chief pinned. "Oh, I'm pretty sure it's over," Emery responded, picking up her dagger along the way. The currents buzzed and pulsed in her hand. She felt angry and powerful, vengeful and fearless. "It's definitely over for you."

Victor eyed the dagger with contempt. "You wouldn't dare kill me."

She swirled the handle of the dagger in her hands. "Oh, really?"

"You don't have what it takes."

"That's where you're wrong." She drew in a deep breath as her eyes met her father's. He gave her a solemn nod. She lowered her eyes back down to Victor. "You will never see the twisted society you so desperately wanted to create come to life. You will never have the power to oppress humankind. You will never harm another human being again. But most importantly, you will never, *ever* take away our freedom."

She smiled as the words left her mouth. "Alpha, a new beginning for humankind, the one it's always deserved. And Omega, the fall of the Federal Commonwealth, the termination of your reign. Your time here has reached its end."

As Victor opened his mouth to respond, Emery drew the dagger back and plunged it deep into his chest, feeling the electrified blue currents penetrate straight into heart.

His mouth closed as she pressed harder, digging the blade in further.

"You messed with the wrong alpha," she whispered into his ear. She watched as the light left his eyes, his head rolling to the side. His body slumped lifelessly against her father's arms.

Emery pulled away, making sure to leave the pulsing dagger in his chest. She gazed down at her own two hands, surprised by the ferocity that had just overcome her. She looked at her father and Torin, who also appeared to be shocked by her own brash behavior.

"You did the right thing," her father assured. "It had to be done."

Emery nodded slowly as she wiped her hands on her pants.

"Careful, you don't want to leave this behind." Byron grabbed the handle of the dagger and pulled it out of Novak's chest. "I'd say this is a lucky dagger."

Emery turned the blade over in her hands and, for the first time that day, smiled. "I'd say you're right."

Epilogue

Peaceful.

It was the one word that came to mind as her eyes fell on Mason's motionless body. They'd stitched up the gaping hole in his head from the gunshot wound, making it look as though it had never happened. He'd been dressed in a navy blue suit with a pale yellow tie fastened around his neck. His hair had been smoothed down and slicked to the side, far from its usual wavy demeanor. His hands lay across his stomach, one on top of the other, his fingernails perfectly trimmed.

Serene.

Emery leaned her head against the side of the pew as the ceremony music began. Good Day Sunshine by The Beatles. She grabbed her father's hand, squeezing it tight throughout the remainder of the song.

Torin sat one row in front of them with his head bowed. Emery stared at the back of his head, wishing that she could comfort him or that he could comfort her, or that somehow they could comfort each other. But, given the circumstances of Mason's death, she knew this wasn't the time nor the place.

After killing President Novak, she'd walked over to where Mason lay and wept, holding his head in her hands. She'd sobbed until there were no tears left, then slowly closed his eyelids with the tips of her fingers. They'd woken Naia and, albeit her many injuries, traveled downstairs to the underground chamber. Dormants began to emerge from the pods, one by one, and then all at once, looking more frazzled than ever. Emery had tried to locate her mother and sister in the crowd of people, but it'd been nearly impossible.

Byron had called in 7S back-up to assist with the transfer of the civilians back to their homes. He'd decided it'd be best to tell everyone the truth, rather than play off what had happened as yet another failed government experiment. It would take time for the population to resettle and heal after years in a comatose state. It was hard to gauge how long it would take, but one thing was for certain: this new world needed to be one of trust, and that first step started with their leader, with 7S.

Emery turned her attention to the ceremony speaker, Mason's father. It was unfortunate that the first time they'd meet had to be under these circumstances. She'd much rather have met Mason's family when they were close friends. *When he was still alive.*

A single tear rolled down her cheek and splashed onto her lap, leaving a barely discernible wet spot on her black dress. She shifted her focus back over to Torin, who was hastily wiping his face with his hands.

I can't even imagine how he feels right now.

A week before Mason's funeral, Torin had shown up, unannounced, on Emery's doorstep. This was especially confusing seeing as he'd ignored every holomessage and holomail she'd left for him over the past two weeks, since the time they'd deactivated Dormance together. When Emery had opened the door, it was blatantly obvious that Torin hadn't slept in days. The bags under his eyes were a deep purple, and the stubble on his cheeks had transformed into more than just a five o'clock shadow. She'd stood at the door, waiting patiently for him to speak.

"I want to apologize for everything that has happened. For everything I've done." He'd paused, struggling to make eye contact. "I'm sorry for not answering your calls. I just needed time."

Emery had taken a step forward. "I understand," she'd whispered. "But where does this leave us?"

He'd looked at her, shaking his head. "I don't know. But seeing you again for the first time after . . . after . . ."

She'd looked down at her feet and closed her eyes, knowing what was coming next.

"After what I've done, I just can't do it." His voice had cracked. "I can't be around you knowing how much pain I've caused. I'm sorry."

Emery had opened her mouth to speak, but no words came out. What could he possibly do or say to make her feel better? He'd murdered one of her closest friends, someone she'd shared a unique connection with. He could say he was sorry. He could beg for forgiveness. But deep in her heart, Emery knew that it would take time. And without the passing of time, his words meant nothing.

She'd bowed her head as Torin turned and walked away, noticing that he'd dropped the decoy omega pendant at her feet. It wasn't entirely clear if he'd been trying to signal that this was the end of them, but it sure felt that way.

Emery snapped back to reality as Mason's father closed his sermon. The priest returned and led the final prayer. She waited until the final "Amen" was uttered before raising her head, then slowly rose from her seat as people began to file out of the pews, moving gradually toward the casket to say their final good-byes.

She held her breath as Torin's row rose to their feet. He walked by without so much as a glance, his eyes trained on the ground below him. Her row was the next to rise and file into the main aisle. She stayed close behind her father, like a baby duckling too afraid to venture off into deep water. There were exactly ten people in front of her, that she could count, anyway.

What do I say to him when I get there?

The line shrank by two people.

Do I ask for forgiveness? Do I tell him I'm sorry?

Three more people.

Do I tell him it should have been me and not him?

Four people.

Do I tell him that I wish I could have gone with him?

One person.

And then, it was her turn. All the waiting in the world couldn't have properly prepared her for this moment. She approached Mason's casket, her bottom lip quivering.

She stood there for a moment, searching for the right words, but they wouldn't come. Then, as if Mason herself were telling her to, she did something that felt so natural, it had to be right. She unclasped the decoy pendant from around her neck, her finger tracing the shape of the horseshoe.

The words came easily.

"Remember what you told me?" she whispered, her voice shaking as she dropped the pendant into the casket. "Behind every dark cloud is a ray of sunlight waiting to shine through." Emery lowered her head. "Please stay with me," she murmured, more to herself.

With one final look at his innocent face, Emery turned away and walked down the draped aisle. She kept it together long enough to reach the double doors that led outside. A flood of tears ran down her cheeks the moment she pushed them open.

There was such finality in death. A person was only here until they weren't. Whether it was by mistake, on purpose, or part of a greater plan, no one garners the ability to truly embrace death and everything that comes along with it until it actually happens. Until it finally arrives.

And by then, it's always too late.

Emery stepped outside of the chapel and gazed up at the sky. Dark rainclouds threatened the view, and she was certain it was going to storm. *How perfectly the weather matches the tone of this day.*

Then, out of nowhere, a sliver of sunlight emerged from behind one of the clouds, lighting up the sidewalk the same way Mason's smile could light up any room. She extended her arms before her, opening her palms as the light shone brighter. She lifted her head toward the sun, allowing the heat to warm her body from the inside out.

Even though he was no longer living, she could feel him, right there with her. Mason was here.

Behind every dark cloud is a ray of sunlight waiting to shine through.

So long as the sun continued to rise, he would always be right there with her, every step of the way.

And that was all the finality she'd ever need.

ACKNOWLEDGEMENTS

The second book in this series was a very different writing experience than the first. I was presented with different challenges and obstacles to overcome and while it was difficult at times, I'm also reminded that writing is a journey and that in order to succeed, you must enjoy the ride.

First, I'd like to thank God for all of the blessings bestowed upon me. I am eternally grateful.

To the team at Damonza, for their amazing design skills and for creating an incredible second book cover. It's like you can read my mind and know exactly what I'm picturing in my head. Thank you.

To fellow writer, beta reader, critique partner, and friend, Vivien Reis. I am so happy we met and are able to inspire and help each other along our writing journeys. I can't wait for your book to come out. Love you, girl!

Thank you to my sister, Erin Martin, for being such an incredible advocate for the first book and for promoting the heck out of it. Your excitement makes make me even more excited to write. I love you.

I'd like to thank my parents, Barb Marvel and Ed Martin, for being my biggest cheerleaders, no matter what crazy ventures I decide to take on. Your support means the world to me and I wouldn't be half the person I am today if it weren't for both of you. I love you.

To my fiancé, Jonathon Bills. You always push me to grow, be better, and do more. Our late night snuggles and Parks & Rec marathons keep me grounded. I love you.

Last but not least, to YOU, my readers. You guys rock. Your praise and support inspired me to make this second book even better than the first. Thank you for making my dream of being an author come true. It's the best job in the world, and I owe it all to you. So thank you!

DON'T MISS THE FINAL INSTALLMENT IN *THE ALPHA DRIVE* SERIES:

RESTITUTION

The world that Emery Parker grew up in no longer exists—she'd made sure of that. Adjusting to a new lifestyle is no easy feat, but Emery is more than ready to leave the past behind. With the promise of a fresh start and a new beginning, it is a place where she can finally let go of all her painful memories and replace them with better ones.

But Emery's new reality is more unsettling than she ever could have imagined. The sustainability of this world is at risk, and it's up to her to find the solution. To do this, she must follow her intuition and put aside any feelings of guilt and uncertainty, even if it means betraying someone close to her. Once again, Emery must search for new truths and question old ones at the expense of the ones she loves, all while facing conflicting choices about life, death, and love.

TURN THE PAGE FOR A PREVIEW

1

Sixteen.

Sixteen days had passed since Mason's death. Emery had been told that time was supposed to heal. That the more time that went by, the easier things would be. But that was a lie. This was beyond any sort of hell she'd ever experienced.

Emery stood, motionless, in the middle of her living room, in a place that was supposed to be her home, but it certainly didn't feel that way. Her home was back in Dormance, in a world that no longer existed, thanks, in large part, to her.

The house was empty, her mother nor her sister nowhere to be found. Once Dormance had been deactivated, the civilians had broken out in a giant state of frenzy. Those in the FCW's underground lair were released, their bodies weak and frail from being in a comatose state for so long. The Seventh Sanctum had moved fast, releasing statements and press releases to help the masses assimilate back into their societal roles. There was still a lot of work to be done, a lot of broken hearts to mend, and a lot of questions that needed answering.

Emery glanced down at her wrist as the time floated in the air from her holowatch. One o'clock in the afternoon. Her visit to the cemetery was at two. Sighing, she walked over to her mother's room and opened the closet door. *There has to be a black dress hanging in here somewhere.*

She rifled through hanger after hanger of pants, skirts, and blouses, until she finally landed on a lacy black long-sleeved dress. It was perfect. She pulled the dress from the hanger and slipped off her shorts and shirt. The dress fell over her body with ease.

Emery turned toward the bathroom mirror as she smoothed the bottom of her dress. She couldn't help but feel taken aback as her eyes met her reflection. Her face was au natural, her olive complexion paler than usual, her deep crimson hair fastened into a messy bun. Her eyes were tired, and it looked as though she hadn't slept in days. She reached for some blush and mascara, hoping that the two would bring some life to her face. When they didn't, Emery searched through the counter drawers for a red or pink lipstick. She pulled a red one from the drawer and applied it to her lips. It was bright, probably too bright for the occasion, but she didn't care. Mason would have liked it. And that was all that mattered.

A pair of black pumps poked out from underneath her mother's bed. Emery slipped them on and slowly made her way to the T-Port in the living room, dropping the crystal dials onto her wrists along the way. She checked the name of the cemetery again, even though she'd visited every day for the past two weeks. "St. Augustine Cemetery in Burbank, California."

Emery closed her eyes as the familiar tingling took hold, followed by a cool gust of wind. When she opened her eyes, she stood outside a massive wrought iron gate. Looking beyond the gate, she realized that there wasn't a soul in sight. *Good. I can grieve in silence.*

The iron was cool to the touch as she pushed her way through the gates into the lawn area. Tombstone after tombstone lined the grass in neat, orderly rows. Bouquets of wilting white roses sat dejectedly next to a few of the headstones, as if the person who left them there couldn't bear to bring themselves back to the site.

Emery approached her late friend's site, feeling guilty for not bringing her own bouquet. To her surprise, an arrangement of fresh yellow roses sat next to his headstone. She stopped in her tracks, confused, and gazed around at the deserted cemetery. The bouquet was still lined in plastic, the stems sitting in a capsule of water, the price tag clear as day: September, 15, 2055.

That was today's date.

Emery looked around the cemetery again, wondering who would have stopped by to drop off the flowers. A rustling in the distance caught her attention as a tall figure with shaggy brown hair emerged from behind a row of trees, his eyes cast down at his feet. Emery felt her heart stop.

It was Torin.

A mix of emotions welled up inside her chest as he lifted his head, his eyes locking with hers. Anger, fear, hatred, loneliness, sadness.

They didn't speak for a few moments.

Finally, Emery broke the silence. "What are you doing here?" Her lower lip trembled as the words left her mouth.

Torin cleared his throat, then took a cautious step forward. "I wanted to pay my respects."

"Yeah, well, that's nice and all, but I think you've done enough already." She bit her tongue, knowing that her words sounded harsh.

"Emery . . ." Torin began, his eyes brimming with tears.

"No. You don't get to disappear, then come back when you feel like it. Life doesn't work that way." Her voice caught in her throat. "You don't just leave the people you care about to suffer and grieve alone. It's not right."

Torin took another step forward. "I never wanted to leave you. You have to believe me," he pleaded. "I just didn't know how to be around you after what I did." He nodded toward the grave. "I killed him, Emery. I *killed* Mason. Do you understand that? I'm the one responsible for his death."

Emery broke eye contact, unable to look Mason's murderer in the eye. Torin was right. He'd killed Mason. But he'd only done it to save Emery's life.

4

"You may have killed one of my closest friends," she shuddered, "but you saved my life. And for that, I will be forever grateful."

As she turned to leave, his hand landed gently on her shoulder. "I never wanted to leave you alone," Torin whispered, "and I'm sorry. But I'm here now. That's got to count for something."

Emery didn't move, her back still facing him. She bowed her head. "No. No, it doesn't." His grip broke from her shoulder as she made her way back toward the wrought iron gates.

"Emery, please!" Torin shouted after her. "There's so much we need to talk about!"

But Emery wasn't listening. Both her mind and body were engaged in a full-fledged sprint toward the cemetery gates, tears cascading down her face with each and every stride. Just a few more steps. *It should have been me. I should have died.*

Emery stepped onto the T-Port, her voice shaking as she recited her home address. The last thing she saw was Torin running toward her, the expression on his face one of agonizing pain. She closed her eyes as the familiar gust of wind surrounded her.

And, for a few brief moments, she felt nothing.

No pain. No sadness.

Nothing.

2

That went well.

Torin stepped off the platform and walked upstairs to his apartment. He trudged over to the kitchen and turned the faucet on. The water felt cool and refreshing on his face. As he patted his skin dry, a clearing of a throat caught his attention. He lowered the towel so that he could see, his eyes landing on the petite female standing in his living room.

Alexis.

"You were gone for a while," Alexis observed as she took a step closer to the kitchen. "Did you see my sister?"

Torin nodded as he flung the towel onto the countertop. "Yeah. I saw her."

Alexis's eyes lit up. "Really? How is she? Did you tell her?"

Torin gazed at her, unsure how to word what he needed to say next. Her childlike innocence made his guilt drop even deeper in his stomach. "She seems to be doing okay."

"Just okay?" Alexis pressed, her forehead creasing with concern.

"She's been better. We've all been better." Torin sighed. "Listen, I didn't get a chance to tell her. Emery doesn't know that you're here, but I promise that I'll tell her the next time I see her."

"I haven't seen my sister in over a year. The last good memory I have of her is moving her things into her dorm at Darden," Alexis sniffled. "Who knows if it's even a real memory? After all, it did happen in Dormance."

Torin took a step closer, wanting to comfort her. "All of your memories with your sister are real," he reassured, his thoughts drifting back to the day he'd found Alexis.

He'd received orders from 7S to evacuate Novak's underground chamber and instill calmness once the dormants awoke from their comatose state. It had been a no-brainer which two pods he needed to locate first: Emery's mother and sister. They'd been easy enough to find, seeing as they were right next to each other. Alexis woke with ease and, although she was panicked, Torin had found a way to calm her. He'd explained who he was—that he knew Emery and their father—and she'd believed him. Their mother, on the other hand, had been a different story.

Torin snapped back to the present. Alexis was now sitting on the couch with her head in her hands.

"We should probably check on your mom," he said as he walked to the spare bedroom.

Alexis sighed as she pulled herself up from the couch and begrudgingly followed him. A small sliver of sunlight poked through a gap in the curtains. Alexis stepped in front of Torin and took a seat gently on the edge of the bed. She raised her hand to stroke her mother's hair, when, suddenly, she stirred. Alexis paused, her hand in mid-air, as her mother rolled onto her side.

"Let's not wake her," Torin whispered, hoping that he wasn't overstepping.

She nodded, then slowly retreated toward the door, shutting it quietly behind her. "Do you think her memory will come back?"

Torin bowed his head. After finding Alexis, he'd attempted to wake her mother, expecting that the result of the comatose state would be identical in both cases.

He'd been terribly wrong.

Alexis's mother had no idea who her daughter was and so, in order to keep emotions at bay, Torin decided not to tell Alexis about the Federal Commonwealth's microchips or the memory purge—the timing just wasn't right. Hysteria and depression probably weren't good for someone who had been trapped in a pod, unconscious, for almost their entire life. So, he'd decided to keep quiet.

But things were growing progressively worse and he needed Emery's help. It was clear that she was in a bad place mentally and emotionally, still mourning over Mason's death as she should be, but Torin couldn't keep things hidden much longer. The secrets were piling up and he didn't know how much more he could take.

Torin shifted his gaze from his feet to Alexis, realizing he still hadn't answered her question.

"Do you think her memory will come back?" she asked again, quieter this time.

"Yes," he responded, his voice firm. "Your mother's memory will come back."

Kristen Martin is the author of The Alpha Drive trilogy: The Alpha Drive, The Order of Omega, and Restitution. An Arizona native, Kristen currently lives in Texas with her fiancé, two dogs, and cat.

STAY CONNECTED:
www.kristenmartinbooks.com
www.facebook.com/authorkristenmartin
www.youtube.com/authorkristenmartinbooks
Instagram @authorkristenmartin
Twitter @authorkristenm
Snapchat @authorkristenm

Printed in Poland
by Amazon Fulfillment
Poland Sp. z o.o., Wrocław